Praise for t

"A sexy, comical, f … for the next installmen … day

"Deeply satisfying." —*Publishers Weekly*

"Books like this are why I read romance."
—Smart Bitches, Trashy Books

"Funny, sexy, and loving." —Dear Author

"[A] perfect contemporary romance!" —*RT Book Reviews*

"Stacey is an author who knows how to write fun, relevant dialogue within the world of romance." —Harlequin Junkie

"Stacey writes such fun, warm characters with the backdrop of a great small town that I was totally engrossed."
—Smexy Books

"One of the best contemporary romance series . . . Very realistic." —Fiction Vixen

"If you're a fan of big families, cute romances, and friends-to-lovers stories, then this book is definitely for you."
—Under the Covers

Under the Lights

SHANNON STACEY

JOVE BOOKS, NEW YORK

An imprint of Penguin Random House LLC
375 Hudson Street, New York, New York 10014

UNDER THE LIGHTS

A Jove Book / published by arrangement with the author

ISBN: 978-0-515-15584-6

PUBLISHING HISTORY
Jove mass-market edition / June 2015

PRINTED IN THE UNITED STATES OF AMERICA

10 9 8 7 6 5 4 3 2 1

Cover illustration by Danny O'Leary.
Cover photograph of football field © David Lee / Shutterstock.
Cover design by Judith Lagerman.
Text design by Laura K. Corless.

This one's for Meesha. Thank you for being the kind of sister who doesn't judge when I plan to show up for Thanksgiving dinner with a pound-and-a-half-sized bucket of crunchy cheese balls and five cans of cranberry sauce. Thank you for pretending to believe me when I promise to do better next year. And thank you for not being mad when I have to cancel on Thanksgiving morning because snow wiped out our power. Not a day goes by when I'm not thankful you're my sister and my friend.

ACKNOWLEDGMENTS

Thank you to Kate Seaver and everybody at Berkley. I'm so grateful for the enthusiasm and hard work everybody's putting into the Boys of Fall series, and a special nod to the art department for this amazing cover!

My endless gratitude goes out to those who help me in various and invaluable ways—especially to my agent, Kim Whalen, and to Sharon, Lillie and Fatin. And, as always, so much love and so many thanks to Stuart and Jaci. With a husband and a best friend like you guys, there's nothing I can't do, even if I drive us all a little crazy in the process.

01

With his business partner off to who-knew-where with the money he'd drained from their accounts, and his girlfriend currently stripping their apartment of any sign she'd ever lived there, the last thing Chase Sanders wanted to do was answer the damn phone.

It was only nine in the morning and he'd already fielded a call from their lumber supplier, wanting to know why their check had bounced. That was followed up by a call from his girlfriend's new boyfriend, wanting to hash out who owned the television before the guy carried it out to his truck.

Former girlfriend, he corrected himself as the phone kept ringing. Maybe he'd hit the shitty-day jackpot and it was his doctor calling to tell him he might have contracted some horrible disease. Probably from his girlfriend—*ex*-girlfriend—and her new boyfriend.

At the fifth ring he glanced at the caller ID, and the area code snapped him out of his funk—603. And the prefix numbers were from his hometown. Why the hell was anybody calling him from Stewart Mills, New Hampshire?

He tempted fate and picked up the phone. "S and P Builders."

"Chase Sanders, please," said a woman whose voice he didn't recognize, not that he would expect to after fourteen years away. Her tone was warm, and maybe a little sexy, but he braced himself for bad news because that was just how his luck was running at the moment.

"This is Chase."

"My name is Kelly McDonnell." The last name landed a sucker punch to his gut. "You probably don't remember me, but—"

"Don't." Chase was struck by a terrible certainty she was going to tell him Coach—her father—had passed away, and he didn't want to hear it. He had to make her stop talking.

"I'm sorry. Don't what?" She sounded confused, not that he could blame her.

He could deal with Rina reacting to the increase in penny-pinching by finding herself a new guy who wasn't losing his business. He could deal with Seth Poole reacting to the decline in the construction industry by pinching the few pennies they had left and running. But he absolutely couldn't deal with hearing Coach McDonnell was dead. Not today.

"Hello?" she said. "Are you still there?"

What an ass he was. This call couldn't be easy for the man's daughter. "I'm sorry. Go ahead."

"But you said 'don't.' "

"I was talking to my dog." Not that he had a dog. Rina

didn't like dog hair and had refused to budge, even when he'd told her some of those froufrou ankle-biter breeds didn't shed.

"I'm Coach McDonnell's daughter and I'm calling to talk to you about a very special fund-raising festival we have planned for the summer."

Fund-raising festival. "So Coach isn't dead?"

"What?"

"Sorry. Didn't mean to say that out loud."

"Why would you think that?" Her voice was still sexy, but it wasn't warm anymore.

"You're calling me, out of the blue, after fourteen years. I thought you were going to ask me to be a pallbearer or something."

"You've been gone fourteen years, but you think I'd ask you to carry my father's casket? If he was dead, of course. Which he's not."

"You wouldn't ask me to be a pallbearer, but you'll ask me for money?" Not that he had any to give.

"No." He heard her exasperated breath over the phone line. "Can we start over?"

"Sure." Wasn't like the conversation could go any worse.

Chase tried to remember what Coach's daughter looked like. She'd been a sophomore during his senior year, so he probably wouldn't have paid much attention to her if she hadn't always been around because of her dad. Thick, straight blond hair. Not much in the way of a rack, but she'd had killer legs. That was about all he remembered. Oh, and that she hadn't liked him much, for some reason.

"Things are bad in Stewart Mills," Kelly said. He wasn't surprised. Things were bad all over and New Jersey certainly wasn't a picnic at the moment. "The school budget's been whittled down to bare bones and they cut the football team."

He waited a few seconds, but she didn't tell him why she called to tell him that. "And you want me to . . . what, exactly?"

Over the line, he heard her take a deep breath. "I want you to come home."

"I'm not sure what you mean by that, but I *am* home."

"We need to raise enough money to fund the team until the economy swings back around, and we're starting with a two-week-long fund-raising festival. We're hoping to get as many players from the first Stewart Mills Eagles championship team as we can back to Stewart Mills to take part in the events."

"When? For how long?" Not that it mattered.

"Next month. We'd love the whole two weeks and we're hoping for at least the closing weekend, but we'll work around any commitment we can get."

"I wish you all the best, but—"

"Let me tell you some of the events we have planned," Kelly interrupted. "Besides the standard bake sales and traffic tollbooths, we're planning a street fair and—most exciting of all—an exhibition game featuring the alumni players versus the current team. We'll wrap things up with a parade on the Fourth of July before the fireworks."

Getting the crap beat out of him by a bunch of teenagers on the football field wasn't very high on Chase's to-do list. "I have a lot going on. Work and . . . stuff."

"My dad had a lot of work and *stuff* going on, too, but he was there for you. How many hours did he spend with you over the years, making sure you didn't flunk off the team? Bet that college degree came in handy when you were starting your own business."

He leaned back in his chair and groaned. "That's a dirty play."

"There's a lot riding on this. I'll do whatever I have to."

It might be a slight exaggeration to say he owed everything to Coach McDonnell, but not much. Even if Chase's life was currently going to crap, he'd had a lot of opportunities over the years he wouldn't have had without a stubborn old man who refused to give up on him.

"I'll see what I can do." There. That was vague and noncommittal.

"I hope to hear from you soon. Without the Eagles to coach, I don't know what'll keep my dad going."

Even as he recognized her lack of subtlety in laying on the emotional blackmail, his heart twisted and he heard himself say, "I'll be there. I'll make it work."

"Great. I'll be in touch soon with more details and to nail down the dates." She was smart enough to end the call before he could talk himself out of it.

Once he'd hung up, Chase laced his fingers behind his head and stared up at the ceiling. He hadn't thought about Stewart Mills in ages, but now that he had, he couldn't help but crave a little one-on-one time with Coach McDonnell. He loved his parents, but they'd been either unwilling or unable to keep their thumbs on him academically or be a shoulder when he needed one.

He sure as hell could use a shoulder to lean on right now, as well as some pseudo-paternal advice. Besides, if he couldn't straighten out the mess his partner had made in the next month, a couple of weeks wasn't going to hurt. For Coach, he'd make the time.

If there was one thing Kelly McDonnell had learned in her years as the daughter of the Stewart Mills Eagles high school football coach, it was that hesitation got you sacked. If you wanted to win, you had to pick your play and execute it with no second guesses.

And as much as she'd also learned to hate sports analogies during those twenty-eight years, this one she had to take to heart. She was fighting for her dad and for her town, and she couldn't lose, so she had to execute the only play she had left in her book.

It was crazy, though. *She* was crazy. Hail Mary passes didn't even begin to describe the desperate phone calls she'd made. But they were going to work, and that made all the trouble worth it.

She already had several commitments. Alex Murphy, defensive tackle, had been hard to track down but agreed to come back after she reminded him of the many times her father had bailed him out of jail after fights and taught him to channel his aggression into football. The quarterback, Sam Leavitt, was coming all the way from Texas. The son of an abusive drunk, he was probably the kid Coach had cursed the most, loved the most and done the most for. And Chase Sanders, running back, had bowed to her not-so-subtle pressure as well and was driving up from New Jersey.

So, the good news—Chase Sanders was coming back to

town. The bad news—Chase Sanders was coming back to town.

"Officer McDonnell?" Kelly looked up when the school secretary said her name, shoving Sanders to the back of her mind, where he belonged. "Miss Cooper's available now."

Kelly nodded her thanks and made her way through the maze of short hallways—one of the joys of a hundred-plus-year-old brick school—until she came to the guidance counselor's office. She didn't have to worry about getting lost. Besides the fact that she'd walked the same halls as a teenager herself, as a police officer she'd spent a lot of time in Jen Cooper's office. The budget didn't allow for a full-time school resource officer, but Kelly filled the role as best she could anyway.

She'd barely closed the door behind her when Jen pointed at her and said, "You *have* to save football."

Kelly laughed at her best friend's irritation and sat in one of the visitor chairs. "You know I'm trying."

"The boys are already getting into trouble. Since March, when the budget for next school year was decided, they've been sliding, and now, with this school year almost over and finals right around the corner, they're losing their minds." Jen leaned back in her chair, rocking it as she always did when agitated. "Without the threat of August football tryouts to keep them in line, I don't know how some of them will stay on track this summer."

"I'm going to put them to work. If they want to play this fall, they'll have to work for it, even if it's doing car washes every Saturday all summer."

"Hunter Cass hasn't done any homework for over a week.

I had him in today and he told me since he didn't need to maintain at least a C average to keep his sports eligibility, he didn't see the point."

Kelly shook her head, feeling a pang of sadness. Hunter had struggled to keep a D average through middle school, and only the promise of playing football got him to work hard enough to stay above the cutoff. With the help of the peer tutoring program Jen had started, the running back was carrying a B-minus average before they announced the program cuts.

Like Chase Sanders, she realized. Football had inspired him to do better academically, too, and he'd made something of himself. The difference was that Chase had struggled with learning techniques, and Hunter just didn't give a crap.

"When we get a few more details nailed down, we'll be able to start putting the kids to work. Once they can see there's something they can do to save their team, they'll get back on track."

Jen leaned forward so she could prop her elbows on the desk. "What if they put in the time and the work and it's not enough?"

That would be so much worse for the boys, so Kelly was going to make sure that didn't happen. "It'll be enough."

"Where are the alumni going to stay?"

Kelly appreciated the switch to talking about things they *could* control. "To save money, we're boarding them with families in town. It's a little awkward, but since our only motel has plywood on the windows, it would cost a lot to find someplace else for them, and then we'd have to provide transportation, too. My mom decided to ask around, and she's in charge of matching them up."

"Who gets to stay with Coach?"

Kelly rolled her eyes. "Chase Sanders."

She appreciated the battle Jen fought to hide it, but her friend couldn't stop the grin. "Was that your mom's idea . . . or yours?"

"Mom's." Boarding the guy she'd had a crush on in school at her parents' home, where she spent a lot of her time, would never have been her idea. "And I never should have told you I liked him, even though that was a *long* time ago."

Jen picked up her pen and started doodling on a notepad. "He's not married, is he?"

"I don't think so. The only guy who mentioned having to talk to his wife was John Briscoe. Remember him? Tall, skinny, played wide receiver."

"Vaguely." Jen sighed and set the pen down, which was good since she was really burning through the ink, judging by the number of doodles already on the pad. "I'm losing them, Kelly."

"The most important thing is that they see us fighting for them."

Jen nodded, but Kelly wasn't surprised at the lack of conviction on her friend's face. They both had front-row seats to the toll the economic downswing was having on the town's kids. With their parents fighting unemployment, bankruptcy, foreclosure, depression and each other, the children were falling through the cracks. Alcohol-related calls were on the rise, as were domestic calls, and lately the Stewart Mills PD had seen a sharp increase in the number of complaints against teens. Drinking, smoking, trespassing, vandalizing, shoplifting. The kids were doing more of it, there was less tolerance for their behavior and their homes were pressure cookers. Somebody had to fight for them.

Kelly had to make their fund-raiser a success, no matter what, not only for her dad but for the entire town, too. She'd work her butt off and schmooze and beg if she had to. She'd also do her best to ignore the fact that Chase Sanders would be sleeping in the room where she'd spent her teenage years daydreaming about him. She had no idea which task would be more difficult.

Chase managed to bash his knuckles twice on his way down the stairs with the last of Rina's boxes, which did nothing to improve his mood.

She'd moved the bulk of her stuff out already, but as he'd packed his own belongings over the last few weeks, he kept finding things of hers. He'd tossed those items in separate boxes and then, when he was sure he'd gotten everything, he texted her to come and get them. She'd come up with a lame excuse and sent Donny, her new boyfriend, instead.

Nothing soured a day like having to play nice with the guy who'd been banging his girlfriend.

"That's the last one?" Donny asked after Chase tossed the box into the back of the guy's truck.

"Yeah." He was about to walk away, when Donny stuck his hand out. Chase stared at it for a few seconds, debating on punching the guy in the face, but he'd been raised better than that and shook his hand.

"No hard feelings," Donny said.

Chase squeezed, tightening his grip until the man Rina had chosen over him winced. Then he turned and went inside, slamming the door a little harder than was necessary. That was enough playing nice.

With the exception of the duffel bags by the door and a few odds and ends on the kitchen counter, almost everything he owned was in boxes in a storage locker, waiting to be moved to a new, much smaller apartment the weekend after he returned from Stewart Mills.

By downsizing his life, groveling and bargaining, he'd managed to clear up most of his business woes. And, most importantly, he'd sold the engagement ring he'd bought Rina back when times were good and he was feeling flush. Every time he'd thought he was ready to pop the question, though, something had held him back, and the ring had stayed hidden in the bottom of a beer stein from college, under miscellaneous guy debris she had no interest in sifting through.

He wasn't sure why he'd never asked her to be his wife, yet considering she was living with Donny and the ring was paying not only for his trip to Stewart Mills but also the first and last month's rent on a new place once he found one, it was a damn good thing he hadn't.

After one final look around, Chase tossed his stuff into his truck and hit the road. It was a nine-hour drive, so if he pushed straight through, he'd get into Stewart Mills early evening. If he was going to be any later than that, he'd spend the night in a motel and arrive in the morning.

He had one quick stop to make before he left town. When he'd told his parents he was going back to Stewart Mills and why, his old man had called him an idiot, and his mom had told him to swing by and pick up a pie. It was intended as a hostess gift for Mrs. McDonnell, but Chase was afraid if Coach's wife had ever had his mom's pie and remembered the experience, she might not let him in the door with it.

His parents' home was in a small neighborhood made up

mostly of retirees, though his mother still worked. She claimed she enjoyed doing insurance claim work for a large auto body shop, but Chase suspected she couldn't handle her husband 24/7. Nobody could. Today she was home, though, her shiny compact car squeezed into the driveway alongside the massive Cadillac that Bob Sanders had bought back during Clinton's first term in the Oval Office.

His mom was on the sofa when he walked in, watching some kind of cooking show. "Hi, honey. Your father's out back."

It was the standard greeting, but he stopped and kissed her cheek on his way through the house. "Hi, Ma."

His old man was on the tiny dock that matched all the other tiny docks up and down the canal that ran through the neighborhood. He had a bulk package of cheap chicken drumsticks and was shoving a couple of pieces of raw poultry into each of his wire traps. Ma would be making fresh crabmeat-salad sandwiches for lunch.

Chase hated seafood. Especially crab.

"You heading north today?" Bob asked when Chase reached the dock.

"In a few minutes. Ma made a pie for Mrs. McDonnell."

"Lucky her."

Chase grinned and shoved his hands in his pockets, but the smile faded as the silence stretched toward awkward. They'd never had a lot to say to each other, but their relationship was particularly strained at the moment.

Bob Sanders made no bones about being disappointed—and maybe a little embarrassed—by the failure of Chase's business, no matter how much of it was due to the economy and Seth's financial shenanigans rather than mismanagement on Chase's part. Chase's impending return to Stewart Mills had also dredged up his buried resentment that his father had written him off as stupid, and it had taken Coach McDonnell to show him he wasn't.

Bob lowered the last trap into the water, shoved the empty chicken packaging back into the plastic shopping bag and turned to face Chase. "Get everything straightened out?"

"More or less. Got most people willing to wait for pay until the lawyers catch up with Seth. Scraped together enough to stay out of bankruptcy court, and managed to find contractors to handle the jobs I can't afford to do now. Things are tight, but I'll probably get to keep my shirt."

"And you think it's a good idea to go to New Hampshire right now?"

Yeah, he did, because Coach needed him. "Probably not, but I'm going anyway. This mess will still be here when I get back."

Chase followed his dad back to the house and, since the conversation seemed to have run its course, he got the pie and got the hell out of there. He thought about ditching the hostess gift in a rest area trash can, but if his mother tried to call him at the McDonnells' and the pie—or lack of one—came up in conversation, he'd never hear the end of it.

He turned the music up too loud, drove a little too fast and drank way too much coffee, but he pulled into Stewart Mills a little past six. A perfectly respectable time to show up on Coach's doorstep.

As he drove through Stewart Mills, though, he noticed the town had changed a lot, and not necessarily for the better. A lot of For Sale signs. A few bank auction signs. They'd obviously done some restoration work on the historic covered bridge, but it didn't distract from the dark, silent shell of the paper mill looming behind it that used to be the lifeblood of the town.

There was also a new stop sign, he realized *as* he went through the intersection. Without stopping.

And the Stewart Mills Police Department had a fairly new four-wheel-drive SUV, too.

There hadn't been a stop sign at that intersection fourteen years ago, Chase thought as he pulled off to the side of the road, making sure there was plenty of room for both his truck and the SUV with the flashing blue lights.

It was one hell of a welcome home.

02

Kelly untethered her weapon and approached the pickup truck with her hand on the butt of the gun. It wasn't because of the out-of-state license plates—those were common enough due to tourists having to pass through Stewart Mills to get to the four-wheeling and snowmobiling playgrounds farther north—but because it was protocol. The simplest of traffic stops could turn ugly fast if the idiot behind the wheel had something to hide.

She stopped a little behind the driver's window so she could see him, but he would only be able to catch glimpses of her uniform in his mirror. As she opened her mouth to ask for his license and registration, the pieces clicked in her overworked mind and she shut it again. New Jersey plates. The timing. The profile she used to moon over.

Chase Sanders was back in town, and blowing a stop sign was one hell of an entrance.

"License and registration, please."

His head tilted just a little and Kelly rolled her eyes. Here it came—all the cheesy charm men shoveled out when the badge was pinned to a female breast. If he didn't at least make a comment about the handcuffs, she'd do an extra mile on the treadmill.

"Here you go, Officer." He handed the stuff out the window. "How did such a pretty lady end up in law enforcement?"

Gee, that was original. And since he could only see her from neck to waist, and her vest didn't do much for the girls, the fake flattery was wasted. "A guy with no respect for traffic laws broke my heart in high school and this is how I get my revenge."

"Did he have no respect for frisking, too, because I wouldn't mind taking the payback for that one."

Running her hands up and down Chase Sanders's tall, broad body? Maybe burying her fingers in that thick, dark hair? Sure beat the hell out of scrubbing Albert Hough's vomit off her backseat when she didn't get him to the drunk tank fast enough.

He leaned his elbow on his door, craning his head around in an obvious attempt to see her. "If you do need to frisk me, feel free to handcuff me first. I won't struggle . . . much."

Ha! No extra treadmill time. "I don't think handcuffs will be necessary."

"That's too bad, Officer . . ." He was trying to read her name tag, so she stepped forward. "McDonnell?"

She pushed her hat back so he could see her face. "Welcome home, Chase."

"Holy sh— Coach's daughter. Just so you know, I'm not usually this cheesy."

"I'm flattered you dusted it off just for me."

He smiled at her and she remembered the look well from the countless times he'd used it in high school to get his way with teachers, parents and pretty girls. "Flattered enough to skip the ticket?"

She couldn't issue a citation for one of their guests of honor two minutes after he rolled into town. "Just this once."

After he tucked his license back into his wallet and tossed the registration in the glove box, he leaned on the top of the door and looked her over. "So, a cop, huh?"

"A police officer, yes."

"A woman who likes to be in control."

She slapped the side of his truck before handcuffs came up again. "How about if I give you an escort to my parents' house? There's a new stop sign on Dearborn Street I don't want you to miss."

"With lights and sirens?"

"No." Kelly went back to the SUV, wondering if Chase was watching her walk away in the mirror, and feeling like an idiot for caring.

Once she'd buckled up, she steered out around his truck and drove across town. She might have paused a few extra seconds at each of the stop signs, just to be a smart-ass, but he deserved it for the cheesy—and wholly unoriginal—lines.

When they got to the end of Eagles Lane, which had been renamed the year Chase and his teammates won the championship, Kelly flipped on the light bar. No siren, but the flashing blue added a little splash to his arrival.

By the time she'd pulled to the curb and waved Chase

around so he could park in the driveway, her parents were standing on the front porch of the old New Englander–style farmhouse she'd grown up in. Walt, who hadn't been called anything but Coach for as long as Kelly could remember, and Helen McDonnell were healthy and happy as they headed toward their midfifties, but she could see the signs of strain around their eyes.

Coach was trying to keep his spirits up, especially around his team, but his faith in Kelly's Hail Mary plan was shaky.

"Sanders!" Her dad met their guest at the halfway point of the walkway and enveloped him in a hug. "How the hell are you, boy?"

"Good to see you, Coach."

There was some manly back-thumping, and then Chase moved to her mother. "Thank you for inviting me to stay with you, Mrs. McDonnell."

"It means so much that you came." She accepted his hug and kissed his cheek. "And don't you think it's time you call me Helen?"

"Not quite yet, Mrs. McDonnell."

"Well, grab your things and we'll get you settled in."

"I should warn you, my mother sent a pie."

Kelly admired the way her mother didn't grimace, though she'd probably cringed on the inside. Kelly remembered the pies Mrs. Sanders had contributed to the football team's bake sale fund-raisers back in high school. She was pretty sure some generous supporter had paid to make those pies disappear, leaving filling-smeared empty pans behind to save Mrs. Sanders's feelings.

"You coming in for a while?" Coach asked her.

"Can't. I'm on duty until eleven and I have to be in for

eight tomorrow morning. In between, I have to shower, eat and hopefully sleep." She wasn't complaining, though. She'd been lucky enough to keep her job when budget cuts downsized the department.

"O'Rourke's at nine?"

"If nothing comes up." She let Coach kiss her cheek, then waved to her mom. "I'll call you when I get a chance."

"Nice to see you again, Kelly," Chase said.

She faced him, fixing on her "work" smile. "You, too. We really appreciate you coming back, and Coach can give you my cell number if you don't have it. If you need anything, just call."

"And somebody will tell me what I'm supposed to be doing?"

"You're a couple of days early so, for now, just relax and make yourself at home."

She got out of there before any of them got the idea to twist her arm into eating her share of the pie Mrs. Sanders had sent.

The rest of her shift was quiet, which was good. A call after regular business hours usually meant the teens were up to no good, or a domestic situation had gone bad.

The downside was how much time her mind had to wander, and the way it kept wandering to Chase Sanders. Until the idea for the fund-raiser had come to her, she hadn't really thought about him in years. But she'd thought about him in high school. A lot.

She'd been around the team all the time, helping Coach however she could—being water girl or equipment manager or keeping stats—despite his desire that she shake her pompoms for the Eagles. Once the nurses had confirmed his wife hadn't given birth to a future quarterback, Coach gave his newborn daughter the most cheerleader-like name he could think of.

Kelly wasn't the pom-pom type, though, so she'd divided her time between the library and hanging around the fringes of the team. Since Chase never seemed to notice her, she'd pretended to dislike him so nobody would ever guess how she felt about him. As far as she knew, nobody had ever figured it out, except her closest friends.

She was a lot older and wiser now, and no longer the type to fall for a pretty face and cheesy lines. She'd done it once, falling for a guy who was a lot like Chase Sanders, and the crashing and burning of her marriage had taught her a thing or two about relationships. Think first, then think again, and *then* consider sexual chemistry.

So far, only one of the guys had gotten past thinking first, and that one didn't get past the thinking again. Even if her body waxed nostalgic about her long-ago yearnings for Chase, she had no doubt any lingering attraction wouldn't survive a liberal dose of logic.

Walking into Coach's house took Chase back fourteen years to his senior year of high school.

The décor had changed. Rich cream-colored paint had replaced the floral wallpaper, and the furniture was different, even if no longer new. The picture of Kelly in her police uniform, standing between Coach and her mother at what appeared to be some kind of graduation, was definitely a new addition. Just as it had been tonight, her blond hair was in one of those fancy braids that ended below her collar, and her legs still went on forever. Since she wasn't wearing the boob-smashing vest in the picture, he could see she'd blossomed a little in that department while he'd been ignoring her, too.

But the warm, welcoming feel of the McDonnell home wasn't new, enveloping him just as it had the first time Coach dragged teen Chase home with him.

Since he was carrying a pie, it made sense for him to follow Mrs. McDonnell into the kitchen, and that's where the memories really reared up in his mind. The old, sturdy oak table was still there. He couldn't even count the number of hours he'd spent at that table, doing his homework. Whenever he got confused and frustrated, Coach or Mrs. McDonnell would pull out the chair next to his and talk him through the problem, no matter how long it took. Sometimes Kelly would come downstairs when she was done with her own homework and help him, though not often. He always suspected the McDonnells knew his academic struggles would be more embarrassing with her around to watch.

He had no idea how he would have turned out if not for the two people currently dishing up his mother's pie. He wouldn't have gone to college, that was for damn sure. Maybe he never would have left Stewart Mills, and his sister would never have visited him on campus and fallen in love—and pregnancy—with a local boy, which had led to his parents' move and the entire family ending up in New Jersey.

His life may be in chaos, but it beat a dead-end job in a dead-end town.

"We turned the guest room into Coach's office years ago," Mrs. McDonnell was saying. "I hope you won't mind staying in Kelly's old room."

"Of course not." He really hoped Kelly hadn't been a frilly and pink kind of girl. Spooning with stuffed unicorns wasn't his thing.

"I was going to turn it into a craft room—"

"You mean a room with your own TV," Coach interrupted.

"But before I made up my mind, Kelly was going through the divorce, and she moved back in for a while."

So Kelly had been married? He wasn't sure why that piqued his interest, but he was smart enough not to ask any questions about it. Looking like he was trying to hook up with Coach's daughter would be even worse than running a stop sign, as far as being welcomed back went.

"How are your parents?" Coach asked as they pulled out chairs to sit in front of the pie slices his wife set on the table.

"Good." He flailed around in his head, trying to come up with more to say. "They're good."

"And your sister?" Mrs. McDonnell added. "Kathleen, right?"

"Kathy's good, too. She and her husband own a secondhand furniture store and have three daughters."

"No kids for you yet?"

Chase shrugged. "Not yet. Almost had a wife, but it didn't work out."

They caught up a little over his mother's pie, all of them going a little heavy on the milk to wash it down, and Chase noticed that not only did he skirt around the issue of his company's woes, but Coach didn't seem too inclined to delve into the town's problems, either, or his own.

After pie, he grabbed his bag and followed Mrs. McDonnell up the stairs to the small bedroom at the back of the house. No pink, thankfully, or boy band posters on the wall. The room was mostly creams and whites, with a funky, homemade-looking quilt on the twin bed and a rag rug in the middle of the hardwood floor. Either Kelly had been a neat freak in her teens, or most of her childhood history had been boxed up.

A few hours later, when he'd gone to bed simply because it was obvious the McDonnells were already up past their bedtime, he stared at the ceiling and tried not to think about Kelly McDonnell. Actually, thinking about Kelly wasn't the problem. It was trying not to think about her handcuffs that was causing him problems. He couldn't figure out what it was about her that had him tossing and turning, so he chalked it up to his body looking for some stress relief. He wasn't comfortable with relieving that stress by hand, so to speak, under Coach's roof, so he gritted his teeth and suffered.

Chase woke up the next morning, disoriented and with a heaviness in his gut he suspected might be his mother's pie. Light on the breakfast, he told himself as he pulled on some clothes to walk down the hall to the bathroom. When he got downstairs, Mrs. McDonnell shoved a full coffee mug into his hand, and he struggled to wake up while his hosts went through their morning routine.

"I'm heading to O'Rourke's in a few minutes," Coach told him. "The missus doesn't make breakfast on days I go there, so if you're hungry, you'd best come along."

Not nearly enough minutes later, and still suffering a caffeine shortage, Chase slid into a booth across from Coach and tried to decide what his stomach was up to dealing with. He would have thought the laminated menu was the same one he'd looked at the last time he'd been in O'Rourke's, except the prices were higher.

Don and Cassandra Jones had opened the restaurant in 1984 and, according to the anecdotal history of Stewart Mills, they were going to use their own last name. After half the town got sucked into a two-week-long battle over apostrophe placement, Cassandra had gotten mad and ordered a sign with her maiden name, so O'Rourke's Family Restaurant was born in a town that didn't have a single O'Rourke in the telephone book.

Coach ran his finger down the menu, making sounds of indecision as he read. "I usually have the hash and cheese omelet since the wife won't let me have them after my cholesterol check, but I'm not that hungry this morning."

"Me neither, to tell you the truth."

Amusement crinkled the corners of Coach's eyes. "Make sure you tell your mom we said thanks for the pie."

"The gift that keeps on giving," Chase muttered, but his mood brightened considerably when their waitress set an oversized mug of coffee in front of him. No dainty teacups for O'Rourke's.

Then he looked toward the door and saw Kelly McDonnell walking toward them. Either the caffeine chose that second to hit his bloodstream, or he had a serious, previously undiscovered thing for women in uniform.

Or maybe just *this* woman in uniform. She still had those killer legs, and the rest of her wasn't bad, either. The hat was left somewhere, probably in the cruiser, and her hair was braided so tightly he was surprised she wasn't squinting.

There were a few seconds of awkwardness because Chase and Coach were both sitting in the center of their booth seats, but Coach took care of that. "Slide over, Chase, and let my daughter sit."

Kelly smelled as good as her legs looked in the navy pants, and Chase lifted his mug to his mouth so the coffee aroma could block out the surprisingly sweet and slightly fruity cop smell.

"Glad you could make it," Coach told her.

"It's pretty quiet this morning."

Chase chuckled. "Like Stewart Mills becomes a hotbed of crime in the afternoon. New Hampshire's very own Gotham City."

When neither of his breakfast companions laughed, he realized he may have stepped in it. Rather than sink further into the conversational muck trying to talk his way out of it, he gulped some more coffee.

"You've been gone a long time," Kelly said as she stirred cream and sugar into her coffee. "And the worse things get for people financially, the more desperate they get. Shoplifting, burglary, domestic violence. All of it sees an increase."

He knew all about things getting tight, and Seth had shown him how good people did shitty things when they got desperate. But Chase knew, as bad as it was, he was luckier than many. Not only did it look like he'd be able to tread water, but he also didn't have a wife and kids to worry about dragging down with him if he sank.

"And the kids are acting out?" he asked.

Coach nodded. "Yeah. And some of them only walked the straight and narrow because they knew I'd kick their butts off the team if they didn't. If they know there won't be tryouts come August—"

"There will be," Kelly interrupted. Her voice was low

and firm, and Chase wondered if she used that voice while handcuffing miscreants, which led him to wonder if she'd use that voice being bossy in bed. Then he wondered if she'd notice if he squirmed in his seat. "Stewart Mills is coming together to save the team. They'll dig deep."

"Digging deep doesn't do much good if all you've got in your pockets is lint. School spirit and good intentions won't pay the bills."

The man sounded defeated, and that started an ache in Chase's chest. The coach who had changed his life had been inspiring and tough, and he'd refused to give up on anything. Not on his unlikely dream of a state championship. Not on a group of misfit boys who weren't an easy bunch to wrangle. But it sounded like the fight was going out of him.

The waitress showed up to take their order and then stopped back to top off their coffees. Kelly shifted on the hard bench seat, and her knee bumped his leg.

"Sorry," she muttered.

He didn't mind at all. He didn't mind when her leg brushed his ten minutes later, either, or when they both reached for the salt at the same time and almost ended up holding hands.

What he did mind, though, was sitting across from the man he respected more than any other in the world, thinking increasingly inappropriate thoughts about that man's only child.

Coach's daughter was so off-limits for a rebound fling she might as well get a roll of police tape out of her trunk and wrap herself in it. And a rebound fling was all he had to offer *any* woman. Even though he hadn't been ready to put a ring on Rina's finger, Chase had been with her a long time, and it still stung pretty badly that she'd left him for another guy when the going got a little rough. Whether it stung his heart or his pride more, Chase couldn't quite say, but he knew one thing—he had to clean up his own life before he even thought about another relationship. He had to at least have something to offer.

If Coach caught a whiff of Chase's attraction to Kelly and asked what his intentions were, the only answer would be *nothing honorable*. Chase had to stop looking at Kelly McDonnell like a smoking-hot police officer with the sexy voice and the really sexy handcuffs, and start looking at her as Coach's daughter.

That fruity scent of hers was the smell of forbidden fruit, and Chase Sanders wasn't going to bite. No matter how strong the temptation.

Organized chaos Kelly could deal with, but the Eagles Fest meeting was the chaos without the organization. The teens, who were supposed to be doing the bulk of the work, were huddled in the back of the high school art room, giggling and talking and in general trying to look cool.

At least they'd shown up. Half the adults on her list either weren't going to show up, or they were going to be late and claim they were stuck in the first random traffic jam in Stewart Mills history. Now, mere days before the festival kickoff, wasn't the time for volunteers to run out of steam.

When she nodded at Coach, he put two fingers in his mouth and gave a whistle that put the silver kind hanging around his neck at practices to shame. The teenage boys in the room snapped to attention, with the others at least falling silent. "Let's get started."

They'd all finally settled in the metal chairs they had permission to use in the music room, and she was opening her mouth to start the meeting, when the door opened and Chase walked in. It was a good thing everybody turned to look at him because her train of thought ran right off the rails.

In the weeks between her phone call to Chase and his running the stop sign, she'd thought a little bit about what it might be like to see him, but in her mind, he'd looked like the teen she'd daydreamed about, with maybe a little of that computer-generated aging process applied. Her imagination had underestimated him.

Whether it was the years, the construction or both, something had definitely made the boy a man. A ruggedly handsome man in jeans and a T-shirt that drew attention to his tanned, leanly muscled arms, with that smile hinting he could still get up to no good from time to time.

She'd felt like getting up to no good herself when they kept accidentally touching at breakfast. It was a sign she'd been neglecting certain needs when a man's leg bumping hers or his hand almost brushing hers was enough to trigger a tingly hot flash.

Coach's voice boomed over the murmuring crowd, breaking into her thoughts. "Everybody, this is Chase Sanders, one of the greatest running backs to ever play for the Eagles and a member of our first championship team!"

As they all clapped and Chase waved, Kelly didn't miss the way Hunter Cass's mouth twisted into what was more grimace than smile. The current Eagles running back didn't look thrilled to see one of the school's legends in the flesh.

Whether Hunter didn't like sharing the limelight or Coach's attention, she couldn't tell, but she'd be keeping an eye on the boy. He needed to grasp the fact that Chase and the other guys were there to help save the football program.

"Kelly?"

She realized Coach had been prompting her and shoved the two running backs out of her mind so she could focus on the business at hand. "Thank you for coming, everybody. We have a lot to cover, so let's get started."

Chase couldn't sit off to the side somewhere where she could ignore him. No, he had to find a seat toward the back, directly in her line of sight, and every time she looked up, he was watching her. They were all watching her, of course, since she was doing the talking, but there was something about the way he was doing it that made her wonder if *his* mind was on the agenda at hand.

"Saturday and Sunday we're kicking things off with the town yard sale," she said, keeping her gaze on the paper in front of her. "Gretchen Walker and her grandmother have been accepting donations at the farm for the last month, and some of Mrs. Walker's friends have been helping them sort and tag the items. I still need volunteers to get up at the butt-crack of dawn Saturday morning and move the boxes to the town square. We decided to have it there instead of at the farm because it's on the main road, and we're hoping to nab some tourists on their way home Sunday."

Chase raised his hand and she nodded at him. "Chase?"

"I have a truck, so if you tell the boys on the team what time to show up, I'll handle getting everything moved."

Everybody heard Hunter's snort. "Butt-crack of dawn? No thanks."

Before Coach could say anything, Chase pinned the boy with a hard stare. "Then turn your jersey in and whichever guy who shows up at the Walker farm and runs the fastest gets to be running back come August."

Kelly wasn't surprised when Hunter sneered. "Screw you, man. Just because you won a few games like forever ago don't make you shit now."

"Hunter," Jen, who was sitting close to the boy, snapped.

"Sorry, Ms. Cooper," Hunter told his guidance counselor. Then he looked back at Chase. "*Doesn't* make you shit now."

His teen cohorts snickered, but they quit when Coach crossed the room to stand in front of Hunter. "You want to keep playing ball for me, son, you'll watch your language. And you'll be at the Walker farm at the butt-crack of dawn on Saturday morning."

"I can't be there that early, Coach."

"If the folks putting themselves out to help raise money for the team can be there, so can you."

A red flush spread over Hunter's face, and Kelly stepped out from behind the podium just in case he was about to lose his temper. She hadn't had time to change out of her uniform before the meeting, so hopefully being reminded there was a police officer in the room would be enough to keep him in line. But he didn't raise his voice. Instead, it was so low she could barely hear him. "Since my dad isn't working, my parents don't get up early and we only have the one car. I have to walk and it's a dangerous road to walk in the dark."

Kelly knew Tony Cass had been drowning his unemployment sorrows in cheap beer, and she guessed he wouldn't react well to his son's trying to drag him out of bed at dawn.

Not that it excused Hunter's behavior, but she tried to keep in mind every day that the attitude and hostility they were seeing more and more of in the kids were coping mechanisms.

"I'll come and get you," Coach said. "Be ready at six."

"Yes, sir."

When Coach returned to his spot beside her, Kelly turned her attention back to the paper. "Tomorrow evening we'll finish painting the signs. The art classes have made some great banners for the street fair next weekend. And Jen's idea to have a contest for the best Eagles Fest display was brilliant. You've probably seen the homemade signs popping up all over town. We'll announce the winner before the alumni game, I think, though we're taking photos as they go up in case some of them aren't weatherproof."

She went down the items on her agenda—the status of different vendors for the street fair, details on the spaghetti dinner in the works, the bake sale, the tollbooths, the parade—talking for what seemed like forever. And every time she looked up, she looked right into Chase Sanders's eyes.

When the meeting finally ended, Kelly wished she could be the first out the door, but she had to stay. Jen, who had the key, would be last out, and Kelly wouldn't leave her to lock up alone.

Maybe she'd get lucky and Chase wouldn't linger. This weird attraction of hers annoyed the hell out of her. She didn't trust guys with charming smiles and cheesy lines. Men who easily had their way with the ladies tended to find that a hard habit to break, in her experience. Derek certainly hadn't been able to break it, even with a wedding band inscribed with Kelly's name on his finger.

"Your mother's holding dinner for me and Chase." Coach draped his arm around her shoulder. "You gonna come over?"

As tempting as her mom's cooking was, she was exhausted and, truth be told, she wanted to soak in the tub, pop in a DVD and not think about the Stewart Mills Eagles for at least ten hours. Twelve if she was lucky. "Not tonight, but dibs on any leftovers."

After Coach headed for the door, she turned toward the coffee urn to start cleaning up, but almost ran smack into Chase.

"Officer McDonnell," he said in a low voice not meant to be overheard.

"I think you can call me Kelly."

"I think I like calling you Officer McDonnell." The smile that went with the words was so naughty it should have its own police radio code. "So I'm not going to see you at dinner tonight?"

The last thing she needed right now was more of her body parts brushing against his body parts under the table. Her *parents'* table, no less. "Nope, but I'll see you Saturday morning if not tomorrow. Thanks for volunteering, by the way."

She stepped around him before he could say anything else, even though she knew she was being rude. He'd put himself out coming back to Stewart Mills to help her dad, so she should be schmoozing him or something. Unfortunately, it wasn't schmoozing she felt like doing to him, and that was a problem.

Wearing a badge in the town you grew up in, especially as Coach's daughter, meant fighting every day to be respected as an officer of the law. Giving a speeding ticket to a woman who gave you half her sandwich in first grade wasn't easy, but she did it, and Stewart Mills eventually came to respect her and the badge she wore. Sleeping with the prodigal golden boy was not only a bad idea personally, it could be ugly professionally, too. Whispers and wink-wink nudge-nudges while on the job, she could do without.

And that meant doing without lusting after her parents' houseguest. Once Eagles Fest was over, she'd wave good-bye and he'd go back to being nothing but a memory.

03

Chase walked down the stairs the following morning to find the house empty and a note from Mrs. McDonnell propped next to the coffeemaker. Smart woman. He wouldn't miss it there, for sure.

We're off to work this morning, but we'll probably be home by early afternoon. Make yourself at home, and there are fresh blueberry muffins in the basket with the blue towel over it. Helen.

Three cups of coffee, two muffins and a few minutes washing dishes later, Chase stood in the middle of the living room and wondered what he was supposed to do all day. Kelly had made it pretty clear nothing was needed from him until tomorrow morning, but he wasn't used to sitting around watching television while the sun was shining.

He would have given Coach a hand if he'd gotten up early enough. Unlike many high school coaches, Coach wasn't a school staffer who happened to know enough about a sport to coach it. He'd owned his own plumbing business for as long as Chase could remember, and Mrs. McDonnell worked in his office. When the community had begun making noise about starting a football team, they'd asked Walt McDonnell to coach because he'd played in college back in the day, and nobody else had that kind of practical experience.

Chase was a builder, not a plumber, but he could lug tools and hand over wrenches as well as any guy. He'd missed the boat, though, so he was going to have to amuse himself until the afternoon, at least.

He decided to cruise around and reacquaint himself with the town, keeping an eye out for unexpected stop signs. Besides the For Sale signs and the depressing bank auction signs, Chase saw a lot of empty storefronts along Main Street, and it seemed like every building in town needed a fresh coat of paint.

He'd turned off Main Street, planning to loop around to the public parking area and go for a walk, when he hit the brakes so hard the tires chirped, and stared at the sign. Decker's Wreckers. It couldn't be. But who else would slap that name on a business?

He turned in to the lot, trying to remember what name used to be on the old brick garage, but it eluded him. Parking between two tow trucks that weren't in much better shape than the garage, he got out and went into the office. Nobody came to greet him, so he poked his head into the garage area. Two legs like tree trunks stuck out from under a pickup.

"Hey," Chase said.

The creeper wheels squealed in protest as the rest of the man emerged, and Chase grinned. Paul "Deck" Decker had been a big guy in high school, but years, a lot of good eating and probably more than his fair share of beer had added quite a bit of girth. If he wanted to slide under a car, the car would have to be on a lift.

"Hey, Deck."

Deck pushed himself to his feet and wiped his hand on his pants before extending it. "Sanders. No shit. Heard you were coming back."

"Rumor is we're going to wipe up the field with some young rookies. Couldn't let you have all the fun."

"When Kelly asked me to play, I almost laughed her out of my office. I haven't played in years."

"None of us have. At least you just have to stand there and hit people. I'm the goddamn running back. Last time I ran anywhere, my truck popped out of gear and started rolling. Took off after it and got maybe seven or eight yards before I said 'fuck it' and let it hit a tree."

Deck shook his head. "When I laughed at her, Kelly reminded me Coach didn't laugh when he sat down with Ma and helped her fill out all of those government forms so my little brothers and sisters could get free hot lunches at school."

"She plays hardball, that's for damn sure."

"Knows which buttons to push." Deck shrugged. "I'd have given in anyway. I live here and it's Coach, you know?"

"Yeah, I know."

"Plus I've got boys who are eleven and nine, and they've been counting the years until they can be Eagles like their old man. What else are they going to do when they're teenagers? Cruise the back roads, drinking?"

Chase figured pointing out they'd had their share of doing just that despite being Eagles was a bit of nostalgia he'd keep to himself. "I guess Officer McDonnell will keep them in line, huh? Never would have guessed Kelly would grow up to be a cop."

"I don't think anybody did. She went off to college and got married, I guess. Somewhere in there she became a cop, then she got divorced and moved back. Got a job with our police department."

Interesting. And maybe a little disappointing. If her marriage and divorce had happened away from Stewart Mills, there was a good chance only her parents and best girlfriends knew the whole story, and he couldn't very well ask them. Not that it was important, really. Just mild curiosity about Coach's daughter.

"So what's going on in your life?" Deck asked him. "Things must be good if you can take off a couple of weeks to come back."

Or so bad it didn't matter what he did. "Making do, I guess. How 'bout you?"

"Things are tight. People are trying to squeak a few more miles out of their tires and stretching between oil changes. Turning the radio up and ignoring the knocks and bangs."

"You get them in the long run, though, when they push it too far and need a wrecker."

"True enough. And I do the roadside assistance calls for the tourists passing through, which is what's kept us in the black for the last couple of years. Barely, but we've got a roof over our heads and food on the table, so I'm doing better than some."

"You really think this fund-raiser will work? Sounds like even if people wanted to give money, there's not much to give."

"If anybody can save the Eagles, it's Kelly and Jen and Gretchen. If those three women got it in their heads to take over the world, we'd all be in trouble. Plus, they've got some of the stuff planned out so the tourists will stop and chip in. The big yard sale and the tollbooths and stuff."

"As long as there's no kissing booth," Chase said, but even as the words came out of his mouth, he wondered how much he'd cough up if Officer McDonnell were selling off kisses.

"There was talk of one," Deck said. "Guess the high school kids were all for it, but Edna Beecher said it was prostitution, and if she saw anybody offering intimate favors in exchange for money, as she put it, she'd call the FBI."

"Edna Beecher? Shit, she was old as dirt as far back as I can remember. Threatened to call the FBI on my old man, too, because he carried a .38 in the car."

"If she called them half as often as she threatened to, they'd have taken her out by now."

Both men laughed, and Chase shook his head as he thought of all the times Edna Beecher—often called the Wicked Witch of Stewart Mills when people were absolutely sure she wasn't nearby—had given him what for growing up. The thing about Edna, though, was that while she wasn't shy about giving her opinion or laying into anybody she thought was doing wrong, she was generally a decent woman who cared about the town. She was simply more cranky than most.

"You marry a local?" Chase asked, not wanting to think about Edna Beecher anymore.

"Cheryl Hayes."

Hearing the name resurrected a memory of a quiet brunette who usually had her face buried in a book. "Seriously?"

Deck laughed. "You've gotta watch the quiet ones. They sneak up on you while you're not even looking. How about you? Married?"

"Nope. Came close, but we went our separate ways last month."

"Sorry to hear it. It's nice to have a woman to hold your hand during the hard times."

Since Chase had a woman who'd kicked him in the emotional balls when times got hard, he wondered if he should have spent more time in the library and less time at bars back when he'd been looking. "And you've got just the two boys?"

"Yup. They're usually hanging around with me during the summer, learning to turn wrenches, but Cheryl's got them helping her make meatballs for the spaghetti dinner benefit. Good thing we've got a freezer in the basement, because she's made enough freaking meatballs to keep the town alive if the Apocalypse comes."

"When it comes to an all-you-can-eat benefit dinner, I can pack away the meatballs. Whatever she's made, she should double it."

Deck laughed, then looked up at the old-fashioned clock hanging askew on the back wall of the garage. "I'd best get back to work. Promised I'd have this junk done today."

Chase shook his hand again, slapping him on the other shoulder. "Good to see you again, Deck. No doubt I'll see you around all the events. We might even have to practice a little."

Deck snorted. "Like that'll help."

Once he was back in the truck, with no idea where to drive next, Chase put it in drive and waited for a Stewart Mills PD cruiser to go by before pulling out. He couldn't really see the driver, but he could tell by the general build it wasn't Kelly.

Officer McDonnell, he mused, allowing his mind to wander briefly to an image of her slapping handcuffs on him and giving him a *very* thorough pat down.

Very briefly, though. The more he allowed his Officer McDonnell fantasy to grow, the more he was going to think about Kelly, who needed very much not to star in his fantasies. She was Coach's daughter, and Chase was there on a mission, which was to help the man save his job. Then he'd go back to New Jersey and start putting his life back together.

Kelly put the finishing touches on the tollbooth sandwich-board sign and then pushed herself to her feet so she could stretch her back. If she never saw blue, white and gold paint again, it would be too soon. As soon as Gretchen finished the matching sign and Jen wrapped up the massive yard sale signs, they could wash the brushes and call it a night.

They planned to put the tollbooth signs on the yellow line in the center of town, just before the stop sign, and hoped passing drivers would drop donations into football helmets being held out by the players. Friday evenings and Sunday afternoons would yield the most traffic from out of town, and those were generally the people with a little extra cash to spend. The cheerleaders had done it a few years before to raise money for new uniforms and it had been a big success, but things were a lot different then, financially.

"I happened to drive by Deck's place today," Gretchen said, her voice emerging from behind her sandwich board. "Saw Chase Sanders leaving."

"Mmhmm."

"I think he's even hotter now than when we were in high school."

Kelly didn't think that. She *knew* it. Like Albert's homemade dandelion wine, Chase had gotten more delicious and a lot more potent with age.

Jen stood up from behind a yard sale sign and sighed. "Very take-charge kind of guy, based on how he acted with Hunter at the meeting."

Gretchen nodded. "I bet a take-charge kind of guy is just what Kelly needs. A guy who won't put up with that authoritative cop crap and will take her up against the wall if he damn well feels like it."

Even as she shook her head, Kelly felt her cheeks flame and made busy cleaning her brushes so her friends wouldn't see her reaction. She'd never been taken up against a wall, but she'd always thought it sounded hot as hell. "Authoritative cop crap?"

"You're very bossy," Jen said. "So you need a guy who's even bossier than you in bed."

"I'm bossy because you heathens would be racing all

over town, breaking laws left and right, if I wasn't. I swear, I get no respect."

Gretchen put her hand over her heart and tried to look solemn, though she mostly failed. "I respect you, Officer McDonnell. Honest."

Of course, hearing those words made Kelly think of the way Chase had said *Officer McDonnell* in that deep, sexy way, and her face got hot all over again.

Men did seem to be intimidated by her—or the uniform and the gun, at least—and, with her ex-husband and the very few guys since her divorce, that seemed to hold true in the bedroom. Even with the uniform dumped in the clothes hamper and the gun in the lockbox, men always seemed to hold back a little, letting her be the boss. She didn't like being the boss.

Remembering the hard look and the stern tone Chase had used to put Hunter in his place, Kelly shivered. He didn't seem at all intimidated by the badge or the gun, and something about the way he looked at her made her suspect he'd have no trouble taking control between the sheets.

"You know I don't get involved with locals," she reminded her friends. "Getting you people to take me seriously is hard enough without people whispering about my sex life."

"Or Edna calling the FBI to tell them you're corrupt," Gretchen said.

"But," Jen added, "Chase isn't a local anymore."

"Close enough. He's from Stewart Mills, he's back in Stewart Mills and, oh yeah, he's staying with my *parents*."

Jen grinned. "Just makes him easier to find."

Kelly rolled her eyes and started cleaning up in earnest,

hoping to signal the conversation was over. Her friends really had no room to talk, since they both slept alone as often as Kelly did. None of the guys in town lived up to Jen's lofty Prince Charming standards, and working herself to exhaustion keeping the family farm in the black while caring for her grandmother didn't leave Gretchen much time for a social life.

Her cell rang and Kelly sighed when the station's number showed on the caller ID screen. Sometimes it was tempting to pretend she hadn't heard it ring or that she'd been out of service, but she never did. "Hello?"

"Hey, it's Carla." As if she wouldn't recognize the second-shift dispatcher's voice. "You still in uniform?"

"Nope. We're painting signs, plus my uniform's not exactly comfortable, so I changed after my shift. What's up?"

"Some trouble at the Conrad residence. Neighbor called in a domestic dispute that's escalating. Officer Clark is assisting on a motor vehicle accident up by the town line and can't give me an ETA."

"I can run home, change and head out there. Even if Dylan left the scene now, I'd still beat him."

After taking some good-natured ribbing from Jen and Gretchen for sticking them with the cleanup, Kelly swung by her apartment and suited up before heading to the Conrads' home.

She could hear the yelling as soon as she got out of her car, and she hoped yelling was as far as they'd gone. Her knock was firm and loud—her "cop knock" as Jen called it—and she knew they heard her, because the shouting stopped.

She knocked a second time and did some yelling of her own. "Stewart Mills PD. Open the door, please."

When Peter Conrad swung the door open, she could see his flush of anger, but she was happy not to smell alcohol. It had been a bit of a scandal when Doreen left him two years ago because of his drinking, and he'd quit to get his family back. Hopefully the strain wasn't threatening his sobriety.

"It's just an argument," he said. "It got loud, but it's just an argument."

"I'm glad to hear it's not more than that. I'll just say hi to Doreen and then be on my way."

"She's pretty upset. I think she locked herself in the bathroom."

Kelly kept her expression neutral. "Arguments will do that. I'm going to tell it to you straight, Pete. I'm not leaving until I've seen Doreen, so you may as well let me in."

"The kids are in their rooms with their earbud things in, so they don't know what's going on."

She didn't bother telling Pete he was fooling himself. Kids couldn't block out their parents' relationship straining at the seams and getting ready to blow. "I need to talk to Doreen, Pete."

He let her in and she looked around while Pete yelled to Doreen to come out of the bathroom. There was no evidence their argument had turned violent. Nothing overturned or out of place. No crooked pictures on the wall or knocked-over knickknacks.

Pete sank onto the couch and dropped his head into his hands and, a few seconds later, the bathroom door opened.

Doreen's eyes were red and puffy, but she only looked tired instead of scared.

Kelly talked to her in a low voice in the kitchen and, after a few minutes, she was certain Pete had been telling the truth. It was an argument, if a particularly ugly and loud one. Doreen was discouraged, but she wasn't afraid of her husband. Since there had never been a hint of violence in Pete before and her gut told her Doreen had been forthcoming, Kelly decided not to upset the kids further by interviewing them. They were both in the elementary school, so they knew who she was, but she hadn't had as much interaction with the younger kids as with the middle and high school students.

"If your neighbors heard you and were worried enough to call the police, imagine how the kids feel," she told Doreen, and the other woman's eyes filled with tears. "If you and Pete need some help communicating, call Jen Cooper."

"The school guidance counselor?"

"She can't give you marriage counseling, but it's within her job description to help your kids feel secure and happy in their home. She can help."

Doreen took the card Kelly handed her, then Kelly said her good-byes to Pete. "I hope I won't be back anytime soon."

He nodded and Kelly walked back to her truck. Seeing good people she'd known her entire life struggle broke her heart, and it had been a long day. And tomorrow she'd be up at the butt-crack of dawn, as her dad had so eloquently put it, and she'd be seeing Chase.

She threw the truck into gear and headed back toward

her apartment. She'd be seeing a lot of Chase in the near future and she had to be on top of her game. Stewart Mills badly needed a win, and she wasn't going to let old teenage fantasies—or new, *very* adult ones—make things messy with the Eagles running back.

04

Even with a thermos of hot coffee prepared for him by Mrs. McDonnell, Chase wasn't particularly enjoying the butt-crack of dawn. And it wasn't made any more pleasant by the addition of sullen teenagers.

He'd made so many trips between the Walker farm and the town square, he was pretty sure he could make the drive with his eyes closed now. But he didn't try because he'd probably nod off and wreck his truck. Or run a stop sign.

At least Kelly wasn't on duty, so he wouldn't make an ass of himself coughing up cheesy lines trying to charm his way out of a ticket again. He'd caught a few glimpses of her as she moved around the large, grassy square, helping to organize the donations set out on tables and quilts. She was wearing white shorts that made her legs look long and lean and overall perfect for wrapping around his hips. But she was also wearing a blue Eagles T-shirt and a blue and gold ball cap, which were hard-to-miss reminders that she was Coach's daughter, in the unlikely event he was tempted to forget for a few minutes that Kelly McDonnell was off-limits to him.

"Dude, you just blew through a stop sign."

Chase glanced in his rearview mirror, then frowned at his teenage companion—Cody something or other, who played tight end. "Another one? Are you kidding me? Did the town have a budget surplus some year and blow it all on stop signs, or what?"

The kid shrugged. "Whatever, dude."

Chase was really starting to detest being called *dude*, and it was tempting to lecture the kid on respecting his elders. But that meant Chase would be calling himself an elder, and he already felt old enough because of the upcoming alumni game, thank you very much. Hanging around teenage athletes was hard on a man's ability to fool himself into thinking he was still young.

He felt anything but old, though, when he pulled up to the curb and saw Kelly at the corner of the town square. They were trying to hang a tarp, presumably to offer shade for the baked goods and lemonade stands, and she was on her tiptoes with her arms raised over her head.

The way she was stretched out made her legs look even longer, and her T-shirt had lifted enough to leave a gap between its hem and the waistband of her shorts. That teasing glimpse of skin made his mouth dry, and he found himself hoping she'd have to reach just a little bit higher.

"Dude, you're holding up traffic."

Busted. Keeping the curse limited to an under-the-breath mutter because he was trying to set a good example when around the kids, Chase hit the gas and drove around the square until he found a parking space that wouldn't mean carrying the stuff in the bed of the truck too far.

Once the last item—a rocking chair with cushions he guessed had been made during the Carter administration—was deposited with the rest of the donated furnishings, he wiped a light sheen of sweat off his forehead and stretched his back.

"You guys might want to have a few workout sessions before the big game," Kelly said from behind him, and he groaned.

He turned around, shaking his head at the grin on her face. "Don't remind me. I think the Eagles Fest coordinators should take pity on us old folks and make it flag football."

"You know how Coach feels about football. If you're going to play, play it all the way. And you're not old because then I'd be old, too. And I'm not."

No, she certainly wasn't. "What do you want me to do next?"

"I think we're all set. The signs are out letting cars from both directions know there's a town yard sale ahead, and the early bird shoppers are out in force."

"I see that. It's a little ironic, isn't it, that almost the entire town has turned out to support the team when they obviously must have voted to cut the funding at the meeting?"

"I guess it looks that way." She shrugged. "It wasn't personal, though, and very few people *wanted* to cut the team's funding. But something had to give, and it's hard enough to keep good teachers, so we can't and won't make cuts there. Bottom line, it came down to prioritizing academics over athletics."

"Tough choice, but nobody can argue it was the right one, I guess."

"And now we'll try to make up the difference."

He nodded, looking around. "I'll do whatever you need me to do."

"I saw a paint-by-numbers horse on black velvet on a table over by the big maple tree. It would make a great Christmas gift for somebody special in your life."

He grimaced. "I'll do *almost* anything you need me to do."

Kelly laughed. "Mrs. Smith donated some Tupperware. It's slightly spaghetti sauce stained because she didn't clean it with baking soda like Mrs. Donato told her to, but it's still a bargain. Everybody needs Tupperware."

"I'm pretty sure I saw a tools section," he said. "Maybe I'll do a little shopping there."

"Just a heads-up, the reciprocating saw has a bad cord that'll zap the hell out of you. Coach is waiting for its donor to stop hovering, trying to drive up the price, so he can make it disappear."

"Sometimes I forget how much I love this town."

"I can't tell if you're being sarcastic."

He shrugged, not sure himself. "A little bit yes and a little bit no, I guess. It's weird because I feel like a visitor, but as soon as you said her name, I remembered the day Mrs. Donato forgot to put her car in park before she got out, and it almost crashed through the front window of the drugstore."

"You're not a visitor. You're one of the golden boys of fall."

"You almost said that with a straight face." He liked the hint of mocking in her voice. It mirrored how he felt about the whole thing. He wasn't a golden boy, by any means.

"Go get a coffee, golden boy," she said. "And grab one of Mimi Dodge's muffins before the bake sale table runs out. They're that good."

She walked away before he thought to suggest they have coffee and muffins together, which was probably for the best. Since he was having one hell of a time keeping his eyes off her legs and they were surrounded by most of Stewart Mills, it was best if he kept moving and found other things to look at. Like horses painted on black velvet.

Kelly lost track of time as she moved through the crowd in the town square. Sometimes she was helping to drive up prices in a friendly way, even managing to start a bidding war over a DVD player with a missing remote, and sometimes taking turns behind the tables so their volunteer cashiers could have breaks.

She never managed to totally lose track of Chase, though, no matter how distracted she was. She tried to convince herself it was because he was tall, but she felt as if her gaze just naturally homed in on him somehow, as if magically drawn to him.

He looked relaxed and happy as he reconnected with people he'd known his entire life but hadn't seen in almost a decade and a half. And he looked sexy as hell, too, in faded jeans and an equally well-worn Boston Celtics T-shirt. It didn't look like he'd forsaken his hometown sports teams while down in New Jersey.

"How's my best girl?"

Kelly whirled to face her dad, embarrassed to have been caught watching Chase, even though Coach probably had no idea that's what she'd been doing. "I'm good. And so is the turnout, don't you think?"

"I'm starting to think you girls might pull this off, after all."

By *you girls*, he meant her, Jen and Gretchen, even though Eagles Fest was happening thanks to a hell of a lot more than just three people. But it had been Jen, out of affection and concern for the kids, and Kelly—who had the double emotional whammy of caring about the kids *and* her dad—who had stood in the parking lot after the town vote slashed the team, and started coming up with a plan. Gretchen had joined them because what one did, they all tended to do. She wasn't going to let Jen and Kelly take on a project like Eagles Fest alone.

"We only need a few thousand dollars more," Kelly said. "I think we can do it. We'll take in a few hundred dollars, at least, this weekend with the sale. Maybe we'll even hit a thousand if we add in the tollbooth tomorrow."

"I don't want you to beat yourself up too much if the money comes up short," he said, concern deepening the wrinkles around his eyes. "Sometimes the odds are just against you."

It would break her heart if their efforts to keep the team intact failed, but she gave him a confident smile. "I hope you give better pep talks on the sidelines, Coach."

He laughed, and the rich sound was like music to her ears. There hadn't been enough of that lately. "I'm going to go wander around. I'm trying to convince Paul he needs that old canoe over there. You look hot, honey. Go grab a lemonade and find some shade for a while."

That sounded like a good idea, so she kissed his cheek and headed toward the food and beverage area they'd set up.

She should probably have lunch, but the line for burgers and dogs at the grill, which was being manned by the high school principal, was long enough that she'd settle for a drink for now. Later, once the food rush died down, she'd see if they had a hot dog left over.

She took her lemonade to the shade offered by the old covered bridge. A lot of other people had had the same idea, so there was a crowd, and the picnic tables that lined one side were full. Kelly didn't mind, though. Habit took her to the spot where a massive support beam dropped down at an angle to meet the horizontal bridge structure, which formed a rough-hewn bench of sorts.

She sat and sipped her lemonade, smiling and waving at people who greeted her. Because she'd chosen to sit alone, she was mostly left to herself, which suited her just fine. After a few minutes, she reached her right hand down behind the beam and felt around for the heart she'd carved into the wood as a teenager. Inside were the letters *C* and *S*—for Chase Sanders—though they weren't carved as deeply as the heart.

She hadn't dared add her initials because at the time she did it, she hadn't been able to think of another *KM* in their school off the top of her head, and she didn't want anybody to ever know the coach's daughter had a crush on the star running back. The angle had been awkward, making it hard to see as she'd gouged the wood with her knife, but she wanted it to be a secret. There were hearts and initials and a few less savory things carved all over the bridge, but nobody would see her heart unless they already knew it was there. And nobody but Kelly knew. Not even Gretchen and Jen.

And speak of the devil. She drank more of her lemonade and then smiled as Gretchen approached. Her friend worked too hard, trying to keep the family farm in the family, and the genial atmosphere of the day was doing her good. She was even smiling and had a little color in her cheeks, as well as a plastic cup of lemonade in her hand.

"This town loves a yard sale," Gretchen said, sitting next to her on the beam.

"I think they love poking around in each other's belongings, secretly judging."

"No doubt about that. But it's also a buying frenzy. I think I saw Mrs. Tobin buy back a toaster she donated herself."

Kelly laughed. "Whatever gets money into the Eagles' coffers."

"Hopefully it'll be a lot. At the rate the sale's going, there won't be much left by the end of tomorrow."

"If you don't mind storing the remainders," Kelly said, "I was thinking we could try to drum up some more donations over the next week and have a yard sale table during the street fair. Assuming we're not down to stuff that would be better off thrown away."

"I don't mind at all. And every dollar counts, even if it comes a quarter at a time. Which it is, by the way. We're going to have a blast coming up with a total." She leaned closer and lowered her voice. "You're doing a really bad job of not watching Chase Sanders, by the way."

Kelly felt her cheeks get hot. "He's one of our special guests. I'm just doing my part to make sure he's having a good time and doesn't need anything."

"So Alex Murphy and Sam Leavitt and the other guys will get that same level of attention?"

Not unless they turned her head in a way they never had in high school. She'd always been all about Chase. "Of course."

"Yeah, right." Gretchen took a drink of her lemonade as a woman walked by within earshot. "Do we have enough tarps to cover all the tables overnight? Tell me we're not bringing everything back to the farm and then back out here again in the morning."

Thankful for the change in subject, Kelly nodded. "We'll drag some stuff together into tighter groups, especially the furniture, but we should be all set. One of the defensive players has a dad who's a painter, so he let us borrow his tarps. And between residents who can see the square from their windows and Dylan doing some extra drive-bys around dusk, I don't think anybody will mess with it."

"Let's face it," Gretchen said. "Our older generations went all out for this. The generation most likely to try to steal something doesn't want anything out there."

They talked about the upcoming events for a few minutes before heading their separate ways to see who needed a break or assistance with something. It was tiring, but neither of them would complain. This was the first day of a long two weeks, and the only way to get through it was to keep on pushing.

Kelly was especially careful to keep her mind on the job and her eyes off of Chase.

On Sunday morning, Chase volunteered to offer up a shift at the tollbooth. He'd never taken part in one, since it wasn't something they'd done back when he was in high school, but it didn't sound too hard. They were basically panhandling on the side of the road.

The theory seemed to be that traffic would be heavy midmorning through later afternoon as tourists headed home from their visits up north. The main road cut out most of the downtown businesses, since it was the truck route, but there was a short segment that required traffic going in both directions to stop. They hoped the signs announcing the impending tollbooth and its purpose, which Kelly had placed a half mile out in each direction, would give travelers time to pull cash out of their wallets or at least scoop the loose change out of their center consoles.

The boys would be doing the work, holding their helmets out to accept the donations from passing motorists, but there had to be adults on the scene, as well. Not only did they want to make sure the team didn't get too obnoxious in their pleas or harass drivers who didn't offer up money, but there was also always a chance an impatient driver would cause a scene.

They'd been right about the heavy traffic. He barely had time to make small talk with the teenagers since the constantly stopping cars kept them hopping. Time flew by as he accepted half-full helmets to empty into buckets Jen had given him and handed the empty helmets back to the boys.

Some of the kids had a real flair for charm, and Chase thought, by the time they handed the football helmets and safety vests off to the next shift, that they'd taken in at least several hundred dollars, if not more. Once they'd turned the cash—mostly in dollar bills and loose change—over to Jen, who was managing the money that day, he grabbed a hot dog and found a spot at a picnic table to wait for the yard sale to wrap up. He'd volunteered to help haul leftover donations back to the Walker farm when they felt as if they'd run out of buyers for the weekend. He guessed it wouldn't be long, since the people of Stewart Mills had already picked it over like vultures, and there wasn't enough left on display to lure the vehicles passing through town into stopping.

When he saw the three women—Kelly, Jen and Gretchen—standing in the center of the square and looking around, he knew the end was near, so he walked back to his truck so he could park it illegally on the edge of the town square's grass. He was hot and tired and, if Officer McDonnell had a problem with his parking, she could move her own yard sale leftovers.

Other than giving him an arched eyebrow look, Kelly said nothing. Under the direction of the women, the players got everything they deemed not trash into the back of his truck, and it looked like he'd only have to make one trip, which he was grateful for. Besides being tired, he was starting to think his biggest donation to the Eagles Fest cause would be the money he was pumping into his gas tank.

"I'll ride with you and help you unload this crap," Kelly said. "Gretchen has to do some errands before she heads home. Assuming you don't mind bringing me back into town after?"

"Of course I don't mind. I have to go by here to get back to Eagles Lane, anyway."

"Okay. I just need to help fold up these tables and make sure they're all tagged with their owners' names, and then I'll be ready to go."

"I'm going to get off the town's lawn before the local law enforcement notices, and get some gas. You want a soda or something while I'm at the store?"

"I helped finish off the last of the lemonade stand, so I

don't need a drink." She laughed. "The sugar had settled to the bottom, too, so I won't need sleep for a while, either."

Once he'd managed to get off the town square's grass and to the gas station without anything blowing or bouncing out of the back of his truck, Chase swiped his card at the pump and watched the dollar amount climb. Then he pulled the truck into a parking spot and went inside for a soda.

"Well, if it isn't Chase Sanders."

People had been saying his name in that *hey, I know you* voice all day, but there was something different about the way the woman behind the counter said it. She hadn't been working the last time he'd been in, so it was the first time he'd seen her, and it took him a few seconds to place her.

"Janie Vestal." They'd dated most of high school, not out of any great affection, but because football players dated cheerleaders, and they'd liked each other well enough. He suspected she was as relieved as he was when they parted ways before going to college, even if neither of them had admitted it at the time.

The years had been kind to her. With her blond hair in a soft ponytail instead of teased and sprayed to its breaking point and her face free of heavy makeup, he thought she was prettier than she'd been as a teenager. He knew women well enough not to say it aloud, because she wouldn't believe him anyway, and might even think he was saying she hadn't been pretty enough in high school.

"How have you been?" he asked her, leaning against the counter since there was nobody in line. Even if they hadn't been true high school sweethearts, she'd meant a lot to him in his younger years and he was curious.

"I've been really good, all things considered. I've been

married ten years to a guy I met at college. We moved back when my mom was diagnosed with breast cancer and, thank God, she beat it. And I have a seven-year-old daughter and a five-year-old son." Her face softened when she talked about her family, and he was genuinely happy for her. "How about you?"

Well, he had a pretty decent truck in the parking lot and a storage locker in New Jersey. "I'm good. I still live in Jersey and I'm a builder."

"The whole town appreciates you guys coming back for the Eagles Fest," she said. "Without football, I don't think Stewart Mills would have anything to cheer about at all."

"You know what Coach means to me." He knew she did because she'd been the one he'd confided in. Not everything, because their relationship wasn't exactly deep, but enough.

"Everybody loves Coach."

A customer stepped up behind him, so Chase took the opportunity to exit the conversation and hit the soda case. He grabbed a couple of bottles, figuring he'd drain the first one pretty quickly, and then stepped back into line.

"It was good to see you," Janie said as she handed him his change.

"You, too. I'm glad you're happy."

She smiled and nodded. "I am. I hope you are, too."

He smiled back, but it faded as soon as he was through the swinging glass door to the parking lot. Was he happy? He didn't consider himself *unhappy*, exactly, but happy seemed like a little bit of a stretch.

When he pulled up to the town square, Kelly jogged over to the curb, and he had to admit watching her run made him a little happier. He even managed to tear his gaze from her legs long enough to appreciate the entire package. Officer McDonnell was in really nice shape.

Chase took a swig of soda, hoping to cool himself off a bit as she went around to the passenger door. He needed to stop thinking of her as Officer McDonnell, which brought to mind that fruity cop smell of hers, and think of her as Coach's daughter. That was better than a cold shower or a cool drink any day of the week.

05

Kelly took a deep breath before opening the passenger door of the truck. She'd already proven she could handle a little close proximity to Chase without making a fool of herself, but she needed to stop tempting herself like this. She should have begged off and let somebody else help him lug stuff back to the Walker farm.

She opened the door and then laughed. "Did somebody dump their garbage in your truck as a prank?"

He looked around, not seeming to grasp what she was talking about. "Where?"

"Seriously? Chase, it looks like a Dumpster exploded in here."

He frowned and then brushed a straw wrapper from the passenger seat onto the floor. "Sorry. I should probably clean it out."

"Or you could just set it on fire and start over."

He rolled his eyes and gestured for her to get in. "It's a few papers. I suppose you're one of those people who alphabetizes their spices."

"Of course not. They're shelved near my stove in order of how frequently I use them."

"But they have an order."

She climbed up into the seat and rested her feet on a pile of bank slips, torn notebook pages and who knew what else. "You're a very messy person."

"You have no idea," he muttered.

"What's that supposed to mean?"

"Nothing."

She kicked at the pile of crap under her feet. "Did you lose your dog under here?"

"What dog?" He glanced over his shoulder and then pulled the truck away from the curb. "I don't have a dog."

"The first time I called you, you said you were talking to your dog."

"Oh." He gave her a look of chagrin before turning back to the road. "I was having a bad day and was mostly talking to myself, but I didn't want you to think I was crazy, so I lied. Rina wouldn't let me have a dog."

"Rina?"

"My ex. She really hated dog hair, for some reason."

His ex, but ex what? Fiancée? Wife? "Your ex . . . ?"

"Girlfriend. Ex-girlfriend. When you called me, I'd already been on the phone with her new boyfriend and also with some people who were really unhappy with my business partner, so I wasn't at my best."

"Yeah, that sounds like a bad day."

As he drove, he told her about how things had gone to crap for him, from business being slow to his girlfriend cheating to his business partner absconding with their money. While his tone didn't really change, offering up his story in a nonchalant, no-big-deal kind of way, she didn't miss the way his fingers tightened on the steering wheel.

She guessed this all had something to do with the *you have no idea* when she'd said he was a messy person. His entire life was a mess.

"How about you?" he asked. "I've heard there's an ex in your life, too."

"Ex-husband," she said, wishing she could pull off his casual tone. "We got married, discovered we had irreconcilable differences and then went our separate ways."

"That's it?"

No, that was far from it, but she didn't care to dissect her failed marriage for Chase. "He was too charming for his own good, or for *my* own good. Kind of like you, actually."

He nudged her with his elbow so she'd look at him. "You think I'm charming?"

"It wasn't really a compliment."

"I take what I can get."

Somehow she doubted Chase was lacking in self-confidence and needed an ego boost from her. "Now that she's your ex, you could get a dog."

"I should probably get a place to live first since I've got nothing at all to offer a dog at the moment. But I've been meaning to ask you, when are the other guys coming in?"

Not the smoothest subject change she'd ever heard. "Alex Murphy and Sam Leavitt are coming on Friday, the day before the street fair. They're both flying into Boston, so

Alex is going to rent a car and then wait for Sam's plane and they'll drive up together. The others can't come for as long, but they'll all be here for the alumni game and parade. We're still working out some of the details."

"Is Sam staying with his mom?"

"No." They wouldn't even have considered asking Sheila Leavitt about the possibility, even if Sam hadn't told them he preferred to board with a team family, like the others. There was too much history there, and none of it was pretty. "He's staying with Cody. You know, the kid who plays tight end?"

"Yes, I know Cody. I hope Sam doesn't mind being called *dude*."

"I wish Cody was the only offender, there. I hate that. But anyway, Mimi Dodge is his grandmother and he's been living with her for several years, so Sam will be at the Dodge house."

"What happened to the kid's parents? Bill Dodge was older than me, but I kind of remember him."

Kelly hesitated. "I can't discuss Cody's parents. Alex is staying with JJ Barton's family. John Briscoe's bringing his wife and kids, so they'll stay with his parents. Killing two birds with one stone, he said, since they haven't been back to visit for a while. Deck and Phil Parson still live in town, obviously. Phil's out of town, but he'll be back soon."

"So nobody's staying with the running back? Hunter, I think his name is."

"Hunter Cass. And no, nobody's staying with him." There were several families connected to the team who couldn't take the strain of a guest, either financially or emotionally. "We didn't have to ask too many families, since those are the only commitments we could get from the guys we could find. Just the six of you."

"I think you did pretty good, actually."

She smiled at the praise in his tone. "Thanks. I just hope it's enough."

"Even if it's not, I know how much it means to a guy that age to have somebody believe in you and fight for you." He gave a little shrug, and then chuckled. "Which you know, since you didn't hesitate to use it against me."

She felt a pang of guilt. "That was harsh, actually, and I'm sorry I had to do it. But he's my dad. And he knows he's more to the team than just their coach."

"That he is."

Chase turned onto the bumpy dirt road that led back to the big, white farmhouse that had seen better days. Gretchen was doing her best, but without being able to pay for labor, she and her grandmother were on their own. He drove past the house and hooked a left onto an even worse track of dirt that led to the barn. It took them only a few minutes to unload the bed of his truck, and then he drove her back into town, stopping at the curb in front of her apartment.

"I guess I'll run into you soon," he said.

"Very soon. I'm going to run home and take a shower, and then I have to get to my parents' house for dinner." When he gave her a blank look, she cocked her head. "It's Father's Day, remember?"

"Oh. Sure." He clearly hadn't remembered. "I'll probably go to O'Rourke's or something. Maybe grab a pizza. But I'll get out of the way."

"Coach specifically mentioned looking forward to both of us being there for his Father's Day dinner."

He shrugged, but she could see the tension around his eyes. "Okay. I'd rather eat your mom's cooking, anyway."

Kelly didn't bother asking him if he'd called his dad or not. She suspected Father's Day wasn't a big deal for the Sanders family, not only because Chase had clearly forgotten the holiday, but because she knew Chase and his dad had always had a rocky relationship.

None of her business, she told herself as she got out of his truck and gave him a wave. Nothing about Chase's personal life was her business, and what she did know wasn't good. His life was a mess and, if there was one thing Kelly didn't want in her life, it was another mess.

Chase put what must have been the tenth card he'd read back on the greeting card rack in the drugstore. Coach wasn't his dad, grandfather or uncle, so card shopping wasn't going too well. There didn't seem to be a *Dear Coach, thank you for making me the man I am today* sentiment in the bunch.

Of course, Chase would rather be the man he was six months ago, with a successful business and a wonderful girlfriend he thought loved him. Coach would have been damn proud of that man. Now? Chase wasn't sure what was next for him but, whatever it was, he'd be going into it with his debts paid and his head held high. He guessed Coach would be pretty proud of that guy, too.

He finally settled on a blank card with a funny picture of a pug in a bow tie on the front. He'd write his own message, which would probably be something along the lines of *Happy Father's Day, Coach. From Chase.*

Since he was there, he grabbed a few magazines to keep him occupied in the guest room after Coach and Mrs. McDonnell retired for the evening, along with some candy to stash away. Then he grabbed a tube of toothpaste and a box of condoms. Not that he thought he'd need them in the near future, but a man should be prepared in case opportunity knocked.

When he pulled into Coach's driveway, he pulled the card out of the bag and shoved the rest under the seat to bring in later. After digging around his center console for a few minutes, he found a pen and—ignoring the pang caused by seeing *S & P Builders* on the side of it—wrote a quick note inside the card and sealed it.

In the side mirror, he caught sight of Kelly walking up the driveway and got out of his truck, thankful she hadn't caught him holding the almost transparent bag with the brightly colored condom box inside.

"Did your car break down?" he asked, realizing she hadn't driven into the driveway and there were no vehicles parked along Eagles Lane.

"I walk whenever I can," she said, falling into step beside him as they made their way toward the door. "Stewart Mills doesn't have a gym, and I don't have the space or self-discipline for home workout equipment, so walking is my way of staying in shape."

"It's definitely working for you," he said without thinking.

She tilted her head to look sideways at him, her expression unreadable. "Thank you."

He couldn't think of anything else to say, but it didn't matter because Coach opened his front door at that moment and stepped outside. "Thank God you two are here. Helen made a roast in the slow cooker and, after smelling it for hours, I'm absolutely starving."

He wasn't kidding. As soon as he stepped into the foyer, Chase was hit by the aroma of seasoned beef, and his stomach growled in response. When he winced and put his hand over his abdomen, Kelly laughed.

"Mom's cooking has that effect on people, remember?"

He definitely remembered. Most of the time he spent at the McDonnell table, he'd been struggling through homework, but sometimes Mrs. McDonnell would invite him to stay for supper, and those had been the best meals. Not that his mom couldn't cook—baked goods being a notable exception—but there was something about the meals Coach's wife put on the table that made him think of family and home and television shows like *The Waltons* and *The Cosby Show*.

As they dug into the roast, buttery corn and some creamy mashed potatoes with gravy that didn't come from a jar, Chase tried to keep his eyes on his food for the most part. It wasn't easy, since he was sitting across from Kelly. The V-neck shirt she was wearing accented the fact that her breasts weren't large but were probably the perfect size to cup in his hands, and he'd really like to test that theory.

Then he was afraid decidedly *not* looking at her would be as weird and noticeable as looking at her too much, so he stopped staring at his plate and tried to divide his attention among the three McDonnells as naturally as possible.

"Chase, your mom called today," Mrs. McDonnell said, which definitely got *all* of his attention. "She wanted to see how you were doing, but she said you weren't answering your cell phone."

"The battery died and I couldn't find my car charger in my truck. For all I know it was sold in the yard sale."

"Or the trash on your floor ate it," Kelly muttered, and she smiled when he frowned at her.

"She just wanted to see how you liked being back, and she asked how the fund-raising was going. I told her I'd have you give her a call when you came in."

His mom cared a lot more about reminding him it was Father's Day than she did checking in on Eagles Fest, but he didn't say so. Denial was definitely his mother's state of mind when it came to the relationship between her husband and their son. "I'll call her in a little while. Thanks."

When they were done eating, Chase helped clear the table, but he wasn't surprised when Mrs. McDonnell shooed him and Coach out of the kitchen. "It's Father's Day. You two go relive the glory days for a little while we clean up and then we'll have pie."

"Hey! He's *my* father," Kelly said, her hands on her hips. "How come I don't get to go relive the glory days while Chase washes the dishes?"

He would have teased her about being a girl, but she'd probably had some kind of hand-to-hand combat training in the police academy, and getting his ass kicked in Coach's kitchen would be the highlight of the entire Eagles Fest. For everybody else, of course. Not so much for him.

"Because you get every Father's Day with him, and Chase has been gone a long time." Mrs. McDonnell handed her daughter a sponge. "And he's company."

"Did I tell you Chase volunteered to do a double shift in the dunking booth at the street fair?" Kelly's voice was all sweetness and light as she lied to her mother, but the look she gave him when Mrs. McDonnell's back was turned almost made him laugh out loud. And there was going to be a dunking booth? She hadn't told him that part on the phone.

"If you let me off with one dunking booth shift, I'll wash the dessert dishes," he offered, hoping for peach cobbler.

"If you *don't* wash the dessert dishes, I'm going to tell Edna Beecher I saw a 9-millimeter casing on the floor of your truck. You know how she feels about guns and, yes, she still has the FBI on speed dial."

"That's low. And I don't have a 9-millimeter casing in my truck."

She smirked. "Yeah, but it'll take you three days to clean your truck out enough to prove it to her."

"Kelly Ann McDonnell," her mother said, and he felt a rush of smug satisfaction at hearing her middle-named. "It's not nice to threaten people with Edna. Especially guests in our home."

"Sanders, the longer you keep the women talking, the longer I have to wait for that blueberry pie," Coach called from the living room. "If you're going to stay in the kitchen, wash the damn dishes."

After a final glance at Kelly, who was trying not to laugh, Chase retrieved the card he'd set on the foyer table and went to relive some glory days with Coach. It was one of the better Father's Days in his life, and he was sorry he and his dad had never been able to connect the way Chase did with Coach.

He glanced at the clock and figured he had about ten minutes left before Mrs. McDonnell broke out the blueberry pie. That was a perfect amount of time for a phone call home. He could tell his mom how Stewart Mills was so far, wish his dad a happy Father's Day and have a concrete reason for ending the call, rather than letting it die the slow, painful death of awkward pauses as it usually did.

"I'm going to go make a call," he told Coach, whose head kept tilting sideways in his recliner as he fought a post-dinner nap. "I'll be right back."

"Tell your parents I said hello. Especially your old man. We had a lot of conversations about your games back in the day. He was proud of you."

A lump seemed to settle in Chase's throat, so all he did was nod before going out onto the front porch to make the call. Maybe if, just once, his dad had told *him* he was proud, rather than telling Coach, he wouldn't be planning his exit from a call he hadn't even made yet.

Kelly could see Chase from the window over the sink, and he looked like a man who *really* didn't want to be on the phone. She couldn't imagine what it would be like having a strained relationship with her parents. As he leaned against the porch post and did more listening than talking, she idly wiped at the dirty plate in her hand.

"That boy has more baggage than a luggage carousel at the airport," her mom said, moving closer to Kelly so she could see him, too.

"Mr. Sanders always seemed nice, but they're not very close, I guess."

"His mother told me Chase has made quite a mess of his life lately."

Kelly rinsed the soapy water from the plate and set it in the dish rack, sudden anger making her shoulders tense.

Mrs. Sanders had no business calling up a woman she hadn't talked to in many years and telling her personal details about her son's life. Chase had told Kelly enough about what he'd gone through for her to know he'd probably rather keep it private.

"So, after all this time, she just calls you and dumps all Chase's personal problems on you?"

Her mom did a double take at her tone. "It wasn't like that at all. We started talking and, needless to say, we talked about you kids, and she's worried about him."

"I don't think Chase would appreciate his mother telling everybody his business. That's all."

"So I shouldn't put a flyer on the bank's bulletin board?"

Sarcasm from her mom was rare and almost always signaled impatience rather than an attempt at humor, so Kelly didn't push. It was none of her business, anyway. If Chase had an issue with his mother gossiping about him, that was Chase's problem. "How's Dad holding up? Eagles Fest isn't wearing him out, is it?"

"He's doing okay, and it means the world to him, the way everybody's rallied around the team. You know he loves all his boys."

Kelly probably knew that better than anybody. Growing up, there had always been boys from the football team in and out of their house because her dad was more than just their coach. He was like a mentor, or even a father figure for some of them. There had been times she'd resented the attention they got from him, and spent more time than she should have wondering if Coach had wished she was a son.

But, at the same time, she'd also learned a lot about community and offering a hand when somebody was down and out. The way she went about her job as a Stewart Mills police officer was heavily influenced by the way her dad had coached the team, and she was thankful for that.

"How are *you* holding up?" her mom asked. "Even with people volunteering to help, you girls took on a lot with this fund-raising festival."

"It is a lot," she admitted. "But, like you said, we have people volunteering to help."

"Chase certainly dug right in."

The man in question was still on the phone, rubbing the bridge of his nose between his thumb and middle finger. "Yeah, he did."

"He was always one of your father's favorites. It's sad things have gone so badly for him lately."

All that mess, Kelly thought as she watched Chase hit a button on his phone and slide it into his pocket. His business life and personal life were almost as messy as the inside of his truck, which was the opposite of how Kelly liked things. When it came right down to it, the attraction she felt for him made no sense because he was everything she *didn't* want in a man.

"Do you have ice cream for the pie?" she asked, changing the subject.

"Of course." Her mom moved away from the window, leaving Kelly to look out at Chase alone. "French vanilla ice cream on warm blueberry pie is your father's favorite dessert in the world, you know."

Judging by the way Chase wolfed his down once they were all seated around the table, he was pretty fond of it, too. The conversation was relaxed, but she could see some of Chase's tension in the set of his shoulders and lingering tightness around his mouth when he smiled. She didn't know if his conversation with his parents hadn't gone well, if he was just tired or if he wasn't totally comfortable being part of the McDonnell Father's Day dinner.

He cleaned up, as promised, while Kelly visited with her parents in the living room. It only took him a few minutes, since *he* got away with only four plates, four forks, a pie server and an ice cream scoop.

When her mom tried to hide a yawn behind the shawl she was knitting—and had been knitting for at least three years—Kelly stood up and kissed each of her parents on the cheek. "I'm going to head home. I'm covering some odd hours in the next few days, so I need to get some sleep."

Chase followed her to the front door. "Let me give you a ride back to your place."

"Thanks, but I'm fine. I like walking, remember?" When she stepped out onto the porch, he was right behind her.

"It's dark now. You shouldn't be out walking alone after dark."

She laughed. "I'm a police officer, Chase. I can handle it."

He frowned, clearly not wanting to let the subject go. "It just doesn't feel right. Let me walk you home, at least, so I know you got there safely."

Being alone with Chase as close to her bed as her front door was a recipe for disaster, and she shook her head. "But then you'll have to walk back alone, and it's my job to protect and serve, you know."

"I'm not going to win this argument, am I?"

She smiled up at him and was struck by the sudden realization she was standing on her dad's front porch with Chase

Sanders, probably looking for all the world like a woman who expected to be kissed good night.

"Nope." Turning quickly, she almost ran down the steps, tossing him a wave over her shoulder. "Good night."

The cool night air and the walk did her some good, but she still spent too much time thinking about kissing Chase under the porch light instead of sleeping.

06

Chase spent the next few days close to the McDonnell home, helping Coach's wife with some projects around the house and yard. Not only did it give him something to do but, thanks to her busy schedule, it also kept him from crossing paths with the coach's daughter too often.

On Sunday night, when Kelly had smiled up at him under the porch light, he'd wanted so badly to kiss her. He was pretty sure his hand even twitched, as if it was going to reach out for her waist to pull her close. With her hair loose, he could have slid the other hand up the base of her neck and into the soft strands.

"What do you think?"

Chase jerked himself back into the present, which didn't include hot kisses and blond hair tangled in his fingers. Mrs. McDonnell was kneeling in front of the mulch she'd spread around the plants he'd been helping her put in the ground.

He cleared his throat. "It looks great."

"I appreciate the help. I've been after Walter for a month to help me set the bench and put this flower bed in."

It was jarring, hearing Coach's name. As far as he knew, Mrs. McDonnell was the only person who used it at all. He sat on the granite bench he'd assembled for her from the pieces that had been stashed in the garage and admired the flowers she'd put in the holes he dug. They were cheerful looking and all different colors, which was pretty much all he knew about flowers.

"So, how's work going for you?" she asked casually, turning her legs sideways so she was sitting in the grass.

Since she'd talked to his mother on the phone, he suspected Mrs. McDonnell already had a good idea of how work had been going. "I have a couple of jobs to do when I get back. Then we'll see. I'll either try to make a go of it on my own or I'll go find work with a bigger outfit. I haven't decided yet."

"It's hard to have a boss after working for yourself."

"Yeah, but on the flip side, all the worrying belongs to the boss. It'd be nice to just show up, pound some nails and then go home for a change. Let some other guy worry about getting permits and dealing with homeowners and chasing money."

It was something he'd been thinking a lot about. S & P Builders was dead. There was no doubt about that. Even if Seth was waiting when Chase got back to New Jersey, hat in one hand and their joint money in the other, that business relationship was over. But alone, he'd have to cut back on the size of the jobs he could take and some people, including financial institutions, didn't take one-man operations as seriously.

"Walter's been self-employed for decades," Mrs. McDonnell reminded him unnecessarily. "And we've had our ups and downs. Some pretty scary downs a time or two, even. You know you can always go to him for advice."

They'd already had a few conversations about Chase's situation, but Coach wasn't the kind of guy who had or gave the easy answers. He listened and asked questions and let a person work things out on his own. It was an invaluable quality, but not a fast process.

"We've been talking a bit," he said. "I'm trying not to rush into a decision."

"That's always the best approach." She stood and brushed off her jeans. "I'm going to go make some fresh lemonade because I think that's about all I had left on my list."

"I'm going to put the shovel and wheelbarrow and stuff back in the shed."

Being in the McDonnells' backyard, with its white fence and flower beds and big tool shed, made Chase wish he'd bought a house somewhere along the way. He could see the pride they took in their home, and he'd never felt that for any of the apartments he'd lived in. He wasn't sure if it was the fact that they were apartments or that he hadn't owned them, but he felt more of a connection to this place than he had to any of them.

"If it isn't the first champion running back for the Stewart Mills Eagles."

Chase turned and saw a man he didn't recognize at first coming toward him across the yard. Then the guy smiled and there was no doubt who he was.

It was Phil Parson, first champion kicker for the Stewart Mills Eagles. He had a hell of a lot less hair and a few more pounds, but the same goofy smile that made him look drunk even though he rarely touched alcohol.

"Philly!" Chase walked over and shook Phil's hand. "How the hell are you? And where have you been?"

"Mexico, believe it or not. The wife and I left the kids with her mom for a week since we never had a honeymoon. Second day she got so sick I can't even describe it."

"Feel free not to try."

"Ended up paying an ungodly amount to stay an extra day and even at that, the plane ride home was iffy. So I put her to bed and go get the kids because their grandma's had enough of them. I tell them to leave their mother be while I bring their bags in from the car, but they haven't seen her in a week, so I go upstairs and they're all snuggled together in my bed."

Chase didn't need a map to see where that was going. "Oh, no."

"Yeah. All three kids. And if there's one thing I've learned, it's not to leave a woman alone with sick kids to go have a beer with an old friend."

"But now you're back and ready to kick, right?"

"Well, I'm back." Phil grimaced. "As for kicking, I groan when I bend over to tie my shoes, and the last thing I kicked was a flat tire on my wife's minivan."

Chase laughed. "We were counting on you to win this game for us."

"Hell, I was hoping you'd just keep running it into the end zone. Anybody else here yet?"

"No. They're coming in . . ." Chase had to stop and think

about what day it was. "Today's Wednesday, so the day after tomorrow. I'm going to spend the day helping to build stuff for the street fair, and the lucky bastards will miss most of that. I'm going to talk them into dinner, though, before everybody heads off to wherever they're boarding for the week. Briscoe's not coming in until the middle of next week, I think. You in?"

"Hell yeah, I'm in!" Phil paused. "Probably. I should ask the wife. And I've gotta stop by Deck's place, so I'll ask him."

"Sounds like a plan."

"I'm going to head out. Geri's waiting for the stuff on the shopping list she gave me." He gave the goofy smile again. "It's good to see you, Sanders."

"You, too, Philly."

Once the kicker was gone, Chase closed the door to the shed and went inside to see how the lemonade was coming along. It *had* been good to see Phil. And it would be even better to see the rest of them. Once they were all back together, he'd have work to do and guys to talk to, and that would put an end to having time to think about Kelly McDonnell.

Kelly got a discouraging call from dispatch shortly after dark. Two teenagers—one male and one female—were having an argument on the covered bridge and it seemed to be escalating. She didn't bother with the lights and sirens, but parked on the cracked, weed-riddled asphalt that had been the mill's parking lot and walked over.

It was quiet, and for a moment she thought they'd left.

But then she saw a figure sitting on the picnic table and realized only one of them had left. She stepped onto the bridge, knowing the sound of her boots on the wood would signal her approach.

He turned and she saw it was Hunter Cass. With a sinking feeling in the pit of her stomach, Kelly stepped up onto the bench so she could sit next to him on top of the picnic table. He didn't say anything, so she let the silence ride for a bit.

"Molly and I had a fight," he said after a couple of minutes of fidgeting.

"I hear it got a little loud," she said. "Just yelling, right?"

"Yeah. I swear."

She knew him well enough to believe that, but she'd had to ask, anyway. "You want to talk about it?"

When he didn't say no, but only shrugged one shoulder, she waited him out. He wasn't shy about pushing people away or being a jerk, so it was obvious he was ready to confide in somebody. The air had cooled when the sun went down, and the mosquitoes weren't too bad, so she didn't mind sitting on the bridge, listening to the crickets sing.

Finally, he cracked. "I guess there are these charm bracelet things or something that all the girls want, and I told her I couldn't afford one and she got mad. And then she started talking about how much she hates this town and nobody has money to do anything fun anymore since the last mill closed. And how she can't even shop unless her grandparents send her gift cards. And I got mad because at least both of her parents still have jobs, you know?"

Kelly wished Jen were there instead of her. She'd probably know just what to say. "I know things are rough right now, but that makes it even more important to lean on each other.

Sometimes being in a relationship means letting the other person vent, even when you have your own troubles."

"You being an expert on relationships and all."

That hurt, but Kelly didn't allow the impact to show. Of course everybody in town knew about her divorce, and Hunter was just blindly lashing out with whatever weapon he had at hand. "It doesn't have to be a romantic relationship. It's true for family and friends, too."

He hung his head, looking at his hands dangling between his knees. "I'm sorry, Officer McDonnell. That was a shitty thing to say."

"Sometimes people say shitty things when they're hurt or angry or under stress. You do. I do. Molly and your dad do. If you push people away when you're miserable, you're still going to be miserable, but then you'll be alone, too. Trust me, that's worse."

He nodded. "I'll text her later."

"Good. Though make it later enough so you're sure she's home. No texting and driving at the same time."

He actually chuckled. "We know."

"We remind you all the time because we care. Jen . . . uh, Miss Cooper and I and all the other people you accuse of riding your asses, as you like to say, do it because we care. Not because it's our job. If it was just my job, I would have left as soon as I saw there was no more fight. You get that, right?" He nodded.

"I just want to play football." The sorrow in his voice threatened to break her heart. "I know I'm not good enough to play pro ball. Probably not even good enough for a top college. But if I can get a scholarship to one of the smaller schools, I'll be out of here."

"If you're hoping for a scholarship, kid, you can't be getting in trouble. They don't usually go for prospects with criminal records."

He looked at her then, his eyes shimmering with tears. "I don't wanna be like my dad, Officer McDonnell. He's mad all the time now."

"Your dad's a good guy, Hunter. I've known him a long time, so I can say that with certainty. He's going through a rough spot right now, and it's hard on his pride, to say nothing of his stress level. Things will turn around."

"I hope so." He hopped off the picnic table, signifying that he was done talking about it, and Kelly got up a little more slowly. She was getting a bit old for sitting on hard surfaces with no back support.

"I don't see a vehicle. You're not planning on walking, are you?" Not only was it a bad road to walk in the dark, but a teenager in his current frame of mind could get into all kinds of trouble.

"We were in Molly's mom's car, but she took off. I was waiting to see if she'd come back—like maybe she'd drive around and get over it—but I was only going to give it another five minutes or so before I started walking."

"I'll give you a ride home."

He started shaking his head before she even got all the words out, his eyes wide. "If I come home in a cruiser, my dad will sh . . . have a fit."

"You can ride in the front and we'll tell them you were helping me sort through the Eagles Fest decoration contest entries and I drove you home." He didn't look convinced. "I don't want you walking on that road after dark. That's all there is to it."

"Okay," he said, but his reluctance was still obvious.

She waited until they were in the cruiser and on the road—so he couldn't get mad and walk away—before speaking again. "How bad are things at home, Hunter?"

He stared out the passenger window. "They're okay."

"Is your home a safe place for you?"

His head whipped around. "What's that supposed to mean?"

"It's just a question. Are you scared to go home?"

She waited for a smart-ass answer or maybe another cheap shot aimed at her personal life, but he just slumped back in his seat. "No. I mean, I don't want my parents to get pissed a cop brought me home, but I'm not scared. It's not like that."

"Okay. You know you can come to me or Miss Cooper or Coach anytime you need to talk. There won't be any freak-outs or confrontations. Just talking."

"Thanks."

When she pulled into his driveway, the lights were on, but nobody opened the door or—as far as she could tell—even looked through the curtains. Just in case, she swung to the left so anybody watching could clearly see him get out of the front seat. Then she gave him a smile and a wave, waiting until he was inside the house before turning around and heading back out.

After she dropped Hunter off, Kelly drove the roads of Stewart Mills for a while, but all was quiet. The radio was completely silent and her cell didn't ring. Her own thoughts weren't good company at the moment—especially after the shot about her relationship with her ex-husband—so she decided to swing by Eagles Lane and see what her parents were up to. It was a little late for company, but she knew they wouldn't have gone to bed yet. And she wasn't really company, anyway. She even had her own room in the house still, though she regretted that thought because it made her remember Chase was sleeping in her bed.

The garage door was closed, but the porch light was still on, so she pulled in next to Chase's truck and killed the engine. The front door wasn't locked, because no matter how often she lectured them, her parents only locked the house when they were going out of town. And even then, they told half the town where the spare key was hidden, "just in case."

The television was on in the living room, but there was no sign of people, which was surprising. It was definitely the time of night when her dad was in his recliner, pretending to watch TV while he napped, and her mother would be in her chair, pretending to knit while she really just watched TV and held the needles.

When she heard a noise coming from the kitchen, she went that direction and found Chase half in the pantry closet, rummaging around. "She keeps the good stuff in the cabinet above the fridge, behind the light bulbs."

He whirled around and she realized he hadn't heard her come in. She must still be subconsciously avoiding the squeaky spots in the old wood floors.

"Why do they do that?" he asked. "I think all moms hide their stashes behind the light bulbs in the highest cabinet. It's not a very good secret hiding place."

"Women should hide stuff with the extra toilet paper,

because *that's* a secret location. Did my parents go to bed already?"

"No, they went to . . . somebody's house to see pictures of their new grandkid and eat dessert or something."

"With that kind of detail, you should do my police reports for me."

He grinned sheepishly. "Honestly, I mentally checked out at the words *slide show* and *new grandbaby*."

She couldn't say she blamed him. "Did they say when they'd be back?"

"No, but they've been gone awhile and they're not exactly night owls."

"Okay." Awkwardness settled between them. By the time her parents got home, they'd probably be ready to go to bed, so waiting around didn't make a lot of sense. But turning around and walking out on Chase because they weren't home seemed rude.

He held up a bag. "Want some peanuts?"

"All the food my mom has in there and you bring out peanuts?"

"I like peanuts."

It was such a random conversation, she didn't know what to say. "Okay. So do I, but no. I'm all set."

He tossed the bag on the table and sat down. "So what brings you over here so late? Late being relative, of course, but you're obviously on duty."

"Just looking for a pep talk, I guess." She leaned against the counter and crossed one ankle over the other. "You know Coach is good at those."

"Tough night?"

She shrugged one shoulder, but he waited her out. And

he looked sincerely interested—almost concerned—so she found herself telling him about her visit to the bridge. No names, of course, but enough to give him a sense of the discouragement and frustration growing in Stewart Mills.

He got up halfway through and got them each a soda from the fridge, handing her one. She didn't normally drink caffeine except when she first woke up, because she sometimes had to sleep weird hours, but her mouth was dry and she could use the pick-me-up.

"Listening is probably all you can do," he said, leaning his hip against the counter so he was facing her. "It makes a difference, you know. You could have hassled him or ordered him to go home, but you cared enough to let him talk it out. Even if he doesn't consciously know it, it really matters."

"If we can't save the team, it's going to get worse," she said, setting her half-full can down. The caffeine was okay, but the sugar was too much. "Ugh. I'm starting to sound like a broken record."

"No, you sound like a woman who cares a lot about her town and the people living in it, especially the kids."

When he moved closer and put his hand on her shoulder, she stiffened under his touch. Alarm bells went off in her head—she should put some distance between them immediately—but it was a gesture of comfort, and comfort was what she'd come looking for.

Then his hand slid up to cup the back of her neck, while the fingers of his other hand laced through hers, and she knew she was in trouble. Looking into his eyes, there was no doubt he intended to kiss her. But he held back, not tugging at her neck at all while he waited.

To hell with it, she thought, closing the small distance between them and tilting her face up. His mouth closed over hers as she slid her free hand up his back, and the hand on the back of her neck tightened.

When his tongue flicked over her bottom lip, she shivered. He tasted like sugary soda, but she didn't care. All she cared about was his mouth and his tongue dancing over hers and his hand on her neck.

"I've wanted to kiss you since the first night I got here," he said against her lips, his voice low and husky.

Her fingernails bit into his back, but she didn't say anything. She didn't want to talk. She wanted him to keep kissing her until her knees were weak and she couldn't breathe.

"You are so sweet," he murmured, and then he nipped at her lower lip. "I'd like to take you up against the wall right now."

Her breath caught in her throat and she opened her eyes. How could he know how badly she wanted that?

Chase let go of her hand and lifted his hand to her rib cage, only to find the unforgiving hardness of the bulletproof vest under her uniform shirt.

He growled in frustration. "This vest *has* to go. And it can't be comfortable."

"I'm used to it," she said, but the reminder she was on duty sparked horror that burned through the haze of desire. She put her hands on his forearms and pushed them down. What the hell was she doing? "This can't happen."

"You're right." He blew out a breath and shoved his hand through his hair. "You're Coach's daughter."

Anger pushed the lingering frustration of sexual need to the back burner. "Excuse me?"

"I can't mess around with Coach's daughter. And in his own house, for chrissake. You're off-limits to me, but I have a hard time remembering that when I'm around you."

"Flattering, but very wrong. *Coach's daughter* is not my identity, and that's not why this"—she pointed from him to herself—"is not happening. It can't happen because I'm not going to be ground up in the rumor mill because I slept with one of the guys who are basically Stewart Mills' current versions of rock stars. Especially while I'm on duty."

His jaw clenched and released. "Fine. That's your reason this can't happen. My reason it can't happen is that I don't want to disrespect a man who means the world to me."

"Why don't you just leave my dad out of it?"

"That's kind of hard when we're standing in his kitchen."

She shook her head. Sure, she was a little embarrassed to have behaved like that in her parents' house, but that was because they were her parents, not because her dad was *Coach*. "Let me make it easy for you. I'm leaving, so you can stand here in his kitchen all by yourself."

He said her name, but she didn't bother turning back. And she thanked whatever stars kept her parents out late enough that she could get the cruiser out of their neighborhood before they got home. They definitely would have flagged her down, and the last thing she wanted to do was talk to anybody.

She'd had more than enough talking for one night.

07

By Friday afternoon, Chase was questioning whether or not he'd been crazy to agree to come back to Stewart Mills. He was hot and tired, and would happily spend the rest of his life free of teenagers.

He'd reported to the town hall that morning to get instructions from Alice Dubois, who had volunteered to oversee the street fair. Her instructions amounted to explaining to him what she wanted and telling him to go do it, so he'd rounded up the boys and gotten to work.

It had taken them almost two hours just to lug all the booths and tables the town used for Old Home Day out of the storage area, and then they needed to be sorted into the locations Alice had marked on a very badly hand-drawn map before being assembled.

Now he was trying to finish off the assembly of the town's

ancient dunking booth—which Alice had warned him hadn't been used in years—by himself, because he was a sucker and had finally let the boys go dig up a late lunch.

And they didn't have one of those lightweight plastic jobs you could rent for parties. No, Stewart Mills wasn't going to spend money when they had an almost perfectly good monstrosity from the sixties made up of heavy wood and metal.

When he'd finally gotten it placed according to Alice's map, he realized the only way to fill the tank would be with buckets by hand, which would take about two months. After looking around, he found a water spigot, probably used to water the town square if need be, and moved the damn thing so they could use a hose, which he borrowed from the hardware store.

He'd finally gotten the trigger mechanisms to work properly and was up on a ladder, trying to hang the old sign that advertised it was a dunking booth, just in case it wasn't obvious. The sign wasn't really necessary—especially since the thin wood it was made of was drying and splitting, and he was having to work around that—but he had fuzzy memories of the tank being used a time or two when he was a kid, and he liked the old sign.

When he paused, turning his head to stretch his neck, he saw Kelly across the town square, and it looked as though she was looking for somebody. It probably wasn't him, since they hadn't spoken at all since she'd stormed out of Coach's kitchen.

One the one hand, he hoped it *was* him but, on the other, she was in uniform. Official police business was rarely fun.

Through the corner of his eye, he watched her approach.

Maybe it was a combination of the boots, vest and weight of her belt, but she seemed to walk with an extra-sexy sway when in uniform.

When she stopped at the bottom of the ladder, he smiled down at her. "Good afternoon, Officer McDonnell."

She put her hands on her hips and squinted up at him before adjusting the brim of her hat. "I should write you a citation for being disruptive in public."

"Unless Stewart Mills got a noise ordinance along with all those shiny stop signs, this is feeling like harassment."

When she smiled, he felt a rush of relief. Wednesday night had ended so badly, he hadn't been sure how things would go the next time they bumped into each other. Besides the fact that he didn't want to explain to his hosts why he and their daughter weren't speaking, he liked talking to Kelly. He didn't want a kiss—even one that had shaken the hell out of him—to ruin the budding friendship he thought they had.

"Mrs. Clark bumped into Mrs. Davidson, making her drop her eggs, which led to a verbal altercation. According to the complaint, it was your fault."

"I've been on this ladder for an hour, Officer. I'm innocent."

She waved her hand in a gesture that made him look down at himself. Okay, so he was a bit of a mess. He'd taken his T-shirt off a while back and tossed it to the ground. And, because he didn't have his tool belt, the hammer and various other tools hooked on his pockets were dragging his jeans down a little. He swiped at the sweat coating his chest and looked back at Kelly.

Just in time to see the way she was looking at him before

she put her cop face back on. Understanding dawned and he grinned.

"Mrs. Clark wasn't watching where she was going, huh?"

She rolled her eyes. "Don't get yourself too puffed up. She's seventy if she's a day."

Chase had intended to try to get another screw or two into the dunk tank sign, but it was good enough. Since the battery drill he'd borrowed from Coach had run out of juice, he'd been using a regular screwdriver, and he'd had about enough of that. He climbed down the ladder and stood in front of Kelly. "How does it look?"

"Old. Are you sure it's safe?"

"It might look a little shabby, but structurally she's still good to go. I just need to turn on the hose and fill it up while I grab a quick bite to eat. Have you had lunch?"

The amusement on her face changed to uncertainty. "I'm on duty."

"Which I assume includes meal breaks, since you need to keep your strength up if you're going to chase down criminals." He didn't think it had anything to do with being on duty and everything to do with their kiss in the kitchen. "I wasn't asking you out on a date. I planned to grab a couple of steamed hot dogs at the gas station and sit on the picnic table while I watch for leaks in the tank."

Her expression cleared. "I could go for a dog right about now. How about I go get the hot dogs and a couple of sodas while *you* put your damn shirt back on so the women in this town can get back to what they're supposed to be doing instead of watching you."

He grinned. "Yes, ma'am."

As he watched her walk away, appreciating that extra

sway in the hips, he wondered if Officer McDonnell had been one of the women watching him instead of doing what *she* was supposed to be doing.

Snatching his T-shirt off the ground, he walked over to the spigot. Before attaching the hose, though, he turned the water on and stuck his head under the flow to cool himself off. Then he splashed some of the frigid water across his chest before turning it off.

When he pushed his arms through his T-shirt sleeves and tucked his thumbs into the neck hole to pull it over his head, he caught a glimpse of Kelly, who had stopped at the curb and was looking back at him. He grinned and pulled the shirt on, and by the time he could see again, she'd turned away.

Kelly paid for the hot dogs and sodas, calling herself every variation of *idiot* she could think of the entire time. After their kiss in her parents' kitchen, she should be avoiding Chase, not having a picnic lunch with him.

Avoiding him was easier said than done, though. Besides the fact that he was an honored Eagles Fest guest and was staying with her dad, he was in the town square. Not crossing paths with him would be harder than simply pretending the other night had never happened.

For instance, just a few minutes before when she'd started across the square before spotting him, and he'd seen her first. Turning around would have been obvious, and she refused to give him the satisfaction of her running away. Of course he had to be shirtless and glistening with sweat at the time, because that was just her luck.

"Kelly?"

She jerked her attention back to the change being offered to her, embarrassed to have been caught staring out the window, lost in thought. "Sorry. I was just running my to-do list through my head."

The lie made her face feel hot as she realized she'd mixed Chase with *to-do list.* She was not doing Chase. Period.

By the time she made the long walk back to the picnic table where Chase was waiting for her—thankfully fully clothed—Kelly had herself back under control. He was a volunteer, working to make Eagles Fest a success alongside everybody else, and she was bringing him a steamed hot dog. No big deal. She'd do the same for anybody.

She sat on the picnic table bench across from him, but a little offset so they wouldn't find themselves in an accidental game of footsie under the table, and set the two bags in the middle of the table. "I got packets of everything, since I forgot to ask what you like on them."

She pulled the cold sodas out of one bag while he unpacked the hot dogs and made quick work of drowning his in ketchup, mustard and relish. "I would have grabbed extra napkins if I'd known you were going to use *all* of the condiments. You're going to be a mess."

He looked at the hot dog and then grinned. "You're right. Maybe I should take my shirt off while I eat so I don't get mustard stains on it."

"And maybe I should write you up for running that stop sign, after all." He was flirting with her and she had no idea how to handle that. Not while she was still having to make a deliberate effort *not* to think about his kiss and his hand on her neck and how he wanted to take her up against the wall.

"The statute of limitations on something like that is probably about five minutes." He took a bite of the hot dog and then swiped at a dot of mixed condiments on his lip. "I haven't had a steamed dog in ages. I forgot how good they are. So, should we talk about the other night?"

The abrupt change in subject startled her. "No."

"Okay."

They watched the dunk tank filling very slowly with water while they ate their hot dogs, and Kelly felt the awkwardness looming large between them. She hated it. And there was no reason for it. They were two adults and they'd kissed.

"Fine, let's talk about it," she said when Chase had shoved their napkins and empty condiment packages into one of the bags. "Being Coach's daughter is both wonderful and a total pain in the ass at the same time. All my life, it's felt like people . . . I don't know how to explain it. I don't have a different standard, per se, but I feel like I'm more visible. Everybody knows who I am and who my dad is. So when I'm alone with a guy, being called the coach's daughter—having it be the reason I'm pushed away—pisses me off."

"You pushed first, just for the record." Chase stretched his legs out, leaning his elbows on the tabletop. "And I'm sorry I pissed you off, but it's hard for me to separate the two of you, because he means so much to me. When I look at you, I see a sexy, confident woman who's amazing, and I want you so bad it hurts sometimes. But I love your dad, Kelly. I love and respect that man, and you're the most important thing in the world to him. That matters."

Kelly absorbed his words, trying to focus more on the

emotional confession than the fact that he wanted her so badly it hurt. "I guess I can see that."

"Maybe if my life wasn't in the shitter and my intentions were more . . . honorable, I wouldn't have a problem. But you're not a woman I can mess around with lightly, and that's all I've got to offer." He turned his head to look her in the eye. "And even if I could put all that aside, I'm not what you're looking for long-term, and you're not looking to have a fling that'll put you in the gossips' line of fire. Right?"

"Right." She felt as if she should say more, but he'd managed to sum up the situation pretty well.

"So we kissed. It happens."

"It was a great kiss."

His gaze dropped to her mouth. "Yeah, it was."

Just thinking about it made her want to do it again but, even if they hadn't been in one of the most public spots in Stewart Mills, the kissing was over. "How's the street fair coming along?"

He shrugged and looked out across the grass again. "My part's about done. Once the tank is full and I've made sure it doesn't leak, I'll cover it and head back to your parents' house to clean up. I'm looking forward to seeing the guys again. Murphy and Leavitt should be here soon, from what I hear."

She nodded. "Alex texted me when he found Sam, and they were on their way out of the airport. That was about two hours ago, so it'll be at least another hour. Probably more like two, with Friday night traffic."

"Yeah, they're going to meet Jen in the school parking lot so she can take them to where they're staying. Then, after they settle in, they're going to pick me up so we can go out and catch up over supper."

Kelly nodded and then drained the last of her soda. "Break's over, I guess."

"Somebody could be having a verbal altercation over spilled milk right now," he teased, standing and gathering the garbage, which he tossed into the nearby trash.

"You're funny." She tossed the empty can into the recycling bucket next to the garbage and gave him a stern look. "I'll see you later. And keep your shirt on."

"Yes, ma'am."

She really liked the way he said that.

Because Sam texted him when he and Alex hit the town line, Chase was watching for them and stepped out onto the porch when the navy sedan pulled into the driveway.

When the two men got out, Chase felt a surge of emotion he hadn't expected. Sure, they'd been his teammates and his high school buddies, but then they'd all gone their separate ways and eventually lost touch. He hadn't realized he'd missed them until now.

They looked remarkably the same and yet different at the same time. Sam was more rugged than he'd been as their quarterback, and whatever he did for work was obviously physically demanding. His brown hair was cut short enough that the barber probably skipped scissors and went straight for the clippers, and he was wearing at least a day's worth of scruff.

Alex had changed even more than Sam. He'd been a very big guy in high school, the star of their defensive line, but now he looked lean and strong. Where Sam looked like he'd just come off a construction site, in worn jeans and a faded T-shirt, Alex wore a button-down shirt and jeans that looked so new, Chase wondered if he'd bought them just for the trip. His dark hair had what Chase always thought of as a business cut, and he was clean shaven.

Seeing the changes in them made Chase feel old, but he consoled himself with the fact that they looked like they could still kick some ass, so maybe he could, too.

He met them at the curb, and both handshakes turned into a quick hug. "I can't believe it's been so long since I've seen you guys."

Sam scowled. "I can't believe it's been so long since Murph stopped at a bathroom."

"When you travel as much as I do, you get used to holding it for longer than a four-year-old can."

It was like they'd never been apart. They'd all been friends—practically brothers—but the bickering between Murphy and Leavitt was part of the soundtrack of their high school years. "Come on in and see Coach."

That reunion ate up almost a half hour, until Chase was so hungry he couldn't stand it anymore, having burned off the hot dogs a long time ago. He'd already told Mrs. McDonnell they were going out on the town, so she didn't bother with a big dinner. She just kissed each man on the cheek and told them to have a good time and that Chase shouldn't worry about waking them if they were out late.

O'Rourke's offered good food and beer, but they ended up going to the Stewart Mills House of Pizza just because they'd spent so much time there during their teen years. There was something about being all together again that brought out the nostalgia.

Decker and Philly joined them, so the only guy they were waiting on for the big game was John Briscoe. Chase spent a couple of minutes wondering about their other teammates—the ones who hadn't come—but then he put them out of his mind. There were a million reasons a guy couldn't put his life on hold even for a few days to play an exhibition game against a bunch of high school kids, and he wouldn't hold it against them. These were the guys who had come back for Coach's sake and that was all that mattered.

"It feels a little unreal, being back here," Sam said when they'd knocked the hell out of three large pizzas and a pitcher and a half of beer, with sodas for Sam.

Chase wanted to ask him if he'd see his mother while he was in town, but it wasn't the time. They were laughing and reminiscing about their glory days, and Sam's parents didn't fall in the happy memories of Stewart Mills category.

"Brings it all back," Alex said. "I don't know if I've ever had a moment better than the second I realized we'd actually won the damn game."

"When Briscoe caught that pass and you threw that block so he could get in the end zone," Deck said, "I couldn't believe it. Even when they signaled the touchdown. I mean, who the hell thought we could win a championship?"

"Coach did," Sam said quietly.

Chase nodded, then took a swig of his beer. After the final whistle blew and the crowd was going wild, Coach had gathered his team at the bench. *I never doubted you boys for a minute.* It was only the second time in his life Chase felt as if he'd made a person he loved proud. The first time had been busting his ass on an English essay his senior year and getting to hand Mrs. McDonnell the graded paper with a big A minus circled at the top. She'd hugged him hard and then baked a cake for him.

"I wonder if Coach believes we can win *this* game," Alex said, and they all laughed.

"I know I wasn't the best student ever to go through Stewart Mills High, but I count six old guys," Sam said.

"The rest of the *old guys* team will be filled in with school staff and a few dads, I guess," Chase said.

Alex leaned forward. "What about any guys who played for the Eagles and graduated last year? Technically, they're alumni, and if some went away to college, they're home for the summer right now. Let the young kids take the hits."

Chase shook his head. "I tried that. There has to be some affiliation to the championship team, even if they were just sitting in the stands watching the game. The school custodian's going to play. He was in the band the year we won."

"This would be a great high school revenge plot. Luring the jocks home in a secret plan to pummel them on the field they once owned," Sam said. He frowned at Chase. "We didn't piss those girls off in some way back then, did we?"

"I don't think so. And it's a little extravagant for revenge." Although if anybody could come up with a scheme like this, it would be Kelly, Jen and Gretchen.

"Revenge plot or fund-raiser." Alex refilled his mug and then emptied the beer pitcher into Chase's. "Either way, it's going to hurt."

08

After Jen had made sure Alex and Sam were settled with their host families, Kelly, Jen and Gretchen decided to have an unscheduled Eagles Fest meeting at the Walker farm for the simple reason that Gram Walker had made macaroni salad. It was creamy and tangy, with chunks of ham and some secret ingredient that Kelly had never been able to figure out, but really wanted to.

Gram, who still lived her life on a milking schedule even though she'd had neither a husband nor cows for more than a few years, had already eaten and retired to her chair in the TV room to watch the evening news before she went to bed, so the women took heaping bowls of the macaroni salad into the dining room to talk.

"I finally found a printer for the discount cards," Jen said after they'd all enjoyed a few bites. "We'll have them in time for the street fair."

That was a huge relief. It had taken a lot of door-to-door schmoozing to get the local businesses to take part in the discount program. If a person bought the card for ten dollars, with the entire amount going to the Eagles, he or she would get 5 percent off at many places in Stewart Mills until the last day of October. But finding a printer willing to donate services hadn't been as simple.

"You should get a trophy when this is over," Gretchen told Jen.

"Trophies cost money," Jen said. "But when this is over, I won't say no to a really cheap cocktail."

Kelly knew Gretchen wasn't exaggerating. Jen spent hours searching the Internet, looking for forms to fill out to request grants from numerous football-related foundations. She'd emailed the contact person for every current or former NFL player she could find with a connection to the state, or even to New England, and knocked on any door that might lead to a donation.

"Maybe we can buy a used trophy and write your name on it with a Sharpie," Kelly said, and they all laughed.

"I'll leave the trophies to the football team," Jen said. "Unless it's made of chocolate. Then I'll take it."

Kelly swallowed her last bite of macaroni salad and pushed her bowl away. "Speaking of chocolate, did either of you say anything to Chase about my sex life?"

Jen looked shocked, and then her expression changed to offended. "Of course not. I resent that question."

"Sorry," she mumbled.

"I didn't, either," Gretchen said. "But now I'm dying to

know what made you ask us. Especially since, as far as we know, you don't *have* a sex life."

And now Kelly didn't want to tell them. She should have accepted the fact that it was a weird coincidence and kept her mouth shut, but it was too late now. "He said he wanted to take me up against the wall."

Jen sat up straight. "And did you say *yes, please*?"

"Of course not." Kelly smiled. "I might have thought it, though."

"You could have just said *you, up against the wall, right now.*" Jen tilted her head. "Come to think of it, you've probably said that before."

"You're hilarious. And I don't want him up against the wall. I want *me* up against the wall."

Gretchen shook her head. "Since you've obviously given this scenario some thought, I'm seriously sad you threw away the perfect opportunity to make that dirty little fantasy come true."

So was Kelly, though she'd rather not admit it. "You already know I have a good reason for why I won't have sex with Chase."

"No," Jen said. "We know why you don't want a long-term relationship with him. And we know why you *think* you shouldn't have sex with him, but we disagree on it being a good reason."

"What are you girls talking about?"

They all jumped. Partly because they hadn't heard Mrs. Walker come into the room and partly because Gretchen's grandmother had caught them talking about sex. Kelly wasn't sure there was ever an age when that didn't feel awkward.

"Nothing, Gram," they all said at the same time, which was probably even more suspicious than the fact that they'd all jumped when she spoke.

"So boys, then." She looked at each of them in turn, then zeroed in on Kelly. "Any special young man in particular?"

"No, ma'am."

"I heard that Sanders boy is back in town, and he bought condoms at the drugstore."

Kelly was vaguely aware of Jen almost spitting her drink all over Gretchen and barely choking it down in time, but all she could do was try to meet Mrs. Walker's look with a straight face. "I hadn't heard that."

"He's up to no good, that one." Gram nodded. "I'm going to bed to read. You girls clean up after yourselves."

They managed to hold back the giggles until they heard her footsteps reach the top of the stairs and disappear in the direction of her bedroom. Then they laughed, trying to muffle the sound with their hands.

"I can never un-hear your grandmother saying *condoms*," Jen said when they'd regained their composure.

"A whole box of them, even," Kelly said, putting her hand on her stomach because it ached from laughing and eating too much macaroni salad. When both women turned their gazes on her, she shook her head. "Don't look at me."

"Since I've seen *Chase* looking at you," Jen said, "I'm going to guess you're the only woman he was thinking about when he bought them."

Gretchen held up her hand. "Back up for a minute. I want to know the circumstances of him telling you he wanted to take you up against the wall. Did he tell you that over coffee?

Write it on a napkin? Just randomly blurt it out when you walked by?"

"We were . . . kissing." And just the memory of it still made her weak in the knees. "In my parents' kitchen."

"I can't believe you didn't tell us *immediately* that you were kissing him," Jen said, and Gretchen nodded.

"It didn't really end well." She told them how the post-kiss conversation had gone. "He looks at me and sees Coach's daughter and not Kelly."

"It's natural for him to worry about disrespecting your dad because he means so much to Chase," Gretchen said, being her usual reasonable self.

Jen nodded. "But his need to take you up against the wall is going to get the better of him very soon and, when that happens, you need to let him."

"I am not going to have sex with Chase Sanders."

Gretchen snorted. "You just keeping telling yourself that."

Kelly rolled her eyes, but she'd been doing exactly that pretty much since she'd pulled Chase over for blowing the stop sign on his way into town. If she kept saying it to herself over and over, maybe she'd start believing it.

Ordering another pitcher of beer was probably a mistake, Chase thought. As hot and tired as he'd been all day, the alcohol seemed to be hitting him a little harder than usual, and he'd reached that state of pleasant buzzing in which the greatest ideas of all time were spawned.

Deck and Philly had split before the last pitcher because

they had wives and kids waiting for them, but the three that were left weren't ready to call it a night yet. Since there weren't any other options, they were still sitting at the Stewart Mills House of Pizza, drinking and talking.

"I thought by now there'd be something to do in this town," Alex said. "I always thought we hung out and drank beer because we were young. Now I realize it's because there's literally nothing else to do."

"We should head out soon, anyway," Sam said. "We're guests in people's homes, and even though they said they'd leave the doors unlocked, we shouldn't stay out too late."

Chase rocked his chair back onto two legs. "Look who learned some manners while he was . . . where the hell were you, again?"

"Texas. And screw you, Sanders."

"He's right," Alex said. "But a few more minutes won't hurt."

Chase set his chair down with a thump so he could refill his mug. The frost had long since melted off the glass, but he was too lazy to walk up to the counter and get a fresh one.

"I can't believe Coach's daughter is a cop," Sam said. "I always thought she'd be a librarian."

Chase snorted, even as the phrase *Coach's daughter* caught in his mind. Kelly was right. Her identity was always wrapped up with her dad's. "Why the hell would you think that?"

"She was always reading, remember?"

"I remember she didn't like me very much, so I mostly ignored her."

Alex shook his head. "I think she liked you more than you think. And since you were too busy dating cheerleaders, she pretended she didn't like you so nobody would know."

"You've been watching too much afternoon television, my friend," Chase said, but it was an intriguing idea.

Had Kelly McDonnell had a crush on him back in high school? Not that it would have mattered. Even if he hadn't been going steady with Janie Vestal, he would have been too afraid of Coach to risk dating his daughter.

Hell, he was still afraid to date—so to speak—Coach's daughter, as he'd so badly proven in the kitchen. But if she'd had a crush on him then and had thought about him over the years, she probably still wanted him more than she was willing to admit.

There had been no hesitation in her kiss. She'd enjoyed it as much as he had. And he'd seen the heat in her eyes and the hitch in her breath when he'd said he wanted to take her up against the wall. That desire was just as mutual as wanting the kiss.

But they were in a good place right now. They'd talked through the awkwardness and they each acknowledged the other wasn't the right person. It didn't stop him from wanting her, but he hoped like hell it would help keep him from showing it.

"Earth to Sanders," he heard Sam say.

"Huh?"

"Considering the conversation, I'm real interested in where your thoughts went just now."

Chase snorted, as if Sam was totally off base. "I was thinking about football and wondering if any of us remember the old play calls."

"Shit, I barely remember how we line up on the field," Alex said.

Sam laughed. "That's easy for me. I stand behind the guy

squatting over the ball and pray like hell I don't fumble the snap."

"Kelly said we'll have access to the field next week to practice if we want," Chase said. "I think we should take her up on that offer."

"We don't have a chance in hell of beating those kids," Sam said. "But I'd like to not embarrass myself."

"I've heard that before." Chase took a swallow of beer. "We didn't have a chance in hell of beating those kids for the championship back in the day, either, but we did."

Both guys stared at him for a few seconds, then burst out laughing. He joined in because no amount of guts or inspirational speeches would get them past a team of well-coached teenage boys. But that didn't mean he was going to let them steamroll over him, either. So a few years had passed since he and the others had played ball together. Didn't change the fact that they'd been pretty damn good at it once.

"We really do need to get out of here," Alex said. "If we don't leave now, we'll need more beer, and I don't want to forget how to get to the Bartons' house."

"It's a little awkward when everybody goes to bed and you're not tired," Chase warned. "I've got a stash of snacks and magazines in my room to kill time until I'm tired, but hopefully your families aren't the early-to-bed, early-to-rise types."

"I'm a night owl," Alex said, "but I have my laptop, so I can work if they go to bed early."

"I'm one of those early-to-bed types," Sam said, and then looked at the old-fashioned clock that had hung on the wall for as long as they could remember. "Though maybe not this early."

"You know, I have a great idea," Alex said, his voice low so he couldn't be overheard, and Chase leaned in closer. He was in just the right mood for a great idea.

Kelly's cell phone rang mere seconds after she'd finished tying the drawstring waist of her favorite pair of sweats, and she knew without looking at the screen it would be the night dispatcher. "Hello?"

"I know you're not on duty and it's late, but we have a situation and I thought you might want to handle it yourself."

Scenarios began running through her mind. Her parents were first, but dispatch would have opened with that. Hunter Cass, maybe. A break-in at Gretchen's farm. The possibilities were endless. "What's the situation?"

"Earlier tonight, Chase Sanders, Alex Murphy and Sam Leavitt were at the pizza place and they were drinking with a couple of the other guys."

Kelly frowned. Had they gotten in a fight? If any of the guys from town had caused trouble for their guests, she'd ticket the offenders if they so much as jaywalked for the rest of their lives.

"We just got a call," the dispatcher continued, "and it seems like the three of them might be trying to break into the high school."

She dropped her forehead to the palm of her hand with a thud. "You're kidding. Those idiots."

"Yeah. That's why I called you instead of putting out the radio call."

"I appreciate that. I'll take care of it."

She didn't bother putting on her uniform and shoved her

bare feet into her sneakers before grabbing a flashlight. It's not as if she'd be shooting anybody, although she wouldn't mind giving Chase a quick jolt of the stun gun in the ass. What the hell were they thinking?

It was less than a mile to the school and a route she ran regularly, so she jogged to the high school and walked around the perimeter. Since she didn't see the guys, she assumed they'd made it inside. If she didn't find an access point, she'd break down and text Chase, but for now she swept the exterior of the old brick building with her flashlight.

It didn't take her long to find it. In a recessed area where the Dumpsters were parked and the kids were discouraged from going, there were two windows at ground level that went into the mechanical room. They hadn't been updated yet, and the guys had actually managed to pull the ancient window out of its casing.

Shaking her head, she went to the closest door and used her master key to let herself in. After orienting herself and plotting the quickest route to the gym, she jogged through the halls.

She heard them before she saw them, laughing and talking in a low enough rumble so she couldn't make out the words. Switching off the flashlight, she gave her eyes a few seconds to adjust to the moon shining through the scattered and high windows, and then stepped up behind them.

"Police," she said in a stern voice. "Turn around."

They all pivoted at once and she had to bite back a laugh when Chase and Alex bounced off each other in the process. They'd definitely had a couple of drinks too many with their supper.

"Officer McDonnell," Chase said in that low, sexy voice she heard in her dreams. "You're out of uniform."

She pointed to the Stewart Mills PD emblem on the chest of her zip-up hoodie. "Close enough."

Alex Murphy folded his arms over his chest and scowled. "We walked instead of driving, so we didn't do anything wrong."

She raised her eyebrow, forcing herself not to smile. "Really?"

"Yeah. The car's still parked in front of the House of Pizza, so you can just go away."

Sam, who looked sober, elbowed him in the ribs. "You should stop talking now."

"She's giving me the cop look."

Chase snorted and she turned that look on him. "I was about two minutes from curling up on my couch with a bowl of ice cream and the TV remote when I got the call three drunken morons were breaking into the school. Don't push me."

"I don't drink," Sam said. "Only two drunken morons were breaking into the school."

"So your excuse is . . . ?"

He shrugged. "Didn't seem like a good idea to let them come alone."

"So you're just here to chaperone this little criminal trespassing field trip?"

Though it didn't affect her the way Chase's did, Sam's grin had a way of lighting up his hardened face. "Yes, ma'am."

She couldn't hold the smile back anymore. "If you don't drink, why is the car still at the pizza house?"

"In theory, walking here was more stealthy than driving."

"And no stop signs," Chase added.

"Yes, because a failure to stop is totally your biggest concern right now." She sighed and shook her head. "Let's go."

"We haven't seen the trophy case yet," Alex said.

"I'd be happy to bring you here during the day, with the principal's blessing, for a tour of the school."

"We're already here, though," Chase said, with all the sincerity of an intoxicated person whose logic made perfect sense to him.

"Illegally."

"If you'd stop arguing with us, we'd be done already and you could be eating ice cream," Chase continued. Then he gave her a half smile. "I really like ice cream."

Alex seemed very interested in a pep rally poster still taped to the wall, but Kelly didn't miss the way Sam looked from Chase to her and back again.

Chase leaned closer to her. "What law do I have to break to get handcuffed around here?"

"You should probably start exercising your right to remain silent," Sam said.

"She hasn't arrested me yet," Chase argued. "If she arrests me, she has to frisk me first."

"Fine," Kelly said, surrendering to the inevitable. "Let's go see the damn trophy case."

She led them through the dark hallways, using her flashlight to guide the way. When they came to the lobby area outside the gymnasium, the moon was shining through the skylights, so she switched it off and waved toward the trophy case.

The three men gathered in front of it in silence and Kelly

hung back. She didn't need to look, since she walked by it several times a week during her visits to the school. There were a variety of trophies in the case now, but the big one—the first one for football—was on the top shelf, with a framed photo of the team beside it. Mounted to the back of the case were several newspaper clippings.

THE STEWART MILLS EAGLES WIN!

A photo of her dad was in one of the articles, faded to a pale yellow now. He was in his Eagles polo, with his whistle around his neck and a ball cap on, and the joy and pride he'd had in his team shone on his face. It was the same photo she'd had next to her when she started making the phone calls to bring these guys home.

As she looked at the three of them, their heads bowed almost in reverence, she felt warmth seep through her. They'd all put their lives on hold to help her dad, and she wasn't sure she could ever thank them enough for that.

"We should steal the trophy," Alex said in what he probably thought was a low voice.

Idiots. "Okay, guys. Let's see if we can get you back to the car, which Sam is going to drive, by the way."

"You were a lot more fun back in high school," Alex said, and then he frowned. "No, wait. That was Courtney."

She gave him her best cop face and pointed down the hallway. "Go."

She managed to get them outside and, after locking the door behind her, was able to secure the back window with Sam's help. Then she pointed in the direction of the pizza place, and they started walking.

"We could go to the covered bridge and make out," Chase said when they'd gone maybe thirty yards.

"You're not my type," Alex said.

"I was talking to Kelly."

She rolled her eyes. "You have more of a chance with Alex."

"Dude, she's Coach's daughter," Sam said.

Kelly was getting tired of hearing that. Yes, she was proud to be the man's daughter, but she didn't want to be hoisted up onto whatever pedestal they'd put him on. "Right now, the only part of my life relevant to you three is my job. Keep it up and you'll sober up behind bars."

When they reached Alex's rental car, she waited while he pulled the key out of his pocket and handed it over to Sam. "I'll see you gentlemen at the street fair tomorrow. Bright and early."

She took a perverse satisfaction in their groans as she walked away.

09

Chase was a little slow getting out of bed the next morning, and only the mouthwatering scent of frying bacon wafting up to his room made him do it.

Too much beer. A great idea. Breaking into the school. Asking Kelly to go make out with him on the old covered bridge. Tripping up the stairs while trying to sneak into the McDonnell house. Not one of his finer nights.

He made quick work of showering and dressing for the day, choosing cargo shorts and the faded Eagles T-shirt he'd brought with him from New Jersey. He supposed that was a bright spot in his life, being able to fit in a shirt he'd worn in high school.

Coach was just sitting down with his breakfast plate when Chase walked into the kitchen. "Surprised to see you up this early, son."

Ouch. "I apologize again for the noise. And your daughter said she wanted to see the three of us bright and early for the street fair."

"When did you see Kelly?" Mrs. McDonnell asked from the stove, where she was frying eggs. He noticed she didn't fry them in the leftover bacon grease anymore, maybe out of deference to Coach's health, but they still looked delicious.

"Uh . . ." He wasn't awake enough yet to lie. "Last night, when she responded to the call we'd broken into the high school."

Coach almost choked on his coffee. "You do any damage?"

"No, sir. We just wanted to see the trophy again."

He felt like a teenager again, squirming under Coach's steady gaze, but then the man laughed and Chase relaxed. "Seeing you boys together again does an old man's heart good, but I thought you'd all have learned to stay out of trouble by now."

"There was beer."

"How many?"

"Three or four?" Chase replied, but Coach raised that eyebrow at him. "Pitchers."

"Sit down and eat," Mrs. McDonnell said, setting a plate and a cup of coffee in front of his chair. "You have a long day ahead of you, although it doesn't start until ten, no matter what Kelly said."

"Yes, ma'am." He dug in, scooping up egg yolk with the thick-sliced bread she baked at home. When she set a tall glass of orange juice and a couple of painkillers next to his coffee, he smiled his thanks.

To make up for his less-than-graceful entrance the night before, Chase cleared the table and washed the dishes when they were finished with breakfast, waving away Mrs. McDonnell's objections. When he was done, he stuck an Eagles ball cap on his head and walked toward the downtown area, since if Kelly could walk, so could he. And he wouldn't have to worry about parking his truck or it getting blocked in.

The sun was warm without being hot and the humidity was low, so it would be a perfect day for the street fair. He waved to the kids manning the tollbooth, which they were doing again for the weekend, and they all waved back. A lot of people greeted him by name and, for most of them, he could do the same.

There were all sorts of activities going on, and he couldn't help but be impressed by the way the town was pulling together for the football team. There was a garden club booth, with women selling flowers, along with a craft booth. A yard sale booth and a huge book sale. Everything was donated, with all the proceeds going to the Eagles.

The karaoke booth drew him in, as it had many others. It was fifty cents per song to perform, and there was a tip jar that would also go into the football fund at the end of the day. The citizens of Stewart Mills really loved to sing, he thought, though they did so with varying degrees of talent.

The realization that the fate of the Stewart Mills Eagles football team might come down to how much pocket change people could spare was a humbling one. Everybody was working their asses off, scraping for quarters and dollar bills, and they were smiling while they did it.

He saw Alex from a distance, taking pictures as always. The camera looked a lot more sophisticated than the junk one he'd had when they were kids, but Alex had always had an eye for photography. Chase thought it was pretty cool he'd managed to turn his childhood passion into a career.

Hunter and Cody walked by with an older couple, all of them laughing, and he waved. The man looked enough like Hunter for Chase to assume it was the boy's dad. After seeing the kid at the first Eagles Fest meeting he'd attended and then spending time with him off and on, he'd surmised Hunter was probably the boy Kelly had talked to on the covered bridge the other night, and it was good to see him having fun with his family. No matter what happened with the team, Stewart Mills needed a celebration.

After watching a dozen or so people mangle popular songs, Chase went to the lemonade stand, where they were charging a dollar per cup. After the supply costs were recouped, the profit would go in the kitty, too.

He bought a cup and, after wincing at the amount of sugar, walked across the town square to check on the dunk tank. It didn't appear to have sprung any leaks overnight, nor had it been messed with at all. He'd assumed it would be okay, since the kids most likely to mess with it were the kids who most needed it.

"You going to take a turn in that?"

He turned to see Decker with his wife and kids, all of them eating brownies. "I haven't been asked to and I hope to keep it that way. Where did you get the goodies?"

"Bake sale booth," one of Deck's sons muttered around a mouthful of brownie.

"I must have missed that one." A memory surfaced and

Chase's mouth watered in response. "Are there pistachio bars?"

Deck grinned. "The woman who made them when we were kids passed away a few years ago, but her daughter mastered the recipe. I've had two already."

"Nice to see you," he said to the Decker family. "I have to find the bake sale booth before Leavitt does. He inhales those suckers."

"It's over by the guy playing the banjo," Cheryl called after him. "Just follow the music."

Chase did just that, stopping to drop a buck in the banjo player's hat—which had an Eagles Fest sign on it—on his way to the pistachio bars. There was a crowd around the baked goods booth, and he hoped he wasn't too late.

He got in line and saw the back of Sam Leavitt's head several people ahead of him. *Damn.* "Hey, Leavitt!"

The quarterback turned to face him, as did almost everybody else, including the women in front of him. He'd been so focused on the booth he hadn't realized Kelly, Jen and Gretchen were in line.

"What?" Sam called.

"No cutting," Gretchen said.

"What are you ladies after?"

"Brownies," they all said in unison.

"Good." He looked over their heads to Sam. "Don't you dare take all the pistachio bars."

His old friend shrugged. "You gotta be faster, Sanders. Come to think of it, I think I used to say that to you back in high school, too."

Chase wanted to flip him off, but the street fair was a family event. Instead, all he could do was glare and hope there were plenty of pistachio bars left. With the golden cookie-type crust loaded with pistachio pudding and whipped cream, they'd always been his favorite treat at Old Home Day, and now he had his heart set on one.

"How are you feeling today?" Kelly asked, a deceptively innocent smile on her face.

"Fine." He wondered what, if anything, she'd told her best friends, who seemed more interested in whatever they'd been talking about than him. "How 'bout you? Did you have your ice cream?"

"I did. Do you remember last night?"

"Of course." He wasn't *that* drunk. Buzzed enough to break into the high school and try to get her to make out with him on the bridge, but not enough to obliterate his memory.

He wondered if she was aware of the way her question sounded, because Jen and Gretchen both stopped talking. They didn't turn around, but he could tell they were interested now and wanted to listen more than talk.

"I'm sure Alex and Sam appreciate your help as much as I do, Officer McDonnell," he said, just to let the eavesdroppers know they were going to be disappointed if they thought he and Kelly had been up to something else last night.

"You really need to start calling me Kelly," she muttered.

"Off duty today?"

She shrugged. "For about another hour. Then I'll run home and get my uniform on and come back."

"I left you one," he heard Sam say, and he looked up in time to see the guy biting into a pistachio bar, while holding two more on a napkin in his other hand.

The women in front of him each picked up a brownie, and then Kelly's hand hovered over the last pistachio bar.

"Don't do it," he warned.

She grinned. "I'm wondering what you'll do for a pistachio bar."

"Are you going to make me beg?" He dropped his voice, making the question as suggestive as possible in the hopes she'd rather put distance between them than steal his pistachio bar.

"I was thinking more along the lines of cleaning the grout in my bathroom."

He leaned close. "If you take that pistachio bar, I'll tell you in detail, in a very loud voice that carries, exactly what I'd be willing to exchange for it. And it won't include grout."

"Maybe *I* should buy the last pistachio bar," Jen said, and Chase realized both women had given up being stealthy and were blatantly watching them.

"No," Gretchen said, waving her hand between Chase and Kelly. "Please do go on. In detail."

"What's the holdup?" somebody shouted from farther back in the line.

"Enjoy your pistachio bar," Kelly said, tucking her money in her pocket so she could pick up her brownie.

"I think I would have enjoyed trying to get it from you more."

Kelly walked away, but Gretchen stopped to whisper, "She would have, too."

A few hours later, Kelly fell into step beside her mom, wishing she was still in her jeans and T-shirt. It was a beautiful day, but hanging out with her friends had been a lot more fun than patrolling the street fair on foot.

"Hi, honey," her mom said. "Having fun?"

"It was more fun before I went on duty, but everybody's having a good time and the dollars are adding up. Jen and Gretchen have been circling around emptying the fund buckets every so often, and it looks like it'll be worth the work."

"Have I mentioned today how proud I am of you girls?"

"At least twice." Kelly laughed and hooked her arm through her mom's. "Hey, do you have a recipe for pistachio bars?"

"No, but I could get you one. That's an odd request, seeing as how you don't like them."

Busted. "Asking for a friend."

"Mmhmm." They walked in silence for a moment but, as always, it didn't last long. "Chase told me you got the call when they broke into the school to see the trophy."

Kelly stopped in her tracks, her arm sliding free from her mom's. The transition from pistachio bars to Chase made her wonder if Jen and Gretchen had run their mouths. And she was surprised Chase had confessed so quickly. "He told you about that?"

Her mom chuckled. "I asked when he'd seen you, and not many people lie in front of your father. Especially his boys."

That was true. "The dispatcher called me personally even though I was off duty, thankfully. I don't think the guys would have arrested them, either, but this way I don't have to listen to it or owe anybody any favors."

"Speak of the little devils . . ."

Kelly followed her mom's gaze to where the alumni team members were holding court on the steps of the gazebo. Though she couldn't hear them, she saw the men laughing and, of course, she couldn't look away from Chase.

He looked relaxed, standing on the top step and leaning against one of the gazebo's support beams. His mouth moved and she wished she could hear his words as the people around him laughed some more.

"Nothing there but heartache, honey."

Her mother's words were softly spoken, but Kelly heard the message loud and clear. She could have tried to deny she was attracted to Chase, but there was no sense in it. Not with her mom. "Nobody said anything about my heart."

"I've been keeping an eye on you today, and every time you cross paths with him, the chemistry's obvious. But there's affection there, too. You enjoy each other's company, and sex will muddy the waters. Especially if the sex is good."

Kelly felt her cheeks grow hot, and she glanced around to make sure nobody else was in earshot. "Mom!"

"I'm just saying."

The sex would be good. Kelly had no doubt about that. "Now that the other guys are around, we won't see as much of each other."

Even as she said the words, they watched Chase's head turn as he scanned the area until he spotted her. They locked gazes for a long beat, and then he smiled slightly before turning back to the crowd.

"It's time to start the dunking booth," Kelly said before her mother could comment.

It took her a few minutes to find Gretchen, who was definitely the loudest of them, so she could climb up on a picnic table and yell loud enough to be heard that it was dunk tank time. Word spread quickly through the crowd, who moved to gather around.

Coach climbed to the top step of the tank, and it seemed

like everybody sucked in a breath, which made him laugh. "No, I'm not getting in. I just want to make sure everybody can hear me."

Years of yelling over noisy football fans had served him well, and most people could hear him. Kelly wanted to kick herself for not having some kind of microphone system or at least a bullhorn. They probably had one at the station, but by the time she could get there, her dad's speech would be over.

"Everybody having a good time?" he bellowed, and the crowd cheered. "Well, it's about to get better. The highlight of the street fair's about to start, as soon as we get a volunteer. And, because it's so much fun and it takes time to reset the platform, we're going to want five dollars for three balls."

People were already digging in their pockets for the money, which Kelly took as a good sign. They'd almost decided against the tank because it was so much work, but it was probably going to rake in some cash.

"All we need is our first volunteer," her dad announced.

Simon Ward's voice rose over the rest. "I'll write a check for a thousand dollars to the football fund right now if Kelly McDonnell does a half-hour shift in the dunk tank."

Everybody quieted, staring at her, but she shook her head. Simon had had a hair across his ass where she was concerned since she'd had his precious Escalade towed during a blizzard. He had more money than most everybody else in town, so apparently he thought winter parking bans didn't apply to him. And now he thought he would humiliate her in front of the town, but he was going to be disappointed. She couldn't very well ask some random person in the crowd to hold her gun.

"I'm in uniform." As far as she was concerned, that put an end to the subject.

"Come on, Officer McDonnell!" one of the kids yelled. "Do it for Coach!"

"I'm in uniform," she said again, this time more slowly, and she patted her holstered weapon for good measure.

"I'll hold your weapon," the chief said, having come up behind her. "And your belt."

The gathering crowd cheered, which masked the curses Kelly muttered under her breath. If she climbed into that tank, the line to dunk her would probably wrap around the park. And every person in that line would cough up money to see her get wet, which meant even more money into the Eagles' fund.

She spotted Hunter Cass in the crowd and remembered the night he'd opened up to her on the bridge. If letting Simon Ward think he'd gotten the better of her put a thousand dollars of his money into the team's pocket and kept Hunter and the rest of the boys dreaming of their futures instead of giving up, she'd take it.

When she unbuckled her belt, the cheering reached an earsplitting decibel and she knew she'd guessed right about people wanting to see her get dunked. After handing her weapon and belt to the chief, she unbuttoned her short-sleeve uniform shirt and yanked it free of her pants. Once she'd removed her vest so she was in the plain T-shirt she wore under it, she sat on the steps to the tank and took her boots off.

After sweeping everybody with a stern, warning glare that made them laugh, she made a show of slowly climbing the stairs, as if she were going to the gallows. Silence fell on the crowd and then, as she reached the top step and turned, she heard Simon Ward's voice again.

"I'll add fifty dollars for every dunking of Officer McDonnell by a player from the first championship team, up to five hundred dollars!"

Kelly's eyes met Chase's, and her stomach sank when she saw the slow grin that lit up his face. She was going down, multiple times, and he was going to enjoy every minute of it.

10

Chase wasn't accustomed to being booed by anybody, never mind by the entire town of Stewart Mills. *So much for being a hero,* he thought as he missed the dunk tank's smaller-than-it-looked target for the second time.

Kelly laughed at him.

"Hey, I played football, not baseball, and I was a running back," he shouted over his shoulder to his audience. "Catching the ball was my job. Throwing it was Sam's."

"Then get out of the way and let Leavitt try," somebody yelled back.

Like hell he would. Not after he'd shoved and even thrown a few elbows getting to the front of the line. "I was just getting warmed up."

"Last ball, Sanders," Kelly called to him from the tank's platform, her voice taunting.

If he missed his next throw, he'd never live it down. Trying to block out the noise around him, he focused on Kelly's face for a moment. Her lips were tilted up in amusement, and he couldn't miss the challenge in her eyes.

She was going down.

Chase went through an exaggerated pitcher's windup because it made the little kids laugh, and then released the ball.

It hit the center of the target, and he had just enough time to watch her eyes get big before the platform released and she was in the tank. She came up sputtering and everybody cheered.

"That's fifty dollars in the Eagles fund, everybody," Jen yelled. "Sam Leavitt, you're up!"

Sam went two for three and by the time Alex had gone—getting only one hit—Chase could see that Kelly was shivering. When Deck stepped up, the crowd cheered so loudly Chase thought the water in the tank might have rippled. Not only was Deck a member of the championship team, but he'd also stayed in Stewart Mills and was obviously a hometown favorite.

Maybe it was from playing ball with his boys, but Deck had a great arm and put Kelly in the water with all three throws. Philly dunked her once, and then it was Coach's turn.

"Dad, really?"

Coach grinned and Chase joined most of Stewart Mills in cheering him on as he dunked his daughter three times in a row.

Even though there were probably a lot of citizens who'd like the opportunity to dunk one of their police officers, they were after the bounty Simon Ward offered, so Chase found himself up again.

As nice as the day had been, he knew the water in the tank—which had been filled with and was being replenished by the hose—was freezing, and Kelly's lips were chattering now. The taunting challenge he'd seen on her face the first time he'd faced her had been replaced by determination, and he knew she wouldn't quit.

"The half hour is almost up," Jen announced. "Make your throws count, Chase."

He'd been considering deliberately missing, to give her a break, but now the pressure was on again. The first throw was a dead-center hit, and the cheering drowned out the sound of the splash as Kelly hit the water.

The second throw was a somewhat legitimate miss. He might have pulled it sideways just a bit when a shudder wracked Kelly's spine. With a sigh, he took the third ball from Gretchen and looked her in the eye.

Despite the fact that she was freezing, she gave him a slight, shaky smile and arched her eyebrow. She wanted that fifty dollars for the Eagles fund, and what the hell was he waiting for? Still, he hesitated. Under the bravado, she was miserable and he didn't want to add to it.

"Get it over with so she can get out of there," Jen muttered at his side.

Good point. He showboated for a moment, giving the crowd a performance that would hopefully keep interest in the tank high and the five-dollar bills flowing. Then he went through his comedic windup routine and let the ball fly.

She went down like a rock and actually stayed under long enough that he and Coach each took a step forward before she surfaced. After waving to the crowd, who gave her a healthy round of applause, Kelly climbed out of the tank and ducked behind it.

Chase knew her mom had a towel, but he didn't think it would do much to dry her off, never mind warm her up. As Coach and Jen worked the crowd and found a new volunteer to take a dunking, Chase made his way around the contraption and found Mrs. McDonnell squeezing the water from her daughter's scalp and ponytail with a towel while Kelly grabbed bunches of her T-shirt in her hand, trying to wring the water out of it.

"That water was freaking cold," Kelly was saying.

"We probably should have filled it days ago and let the sun warm it," Mrs. McDonnell said. "But every time water splashes out, we have to add more from the hose, anyway."

"You okay?"

Both women looked up at him and Kelly nodded. "Thanks to Simon Ward hating me, we raised a lot more than we anticipated. The spaghetti dinner might actually put us over the top."

Even with her bottom lip trembling with cold, her smile was so proud and triumphant, he had to smile back. "I hope so."

"Good job, Kelly." The chief joined them, still holding the miscellaneous pieces of cop stuff that couldn't get wet. "I'm going to hang around for the duration, so you can end your shift early. Go home and change. Get warm."

"Thanks, Chief." She grimaced as she shoved her feet into her boots, and then she took her belongings from her boss. "That sounds like a great idea."

"They're trying to get your husband in the tank," the chief told Mrs. McDonnell.

"What?" She handed Kelly the towel. "Absolutely not. Honey, I need to go keep an eye on your father before he gets pneumonia. You go home and get warm and I'll talk to you later."

Mrs. McDonnell and the chief—who Chase thought had gone to school together—walked around the dunk tank, leaving Kelly and Chase alone.

"If it's any consolation," he said, "I feel bad about dunking you."

"Don't." She buckled on her belt and secured her weapon, though she skipped the button-down shirt and vest. "Every splash was fifty dollars in the fund."

"Still, you're freezing."

"Not for long. I'm going to do exactly what they said and go home to change."

"I'll walk with you."

She stopped dabbing at her face with the towel to look at him. "That's not necessary."

"You're shaking and you've spent a good chunk of the last half hour under water. I'll end up so worried about you, I'll just follow you anyway." She didn't look convinced. "Just to the door, and I'll carry the vest. It's the least I can do."

"Just to the door," she said finally, holding the vest out to him.

They walked away from the dunk tank, the angle keeping them mostly out of sight of the crowd. The streets were mostly empty since the dunking booth was probably the most exciting thing to happen in town for a long time, and Chase noticed it was cooling off pretty quickly. Kelly had to be freezing.

"So why was Simon Ward willing to cough up a pretty

substantial amount of money to see you get dunked?" he asked.

"I had his Escalade towed during an emergency parking ban during my first blizzard with the Stewart Mills PD." She laughed, and then told him the story. Even the chief had been surprised she had the nerve to do it, but she wasn't going to pick and choose which laws she upheld based on how nice a vehicle the offender drove.

All too soon, they were at the door. She lived over an insurance office, so there was a door at the street level to unlock. After the third time her frozen fingers fumbled the keys, he took them from her and unlocked it. He knew there was probably another door at the top of the stairs, but he didn't push. If she wanted his help, she'd let him know.

"Thanks for walking me home," she said, reaching for the vest.

He let her take it. "You okay to get up the stairs?"

"Yeah." She looked up at him. "You know how to make hot cocoa?"

"Who doesn't? You put a mug of water in the microwave and then dump the envelope in it."

Her laugh was shaky because of the shivering. "I have the gourmet kind with mini marshmallows. You want some?"

"That sounds great."

"Good. You can make it while I take a hot shower."

"At your service, ma'am." He took the vest back and, after making sure the first door locked behind them, followed her up the stairs. He unlocked that one for her, too, and followed her inside.

Her apartment was nice, with cream paint and hardwood floors. The furniture was beige leather and looked comfortable, with a lot of darker colors added with pillows and lampshades and stuff. It wasn't a placeholder apartment like he'd seen from some of his friends in the past. This was her home and it suited her. It was definitely neater than anything he'd ever achieved, which he'd expected, but it still managed to be cozy and welcoming.

"Nice place."

"Thanks. Mugs are in the cabinet over the coffeemaker, and the box of hot cocoa is on the shelf above them. I'll be back in a few minutes."

Of course she'd have all of her hot beverage supplies grouped together. He wanted to check to see if her boxed foods were grouped by primary ingredient or frequent usage and whether the magazines on the table were spread out in alphabetical order, but he didn't. Even when he heard the shower kick on, he focused on the task at hand and resisted the urge to poke around her place.

He listened for the water to shut off and managed to time it so he was just setting the mugs on the table when the bathroom door opened. If he'd made them too soon, all her mini marshmallows would have melted before she was done with her shower. He looked up and couldn't hold back the chuckle.

"That's not going to work, Kelly."

Kelly sighed and looked down at herself. "You can't be serious."

She'd gone to great pains to make herself as unattractive as possible after her shower. The sweatpants were faded and baggy from her police academy days, and the matching sweatshirt she'd worn to paint her apartment when she moved in. Her bulky, white athletic socks were bunched around her ankles, and she'd pulled her wet hair into a messy knot at the back of her head. She wouldn't even get a mug shot taken in the outfit.

He stared at her for what seemed like forever and then shook his head. "I'm trying to imagine what you could do to be less attractive to me and I'm coming up with nothing."

"I have a T-shirt that's worse than this sweatshirt, but it's so thin now, I'm not sure it's decent anymore." She sat and took a sip of her hot cocoa before the mini marshmallows could melt, savoring the warmth that spread through her. "That would probably defeat the purpose."

"Wouldn't matter," he said. "It's you that's attractive, not the clothes. Which is good, when you think about it, since ideally the clothes come off at some point."

She laughed. "That's very true."

They drank their hot chocolate, making small talk about the street fair. She confessed she didn't even like pistachio bars, which made him feign outrage, and he confessed he felt bad about being the first to dunk her after she'd let his small legal infractions go. Then she mentioned the upcoming spaghetti dinner.

"Why Wednesday night?" he asked.

"Everybody knows Wednesday night is spaghetti night."

"Everybody meaning O'Rourke's."

She shrugged. "Wednesday is spaghetti night. We don't question it."

"Okay, then."

Kelly found herself taking smaller sips of her hot cocoa to drag out having Chase in her apartment. Even though she'd been trying to scare him off, she had to admit it was nice to be so comfortable with a man. Ratty sweats, bad hair and he was still looking at her across the table like she was the most beautiful woman he'd ever seen.

It was surprisingly heady stuff and, instead of killing the mood, she'd only managed to make him seem sexier to her.

Maybe she was looking at the problem of sex with Chase all wrong. She was afraid being Coach's daughter and a female police officer required that she live up to to a higher standing, which meant sleeping with Chase could harm her reputation. Instead, maybe it meant she could have a little fling and people would just pretend it wasn't happening.

Somehow she thought it was the former, though. Nothing brought out those New England Puritan roots like a single woman having sex just for fun.

"You are *really* thinking hard about something," Chase said.

"Yup." She swirled the remaining cocoa in her mug, trying to mix in the sludge that had settled at the bottom.

"Okay," he said after a few seconds. "I actually wanted to know *what* you were thinking. Not making it a question was my idea of being sneaky about it."

She laughed, shaking her head. "You're such a goof. But, to answer your sneaky non-question, I was thinking the same thing I've been thinking about since you drove back into town."

"Something along the lines of *why the hell did we put a stop sign there?*"

"No. We put a stop sign there because we want people to stop at that intersection." She set the mug down. "I had a crush on you in high school, but we're different now. Very, very different. I can't even begin to understand why, but I'm still attracted to you."

"I'm right here for the taking and, luckily, I don't need much in the way of flattery."

"But it's a bad idea."

"Maybe, but it's a *great* bad idea." When he stood up and started around the table toward her, she knew they were as good as in bed, because she was out of the will to resist him. "We've both had a rough go of it. What's so bad about having a little fun together?"

"It's hard enough to get respect around here without sleeping with one of the prodigal golden boys."

"I wasn't planning on hanging a banner on the parade float."

"You seem to have forgotten how Stewart Mills works."

He snorted, reaching for her hand. "It's not *that* bad."

"Gretchen's grandmother told Jen, Gretchen and me that you bought a box of condoms at the drugstore, so I guess I don't need to ask if you have protection."

He froze, his eyes wide. "You're kidding. Her *grandmother*? And she told all of you?"

"Never underestimate the small-town grapevine. She also warned me you were up to no good."

Taking her hand, he pulled her to her feet. "Considering I haven't seen her since high school, she's remarkably correct on both counts. I bought a box of condoms, put a couple in my pocket and now I'm up to no good. So what are you going to do about it, Officer McDonnell?"

"I'm not going to handcuff you, Sanders."

He pulled her hard up against his body, and she wrapped her arms around his neck. "How about a little mutual frisking?"

"The cheesy cop innuendoes might have gotten you out of a ticket—and they didn't even do that, technically—but they're not going to get you in my pants, as inviting as these pants might be."

"Oh, I think sweatpants are *very* sexy." He slid his hand just under the waistband at her back. "I'm a fan of elastic."

Her skin heated under his touch, and she pulled up on the bottom of his T-shirt so she could return the favor. His ab muscles tightened when her palms skimmed over them, and he brushed his mouth over hers. Kelly caught his bottom lip between her teeth and chuckled when he moaned.

Then he kissed her, his tongue dancing over hers until she relaxed against his body. Usually she didn't have a lot of patience for the act, but Chase kissed with just the right blend of softness and hunger, and she thought she could happily spend hours just tasting his lips.

His hands were under her sweatshirt, caressing her back, and she could feel the rough edges of his calluses. He was a man who worked with his hands, and the strength and hardness in them felt good.

His mouth left hers and she would have mourned the loss of his kisses, but he nipped at the side of her jaw before moving to her neck. Her sweatshirt was bunching up under her arms, so she grabbed the hem and started tugging it up. Chase backed off enough that she could take it off, and then his mouth was on her breast.

He tugged at her nipple and she hissed. "Do you like that?"

She raked her nails up his back in response, dragging his T-shirt along. He took it from her, yanking it over his head so abruptly, she expected to hear tearing fabric. He flung it, and then turned his attention back to her breasts. First one and then the other was teased by his tongue until she couldn't take it anymore.

Grabbing a fistful of his hair, she dragged his face back to hers so she could kiss him again. His hands slid under the waist of her sweatpants, cupping her ass. When he pushed down, the loose elastic slid over her hips, and he kept pushing until she stepped out of them.

His kisses grew more demanding as he ran his thumbs over her nipples. She touched as much of him as she could reach, from his hair to his back and chest and down over his abdominal muscles.

It took a moment for Kelly to realize he'd slowly been backing her up, and she sucked in a breath when her back hit the wall and she realized his intention. "Chase?"

He grinned and pulled a condom wrapper out of his pocket before shoving his shorts and boxer briefs down so he could step out of them. "What?"

She'd been about to point out she had a bedroom with a perfectly good bed in it, but she changed her mind just in time. She could give him a tour of her perfectly good bed later. "Hurry up."

She heard the crinkle of the condom wrapper and seconds later, his hands and mouth were on her again. Hungrier this time. More demanding.

Moaning, she threw back her head and bared her neck for his mouth. When she trailed her fingertips across his hips to the start of his lower back, the muscles twitched under her touch and made her smile. "Ticklish spot?"

"I didn't think so, but you have those fingernails and—" She ran them over the same spot, and his whole body jerked. "Okay, enough."

As if guessing it would take more than a stern voice to dissuade her from amusing herself, he grabbed her wrists and pinned them against the wall over her head. Heat flooded through her, but she didn't resist.

After a few more kisses, his thigh pressed between hers, the amusement was gone and all she wanted was for him to be inside her. It had been longer than she cared to admit since she'd had an orgasm with a man present, and she wanted one now.

Finally, he released her wrists and draped her hands over his shoulders. Then he grinned as his hands began sliding down her back to the backs of her thighs. Guessing his intention, she tightened her grip just in time for him to hoist her up and brace her against the wall.

"I've been thinking about this since the night I kissed you." His voice was rough, and she knew he wanted this first orgasm to come as hard and as fast as she did.

When he used the wall to hold her so he could reach between their bodies, she almost moaned in anticipation. And then he was sliding into her, slowly, as she released the breath she'd been holding.

He was patient, moving his hips slowly to give her body time to adjust, and she ran her hand up the back of his neck into his hair. When she curled her fingers, tugging a little, he groaned. Then he began to move in earnest, every thrust a little deeper, and she gripped his shoulders.

The angle was just right and, as he rocked his hips, she urged him on with her fingernails biting into his skin and his name on her lips. Faster and harder he drove into her, her shoulder blades pressed against the wall, until her muscles tightened and the orgasm hit. She raked him with her nails, arching her back until he had to slide his hands under her to hold her up.

As the tremors eased, she ran her hands over his shoulders and forearms, loving the feel of those muscles on his body. "Oh, yes."

Chase groaned as he found his own release, and she tightened her fingers in his hair again as he thrust into her over and over until it had passed. Then he kissed her hard, their ragged breaths mingling between them.

After a long moment, he reached between them to hold the condom while sliding free of her body, then slid to his knees, lowering her along with him, before rolling onto his back. Being stretched out on top of his body was pretty comfortable, and she was content to rest her head on his chest and listen to his heartbeat.

Still breathing a little hard, he stroked her back. "When I can walk again, or at least crawl, you can show me that perfectly good bed of yours."

She turned her head to laugh into his shoulder. "Definitely. But not yet. I don't know if I can get up."

"I hate to admit this, but it can't be too long. I remember now why I don't lie around on linoleum very often."

"Since we're doing confessions, there was a second there when I was afraid your knees would give out."

"Trust me, so was I."

An hour later, Chase would have given everything he owned—which admittedly wasn't much, but his truck *was* fairly new—to stay in Kelly's perfectly good bed and keep holding her until they fell asleep. It probably wouldn't take very long.

She was already in that lazy state of sliding in and out

of sleep, and he probably should have gotten up and left a few minutes earlier. The heavier her head got on his arm and the softer her breathing grew, the more he wanted to wake up next to her in the morning.

They'd already used the second condom, but there were ways around that. Some very fun ways, actually, that he'd like to explore with her in the future, whether they had condoms or not. But it had been a long day in the hot sun, capped off for her by repeated immersion in icy water, followed by a hot shower and several orgasms. It was no wonder she was almost asleep.

He was growing increasingly drowsy himself, and he forced himself to slide his arm free. She made a moaning sound that would have turned him on again were he not exhausted, and burrowed deeper under the light blanket. But when he climbed off the bed and the mattress shifted, she rolled to face him, her eyes open.

"You can stay."

"Tempting."

"Because you want more or because you're too tired to walk?"

He laughed and slapped her blanket-covered ass. "I'm not answering that. But maybe a little of both."

"I'll be honest. I'm not really up on the rules of casual, friendly sex, but it's really okay if you want to stay."

He frowned and clicked on the small lamp next to her armchair. "I might have to if I can't find my clothes."

"They're in the kitchen."

"Damn, that's right. Be right back." He went into the kitchen and pulled his clothes on. Then he gathered hers to take into her bedroom.

After setting them on the chair, he knelt on the side of the bed to give her a kiss good-bye. She had almost nodded off again, and she smiled drowsily. "You're stubborn."

"You realize I have to go sneak into Coach's house now, right?"

She waved a hand. "I'm an adult."

He caught the hand in his and kissed her palm. "Yes, you are very much an adult. But since I'm the one sleeping under their roof, in your childhood room no less, and trying to remember where the squeaky floorboards are, I'm not sure I am."

"You are." Her eyelids slid closed, and he knew she was losing the battle to stay awake.

"Do you need your alarm set for the morning?"

"It already is," she muttered.

He kissed her cheek and turned off lights as he walked through her apartment. He made sure the top door locked behind him, and then did the same for the street-level door, hoping like hell he hadn't forgotten anything.

Standing in the dark, chilly air, he took a deep breath. It had been a damn fine evening, and now he could only hope he made it back to Eagles Lane and into Kelly's old bedroom without attracting attention. Since there weren't any taxi services, he started walking.

He wasn't sure whether it counted as a walk of shame if he hadn't actually slept and put on the same clothes but, all the same, it wasn't a walk he'd expected to be making back in Stewart Mills.

11

Chase spent some timc silently lecturing himself in the mirror before heading downstairs to face the McDonnells. It was kind of important he not look like a man who'd had amazing sex the night before, but it would take some effort to hide it.

The kitchen was empty when he finally went down, so he poured himself a cup of coffee. He could hear movement and knew somebody was in the house. After plucking a spoon from the dish drainer, he added sugar and grabbed the milk from the fridge.

"Good morning, Chase," Mrs. McDonnell said when she walked in and saw him at the counter.

"Good morning. I'm sorry I came in a little late last night," he said, maybe taking a little too long to stir his coffee so he had a reason not to look up. "I tried to be quiet, but I ran into an old friend and started catching up and time got away from us."

It wasn't the truth, but it wasn't exactly a lie, either, which he wanted to avoid if at all possible. Maybe it was a stretch to call Kelly an old friend, and he didn't want to admit what they'd been catching up on, but time had definitely gotten away from them.

Was it his imagination or was Mrs. McDonnell's smile a little tight this morning? "I told you, we're pretty sound sleepers."

"Where's Coach?"

"He went out on an emergency call. I think the only thing worse than Sunday morning calls are holiday calls."

"I would have gone with him if I'd known. I could have given him a hand."

She shrugged. "Would you like some breakfast?"

He was starving, but he had too much guilt going on this morning where she was concerned to ask her to cook for him, too. "I'm heading to O'Rourke's, actually, but thank you."

"Give them my best." She took her grocery list pad and a pen and opened the pantry door.

Chase drank the coffee as quickly as he could and got out of there. He knew it was probably his imagination—or guilty conscience, maybe—but Mrs. McDonnell didn't seem as warm as usual. If knowing he'd been with Kelly was at the root of it, he dreaded what Coach's reaction would be.

Once he hit the front porch, he sent texts to the guys, letting them know he was buying breakfast if anybody wanted in, but only Alex and Sam were free. Since they were farther away and he didn't want to go back into the house, Chase killed some time by walking to the restaurant.

Because he had to stop and talk to what seemed like a million people, the guys already had a table when he arrived. He slid into the booth next to Alex, since Sam was wider, and gratefully accepted a full coffee mug from their server.

He looked across the table at Sam, who looked tired as hell. "You look like shit."

"Good morning."

"Yeah, good morning. You look like shit."

Sam shrugged. "Didn't get a lot of sleep last night."

Unlike Chase, who'd slept like a rock once he'd left Kelly's apartment and snuck into Coach's house. "Maybe we'll get lucky and she'll accidentally leave the coffeepot on the table."

Over breakfast, Alex told them stories about some of the places he'd traveled for work. Being a freelance photojournalist, his work varied, and sometimes he was in a quiet town in Italy, capturing the architecture, and sometimes he was in the middle of a violent coup. It sounded like a great life to Chase, except for the fact that he refused to fly. It would take a long damn time to get to the Middle East without a plane.

He kept the conversation going as long as he could, but both guys had made commitments for the day with their host players. Since Chase had a host coach instead of a host player, he made the walk back to the house, hoping Mrs. McDonnell would have something for him to do.

Coach was sitting in a rocker on the front porch when Chase walked up the steps, and the sight of him formed a knot in his stomach so tight he wished he hadn't eaten a huge breakfast. "Morning, Coach."

"Morning. Have a good breakfast?"

"Yes, sir." The man was giving him nothing as far as a possible emotional response. "Cassandra doesn't serve up quite as good a breakfast as Mrs. McDonnell, but it's not half bad."

Coach smiled and the knot in Chase's gut loosened a little. "You know, you're a grown man now, and she's said she doesn't mind if you call her Helen."

"I appreciate that, but it doesn't feel right."

"That's what I figured you'd say. You all had your share of troubles, but you were all good boys at heart."

Guilt reared its ugly head again, but Chase hid it behind a smile. "There were times you were the only person who seemed to believe that."

"It might have felt that way, but I wasn't the only one. And it makes me proud none of you ever disappointed me."

Chase wasn't sure if he was simply reminiscing or if Coach was trying to give him some kind of message, so he just nodded and kept his mouth shut. He figured if Coach knew where Chase had been last night and was mad about it, he'd have let him know by now.

Hell, maybe Coach would even be happy about it. Chase had always been close to him, so maybe the older man was thinking about him as a potential son-in-law. One who was good at heart and had never disappointed him.

But Chase wasn't looking to be anybody's son-in-law anytime soon. And Kelly wouldn't have him if he were. It had been a no-strings bit of fun—maybe even a one-night thing, though he hoped not—and that was it.

He was pretty sure if Coach knew the truth of what was going on, he would be pretty disappointed in Chase, after all.

Because she didn't have a family at home, which made one day more or less like any other, Kelly often worked Sundays. She didn't mind. They were slow days, with most of them spent monitoring the flow of traffic heading south through the town as the tourists went home.

This particular Sunday she would have liked to spend in her bed, basking in the glow of great sex. Instead, she was driving around, trying not to dwell on whether Chase would call her or if she should call him or if there should be any phone call at all. Since she'd never done the casual-fling thing before, she wasn't really sure what the rules were.

The only thing she knew for sure was that she wanted to be alone with him again, and sooner rather than later. They didn't have a lot of time.

She sat on the side of the road into town for a while, watching the noses of vehicles dive as drivers saw her cruiser and hit their brakes. None of them were speeding enough to merit banging a U-turn and pulling anybody over, but she liked slowing the flow of traffic before it hit the main street of Stewart Mills.

When the dispatcher called, she sighed and knew her peaceful morning was probably over. "Go ahead."

"Officer Clark responded to a shoplifting call at the gas station. He has a twelve-year-old female in custody and is requesting a female officer on scene. So, that would be you."

"ID?"

"It's Emily Jenkins."

Her heart sank. "Oh, damn. Tell him I'm on my way."

Emily's mom had been a friend of Kelly's, and they'd lost her two years ago to cancer. Emily seemed to be doing okay, but shoplifting was so out of character for her that Kelly wondered what could have gone wrong.

When she pulled into the gas station, she saw Emily sitting in the back of Dylan's marked sedan, her head bowed and shoulders shaking. Dylan was leaning on the outside of the car, and he gave a shrug of his shoulders when Kelly looked his way.

She decided to start inside so she could get the full story before she talked to Emily. Janie Vestal was behind the counter, and it occurred to Kelly that the woman had been Chase's girlfriend back in high school. Even though it was stupid, she felt awkward all of a sudden and almost forgot why she was there for a second.

Then she took a deep breath and stepped up to the counter. "Hey, Janie. What's going on?"

"I caught her shoplifting feminine hygiene products," she said, almost in a whisper even though the store was empty. "You know, pads."

Oh, the poor child. "Is this the first time you've caught her shoplifting?"

"It is. I called the owner. It's hard, Kelly. I mean, my heart breaks for the child, but with the economy the way it is, we can't be seen as an easy target. If we look the other way when a kid going through a tough time steals from us, we'll be having tough times, too."

"I understand, and I agree. What about pressing charges?"

Janie shook her head. "She's only twelve, and it's not like it was cigarettes or beer or something. The poor girl's having her period and it might even be her first. But we need you to make sure she understands she can't do it again."

"I will." Kelly rubbed the spot between her eyebrows. "You can tell your boss I'm going to speak to her father and that I appreciate being able to handle it. Trying to scare the kids with jail only does more harm than good."

"I know you care about the kids. All this work you're doing for the football team is amazing." Janie cocked her head sideways. "I couldn't believe it when Chase Sanders walked in the other day. I dated him in high school and thought we'd get married someday. I heard his life's a wreck, though, so I sure dodged a bullet there, huh?"

Kelly nodded and smiled, as if she agreed, but she had to fight an urge to defend Chase. So what if he'd fallen on hard times not all entirely of his own making? A woman who'd just had to call the police on a little girl who didn't have money to buy pads for her period should probably be a little more sympathetic.

"I'm going to go see to Emily now." She saw the package of feminine pads on the end of the counter and slid it over to the register as she pulled out her wallet. "I'll pay for these."

After Janie put the package in a paper bag, Kelly walked outside and took a deep breath. Sometimes she wondered what it would be like to be a police officer in a big city. More dangerous, of course, but maybe more impersonal, too. But she supposed community was community no matter the size, and it would always be personal on some level.

"I'm going to take her home," she told Dylan, who looked relieved. "I'll talk to her dad and hopefully that'll be the end of it."

"I wasn't sure what the story was because Emily just kept crying, and then Janie got all choked up and said it was a female issue. I figured with you being a woman and being a friend of her mom, it would be easier for everybody if you came."

"Absolutely." She opened the back door of the sedan. "Come on, honey. I'm going to take you home."

Emily seemed to calm down once she was riding shotgun with Kelly, but she sniffled a little when she handed her the paper bag. "I'm sorry I tried to steal them."

"You got lucky, Em. The man who owns the gas station is a nice guy and Janie went to bat for you, but you can't try to steal from them again or it'll be bad."

"I know. But they're expensive, and Dad's still paying for Mom's medical stuff even though she's not here anymore and I didn't want to ask him for money."

"You'll need these every month, honey, and they're a lot cheaper if you buy them at the big grocery store. He'll just put them on the list and it won't be a big deal."

"It's embarrassing," she mumbled.

Kelly tried to imagine having to go to Coach the first time she'd had her period, but her mind didn't even want to go there. She'd gone to her mom and that had been that. But Emily didn't have a mom. "As you get older, there are going to be things you need to talk to your dad about, honey. And even if you or he or both feels a little uncomfortable, you still need to talk to him. Or at least to somebody. Go to Miss Cooper. Or to me."

"I don't like telling people we don't have a lot of money," Emily said, her mouth setting in a stubborn line.

"Your family's not the only one going through hard times. Trust me. But stealing is not the answer."

"I won't do it again. I promise."

Talking to Emily's dad was as awkward as she'd imagined. Between hearing the news his daughter had shoplifted and learning she was transitioning into young womanhood, he was so flustered he forgot to be mad. After pulling him aside to give him a crash course on how to deal with this new chapter of his daughter's life, Kelly got back in her cruiser with a sigh of relief.

She had to go back to the gas station to fill her tank, and she was thankful the department had cards to swipe at the pump so she didn't have to go inside. And there were other customers, so Janie couldn't do more than give her a quick wave through the window.

She wondered who had been telling tales about Chase's life, but she also thought about Janie's *dodged a bullet* sentiment. It made Kelly wonder how she would have coped if her husband had lost all of their money and his business and their home. Probably not well, because she tended to be very conservative when it came to money and wouldn't do well in financial chaos.

But she already knew Chase wasn't marriage material for her, and she didn't care. She didn't want to marry him. She just wanted him to call her. Or text her.

She got back in her cruiser and, after a glance at her silent phone, went back out on patrol.

Chase sat in the back of the high school cafeteria, which had been chosen for its seating, trying to pay attention to the television that had been wheeled in and hooked up to somebody's laptop. They were all there—the alumni, the football team and a few of the dads and staff members—watching video of the Eagles' previous season.

They were good, he thought. Maybe not great, but they were a solid team, and he recognized some of Coach McDonnell's personal touches in their training. They were positive without being cocky. They communicated with each other rather than constantly looking to the coaching staff as go-betweens. No play was made by one single player, so they celebrated together and they also shared fault together. Whether they ever got to play for a championship or not, the things they learned from Coach and on the field would stay with them forever.

He wished there was an abridged version, though. Sitting in the curved, hard plastic cafeteria chairs wasn't comfortable, and the plays on the screen were all starting to blend together. What really sucked was that it had been his and Alex's idea to do this. They were hoping to fire the boys up in case their energy was flagging only halfway through the fund-raising and, maybe, see what the alumni team was up against.

There was no mystery there. They were up against a team of teenage boys who played good football together and were led by a great coach. Watching game tapes wasn't going to give the older guys an edge.

After a while, Chase pulled up his email on his phone and scrolled through, deleting the spam. There were a few communications from builders he'd talked to about taking over the big jobs he could no longer afford to do, and he went through the slow and painstaking process of responding to them on the phone's small screen.

It was tempting to ask the McDonnells for access to the

computer they had at Coach's office, but then they'd know something was going on and ask him questions about it. Even if they were coming from a place of concern and caring, he didn't really like talking about the mess at home. It felt like a failure on every level.

When he came to an email from his lawyer, he braced himself as he opened it, hoping it wouldn't be some new horror show in the making. It wasn't, but it also wasn't good news. Seth's lawyer had contacted his lawyer, and he was denying he'd taken the money, blaming it on a hacker or computer glitch.

Chase cursed and had to make an effort not to throw the phone across the room. There was no question Seth had taken the money, and it wouldn't be hard to prove he had. But it would take time. And it also meant he'd probably buried the money someplace where they wouldn't easily find it.

"Hey."

Chase looked up and saw that Deck was leaning toward him. "You're making pissed-off noises. Like sighing and growling and shit. And you're getting louder."

He flagged the email to respond to later and closed his email. "Sorry."

"Everything okay?"

"Yeah. Just work crap I'm not in the mood to deal with right now. And I'm getting hungry. How much longer do you think this will go on?"

Deck looked at the screen for a few seconds. "There are two games left and they've started fast-forwarding through a lot of it. Not long."

"Too bad the pizza place doesn't deliver."

"Dude? Pizza?" That was Cody, from the front of the room.

"There's pizza?"

Somehow they ended up walking to the Stewart Mills House of Pizza when the video ended, where the alumni guys all chipped in enough to buy pizzas for everybody. Chase thought he'd had enough of football for the day, but once they carried the pizzas to the town square and were all sitting in the grass with their slices, he didn't mind. The kids were happy to have the free pizza, and there were no surly attitudes in sight.

Hunter even asked him about his time as running back for the Eagles and, the more he spoke, the more Chase warmed up to the topic. He wasn't sure anything had ever come close to replicating the rush that came from running up the sideline, evading defenders without stepping out of bounds, and breaking the plane for the touchdown.

"Did you ever get hurt?"

Chase shook his head. "No, but I was lucky. Just some bad bruises and a lot of sore muscles. I remember a kid on an opposing team tearing up his knee, though. I don't think he ever played again. That's one reason stretching and workouts and listening to Coach matter. A lot of injuries come from poor conditioning."

He missed whatever Hunter said next because a police cruiser was driving slowly down the main street, and Kelly was behind the wheel. Wishing he'd thought to ask her if he'd see her again—alone and up close—before he left the night before, he debated texting her. But even if she hadn't been driving, he wasn't sure what he'd say.

Hey, had fun. Want to do it again?

That was lame. Maybe something simple and not pushy.

I had a great time last night. Or *I'm sitting on the grass eating pizza with a bunch of guys jacked up on football talk and all I can think about is you.*

"You going to eat that piece, dude?"

He realized Cody had moved closer and was talking to him. "No, I'm full. Go ahead."

"I thought it was super lame they were making a big deal out of you guys coming back," he said around a mouthful of cheese and pepperoni, "but it's kinda cool having you around. Like seeing you all went to college and do different jobs and all live in different places and stuff."

They gave the kids hope there was life outside Stewart Mills. Chase thought he probably would have latched onto that, too, if they'd been in a similar situation back in the day. "You thinking about where you want to go to college?"

Cody shrugged. "I thought I'd work at the mill until they shut it down. So I figured I'd drive over to the furniture factory like some people do, but then that closed, too. So I'll probably go to whatever college will take me."

Not the most encouraging of outlooks. "Once school starts, you should make an appointment with Jen . . . uh, Miss Cooper, and talk about your options. That's a big part of her job, you know. Helping you figure out what comes after high school."

"Yeah, she's pretty cool. And hot, too. I'll probably talk to her."

Whatever got him in the guidance office. "Good plan."

The cruiser made a second lap, and this time Kelly beeped and waved. They all waved back, but he wondered if she'd looked for him in the crowd. He really should text her soon, because the longer he waited, the more awkward it would be.

How's your day going? There. That was conversational and friendly, without being about sex. Not that he didn't want to pursue that angle, but he didn't want to be pushy. And it would be a fairly benign message should she not have privacy when she opened it.

He pulled out his phone and punched it in before he could change his mind. A few seconds later, he saw the cruiser's turn signal blink, and it pulled to the curb.

Really? You can actually SEE that I'm driving right now.

Oops. I thought you'd read it later, when you weren't driving.

I'll text you later, when I can. The cruiser pulled back into traffic and turned off on a side road.

Chase leaned back on his hands, grinning. Even if the brief conversation hadn't gone anywhere, he knew one thing. She hadn't been able to wait when she saw a text from him, and had pulled over right away to read it. In his book, that could only mean good things.

12

On Tuesday, the three women all managed to finally have free time together, so they met at Kelly's apartment to deal with the money from the street fair. So much of it was one-dollar bills, or even quarters, they knew they couldn't just show up at the bank with the plastic buckets.

It took a lot of trips to get the buckets upstairs, and then they all sat on the floor and started separating the money. The bank had a sorting machine, but they wanted a rough idea of how much they'd pulled in. Jen had pulled in a couple more monetary gifts from some foundations Kelly had never heard of, and there was a possibility they could close out the spaghetti dinner tomorrow night with the good news the Stewart Mills Eagles would report for tryouts in August.

"I wonder if strippers have to do this every night," Gretchen said.

Kelly laughed. "Hey, the barn has a pole. You could pull in some extra money."

"I think stripping and a wooden barn pole is asking for splinters in bad places."

About halfway through, Kelly stood up to stretch her back and try to get some feelings back in her legs. "I can't believe how much money is here. Not that I'm complaining, but this is crazy."

Jen tossed a handful of quarters into a bucket and made a tally mark on her legal pad. They were going with rough estimates for the coins, or they'd be in her apartment for a week. "After you left, the boys—the current team, I mean—took turns in the booth, since it's to raise money for them. Their girlfriends and siblings were practically begging money from people to dunk them."

"I noticed you didn't come back after your turn, Kelly," Gretchen said. It was a statement, but the nosy tilt at the end made it more of a question.

"By the time I took a hot shower and had some hot cocoa, I was done. I fell into bed." It was the truth.

"Chase disappeared about the same time you did," Gretchen added.

Kelly gathered four twenty-five-dollar piles of one-dollar bills, very meticulously tapped the paper to line up the edges and then slid a paper band around the stack. She didn't want to lie to them, but she didn't really want to talk about it, either.

"Nothing?" Gretchen pushed, and Kelly shrugged.

"I guess that answers that question," Jen said. "Was there a wall involved?"

Kelly couldn't hold back her grin as she nodded. "But I'm not saying anything else."

"That was Saturday night. It's Tuesday. Have you two been filling in the blanks?"

"No. I've barely even seen him, actually. He's been running around with the other alumni players." Thankfully staying on the right side of the law so far.

"The guys have been hanging out with the kids a lot," Jen said. "Offering advice on football and life and stuff in general, I guess."

"It's good for them." Kelly sat back down and dumped another bucket between her legs. "The kids, I mean. Though it gives the men something to do, too."

Not that Chase needed anything to do. He seemed to be so busy she'd barely seen him and, other than a couple of text exchanges, they'd hardly spoken. Not that she was pining for him. But if they were going to have a hot, sexy fling while he was in town, she'd like a little more flinging before he left.

They worked in silence for a while, the excitement of having so much money to sort fading over the course of the actual sorting until, finally, they were done. They made multiple trips back down to Jen's car and she left for the bank, promising to text them the official total once they'd sorted the deposit and called her with the amount.

Gretchen went back upstairs with Kelly, since she'd left her sweatshirt on the back of the kitchen chair. "Does Jen seem off to you?"

"What do you mean?"

Gretchen shrugged. "I don't know. She just didn't seem like herself, and she hardly said anything the whole time."

"Probably just tired." They all were.

"I know what Jen tired looks like and I know it sounds

weird, but she wouldn't look at Sam when we ran into them on the way over here."

That got Kelly's attention. "Sam Leavitt? Come on. He's so far from her type it's not even funny. Maybe something's going on with the school administration or something, because there's no way there's anything going on between Jen and Sam."

It was a crazy thought. They both knew Jen's type—a cashmere sweater, some Shakespeare for fun—and Sam wasn't it. Not that Chase was Kelly's type, either, but that was different. They were just having a fling. She knew Jen was looking for a keeper.

"I have ice cream," she said as Gretchen pulled on her sweatshirt. "You want some?"

"I should get home to Gram. I've been leaving her alone too much lately because of this Eagles Fest thing, and I told her we'd have a nice lunch together."

Kelly sighed. "I'm on duty soon, so maybe I shouldn't have ice cream for lunch."

A few hours later, she was at her desk doing paperwork when the chief loomed over her. She leaned back in her chair, not liking the uncertainty on his face. He was a man who liked being in charge and, even when he had no clue, he moved through his life with utter confidence in himself.

"Hi, Chief."

"McDonnell. You did a good job in the dunk tank the other night."

All she'd done was repeatedly fall into frigid water, but she'd take whatever praise she could get. "Thank you. All for a good cause."

"Yes." He was actually fidgeting with a button on his shirt, and Kelly got nervous. She silently prayed she wasn't about to be a victim of deeper budget cuts. "There's been some talk about . . . so I heard Chase Sanders walked you home."

Kelly didn't like where that was going at all. "Yes, sir. I was cold enough so that he was concerned about my fine motor skills and wanted to be sure I got home okay."

"Oh. And that's it?"

Oh, hell no. "Are you asking me about a personal relationship, sir?"

"No!" His face flushed and he shook his head so hard she was surprised his hat didn't fly off. "Absolutely not. That would be inappropriate. I was just . . . making small talk. Like I said, good job in the dunk tank."

"Thank you, Chief." She looked at the clock over his head. "If that's all, sir, I should head out on patrol."

"Of course. Uh . . . be careful out there."

She refrained from rolling her eyes at her chief's back, but just barely. While respect was important to her and she was a police officer in a small, old-fashioned town, she wasn't going to let her boss cross that line.

Unfortunately, she couldn't shut down the rest of the town. But still, it was only conjecture, since she knew neither Jen nor Gretchen would talk about her. So what if she and Chase had left the street fair at the same time and neither had been seen again? There were credible reasons why that would happen that did not involve their having sex up against her wall.

She'd been driving the roads of Stewart Mills for nearly an hour, with no more excitement than clearing the road of an empty box that had probably blown out of somebody's truck, when her cell phone's text chime dinged. After parking in one of her favorite spots, she pulled it out of its holster.

I'm going crazy.

It was from Chase and, though she waited a few seconds, no more information seemed forthcoming. Dammit, Chase, I'm a police officer, not a doctor.

Very funny. I want to see you again.

You'll see me at the spaghetti dinner tomorrow.

There was a long pause before her phone chimed again. Unless you're naked, that doesn't count.

She laughed, the sound loud in her empty SUV. When scooping dangly pasta out of boiling water, naked is not recommended.

What about after?

Cleanup and I'm covering late shift.

Call in sick.

Sure, because calling in sick to have sex with Chase the day after her boss was having concerns about her having sex with Chase was a brilliant idea. No.

I'm going to explode.

Hand lotion. There was an image that could get a girl through a long, lonely night.

Tried. It's all that scent your mom uses. I need therapy now.

And now so do I.

A car was coming, and Kelly looked up from her phone in time to see a minivan, driven by a tall, thin guy who looked vaguely familiar, run the stop sign.

Gotta go. John Briscoe has arrived.

Since their last trip to the Stewart Mills House of Pizza hadn't ended well and he had his wife and kids with him, the guys joined John Briscoe at his parents' home for a reunion and cookout. They had a huge backyard and a football, so it was inevitable they ended up tossing it around for a while.

Chase had to admit, it felt pretty good. Football was something he'd been good at and, more importantly, it had taught him that the harder he worked, the better he got. It was a lesson that had gotten him through school, then college and into business. The business hadn't ended so well, but that wasn't entirely his fault.

They'd spent countless hours every week on the field, practicing under Coach's watchful eye. They'd been clumsy at first, dropping balls left and right, but they'd learned. Day after day of Sam handing the football off to him until they weren't sloppy anymore. Chase, getting hit from every direction over and over until he learned how to tuck the ball and protect it while he ran.

Briscoe had run sideline routes until he could be fully extended to bring in the catch while still keeping both of his feet inbounds. Scrimmages had pitted Deck and Alex, along with many others, against each other. They'd hit and they'd hit until they could play it strong and clean at the same time.

Coach had given them everything, both on the sidelines and at home, and they'd given him a championship.

"How are things going?" Sam asked Chase when they took a break to have seconds on fruit salad and some cold drinks.

"Pretty good, I guess." He shrugged. "It's weird. I'll have

been here two weeks tomorrow and, in some ways, I feel like I never left and I'm just here. Like sometimes I have to remind myself I have a life—such as it is—waiting for me in New Jersey."

"You could stay. Just go home and pack your shit and bring it back."

"And do what? Stewart Mills isn't exactly having a building boom."

Sam shrugged. "There's stuff within a reasonable commute to the south, and there's been some activity to the north, from what I've heard. Or don't build houses. Do something else."

"Just like that, huh?" Chase knew Sam had switched jobs many times over the years, doing whatever suited him at the time.

"Yeah. You'd figure it out and make it work if you had a strong enough reason to stay."

A reason like Kelly. With the clock ticking down on his stay in Stewart Mills, Chase had to admit he'd been thinking about her a lot. It was hard to believe that when the weekend was over, he'd be heading home and he just wouldn't see her again.

But he could almost see the look on her face if he told her he was spinning his life further into chaos by bringing it all to Stewart Mills, where there was a good chance he'd end up doing small home repairs in exchange for homemade pies and banana bread. He'd probably be the last man she wanted around, and Coach wouldn't be too impressed, either.

"Have you seen your mom?" he asked Sam, not just to change the subject, but because he knew it had been weighing on the guy's mind.

"Yeah." Sam picked at the label on his bottle of water. "Mrs. McDonnell told me she's been sober awhile, so I stopped by. Mostly just to make Mrs. McDonnell happy, because I stopped giving a shit a long time ago."

"How did it go?"

Sam inhaled deeply through his nose and blew out the breath. "She cried. She knew I was in town, but she was afraid to see me, so . . . she cried a lot and kept telling me she was sorry over and over. Like she'd do back when she was drunk."

"But she's not drunk now."

"Happy for her." Sam took a long swig of water. "I gave her my email address."

It was a start. Email was a lot less personal than his phone number or home address, and the messages were easy to ignore or delete, but maybe his mom would at least have the opportunity to open a dialogue.

Not that Chase blamed Sam at all. His childhood had been ugly, filled with alcohol and anger and pain. The entire town had breathed a sigh of relief when Sam's old man had finally taken off for good, but his mom had spiraled even deeper into the cycle.

Without Coach, Sam probably wouldn't have graduated from high school. There was no way he would have stuck it out, and he would either have run away or ended up in jail.

"Say cheese," Sam muttered, and Chase looked up to see Alex pointing his camera their way. They both flipped him off.

A minute later, John Briscoe joined them, popping the top on a can of beer. "I'd ask if you guys started practicing for the game before I got here but, since we've had to retrieve the football from the neighbor's yard twice and almost broke the living room window, I'm thinking no."

"We didn't want you behind the curve," Sam said, and they all laughed. "How's Rhode Island?"

"Not too bad. Things are going well."

Briscoe, as wide receiver, had been an important part of the championship Eagles team, but he hadn't really been one of Coach's boys. He'd grown up in one of the finer houses in town, with nice parents, had done well in school and gone off to college, where he met his wife.

Chase suspected if John and his wife hadn't seen an opportunity for their kids to visit their grandparents, Briscoe would have passed on the Eagles Fest invitation.

"What's next on the agenda?" Alex asked, pulling up a spot on the deck railing.

Chase noticed they all looked at him. "We have to make sure all the decoration contest entries got logged, because tomorrow afternoon's the deadline, I guess. Jen said she'd explain better when I meet her at the school. Spaghetti dinner tomorrow night. We're supposed to judge the decoration contest on Thursday, but that won't be a big deal since it's all photographed. We can just look at the pictures, assuming we don't screw up tomorrow and miss some."

"We should probably practice at some point," Briscoe added.

They all nodded with a notable lack of enthusiasm. "I need to round up the parents and staff members who'll be filling out the roster. We should at least be able to recognize them on the field."

"It's an exhibition game," Alex said. "For fun."

"For Coach," they all said together.

13

Twice a month, Kelly and Jen tried to meet for breakfast to touch base on the kids. It wasn't necessarily in either of their job descriptions, but sometimes they felt like the first line of defense for the community's children, and they'd do what they had to do.

"I don't have a lot of time," Jen said, sliding into the booth across from Kelly. It was a bad booth at O'Rourke's, wedged in a weird way between the kitchen and the alcove for the restrooms, and they always asked for it. If they talked in low voices, it was as private as one could get out in public. "I have to meet Chase at the school in a little while."

"Really?"

"Yes, really. They're doing the final legwork for the decoration contest today, and I have to give him the lists."

Kelly wanted to ask more about Chase, but there were

more important things on the agenda. After the waitress brought them coffee and took their orders, Kelly filled Jen in on what had happened with Emily Jenkins and the feminine hygiene products heist.

Jen's eyes closed for a moment in sympathy. "That poor girl. It's too bad it didn't happen during the school year."

The community was good about buying doubles of some things when they could and donating the extra to the school nurse. Everything from deodorant to toothpaste to pads could be found in her office, free of charge and with utmost discretion. The kids knew that, and it made a difference for a lot of them.

Kelly and Jen's omelets didn't take long since the restaurant wasn't busy, and they talked while they ate. One by one they went through the list of names they'd been keeping tabs on over the summer. Some of them reached out to Jen for advice, and some ended up having to deal with Kelly when they got in trouble, but the two women worked closely on every incident to make sure it was handled as well as they could manage. This meeting didn't seem to offer up any crises, which was a wonderful thing.

"I just don't think there's a lot going on right now," Kelly said. "Since we really started gearing up toward Eagles Fest, the football players have settled down. The domestic calls are on a slight decline, too. I think things are settling a bit, albeit at a shitty level, and the initial panic stress is petering out. Now it's a long grind."

"I agree. There are still a few families I'm in contact with, but everybody's doing okay."

Kelly sighed. "It's harder during the summer. When we don't see them every day and need a reason to have contact, it's hard to keep up with what's going on in their heads. So, that's it?"

Jen made a face and looked around before leaning forward to whisper. "Keep an eye on Spruce Street."

"That's all you can give me?"

"I wasn't given information about anything specific or criminal, but concern was expressed to me about a young person on the street and whether or not the police monitored that neighborhood."

Kelly sighed. "Hypothetically, if this were a TV show, would it star vice or the special victims unit?

"Vice."

So drugs, not sexual abuse. Stewart Mills had managed to avoid a big drug problem, thanks to the overall lack of money and easy availability. But there were still individuals who knew where to get stuff and would make the trip to bring some back. Because it was small amounts and very few people, it was actually hard to pinpoint problems.

"I'll make sure we're patrolling that neighborhood," Kelly assured Jen.

"Thanks. I guess that's all I've got. And just in time, too. I'm off to see Chase."

Lucky lady. "I'll get the tab. I'm going to order another coffee and scroll through the news on my phone, I think. I've been so wrapped up in Eagles Fest, I'm losing touch."

But once Jen was gone, it wasn't news headlines she pulled up on her phone. She'd taken a picture of Alex's photo of Chase, which had been in the paper, and she looked at it until she saw the waitress heading toward her.

Then she flipped to the news and, after fixing her coffee, settled in to scan the headlines. She'd see Chase at the spaghetti dinner, if she got a moment to herself. In the meantime, she needed to drink her coffee and then get to work.

Chase looked at the papers Jen had spread out on her desk, and nodded. "I think we can handle this."

"Are you sure it's not too much? Because you guys are the honored guests, so we really shouldn't be putting you to work."

"If you don't put us to work, we don't have a good excuse not to practice."

She laughed and sorted the papers into three stacks, neatly clipping each one. "If only Coach could hear you now. Are you sure none of you will get lost? I know you're all from here, but it's been a long time."

"We're each taking a kid," he said, and she looked surprised. "Deck has to work and Briscoe has to do a thing with his parents, so I'm taking a kid in my truck. Alex is taking one in his rental, and Philly has to work, but he's lending Sam his car."

"It's really great that you guys are spending time with the boys. They really need it more than you can imagine, even if they don't show it."

He smiled at her. "We know more about that than you might think. And making them help is better than letting them watch others bust their asses to save their team. Keeps them out of trouble and us out of trouble, and hopefully nobody gets lost."

"Before you go," she said, clasping her hands together on her desk. "If any of you should want access to the school—to take a tour or see the trophy case, for example—just let me know and I can arrange access for you. We have keys."

He would have thought she was simply being polite, except for the way the corners of her mouth twitched upward. She knew they'd broken into the high school, which made sense. She was one of Kelly's best friends. But it made him wonder what else Kelly had told her.

"Thanks," was all he said. "We'll let you know."

He walked back out to where the other guys were just pulling in to the lot and handed the sheets around. "Top one is the address of somebody who filled out the card, emailed or called to say they had a decoration up. We have to confirm we have a photo and take one if we don't. There's also several photos whose addresses got lost and addresses with no photos, and we need to match them up. If we see a decoration while driving around, check the address list and make sure it has a photograph number listed for it."

Alex snorted. "This sounds like work. And somebody needs a new camera. Some of these aren't focused clearly."

"I'll note your objection on the file," Chase said, making Sam laugh. "Let's go meet the kids at the bridge and get this over with."

They were mixing it up a bit, since Hunter and a few of the other boys were picking up some work hours for a landscaper nearby. Chase would be hanging out with a kid named PJ, who jumped into the shotgun seat the second the truck came to a complete stop.

"Hey, Mr. Sanders, I'm PJ."

"Call me Chase. Good to meet you."

"You, too. Jeez, your truck's a mess. My parents moved

here after you left, so you didn't go to school with my dad or date my mom or anything."

Chase's head whirled. "Good to know."

"Wouldn't it be funny if you'd dated my mom, though? I could have been your kid. That would be a funny story, if you came back after all this time and found out I was your kid, wouldn't it?"

"Jesus, kid. You can't be saying stuff like that in a town like this." He wondered if this was some kind of prank. "What position do you play, PJ?"

"Cornerback, though I'm not super good at it. But, really, I'm Coach's secret weapon."

It was probably his job to talk so damn much that the other team couldn't hear their own play calls. Chase pulled away from the curb, wondering how they were supposed to concentrate on addresses and decorations, but PJ took the list and scanned it quickly.

"Take a right up there. Have you guys done a lot of practicing since you got back?"

"Not really. We haven't had a lot of time." Chase made the right turn.

"Bummer. So are you using your old playbook from high school? It would make sense, since it won you the championship."

"We're using some old plays, but we have a few new tricks up our sleeves, too." That was a lie, but he had a feeling this kid had more tricks up his sleeve than they did.

"When we were young, like in middle school, we used to pretend we were you guys. It was pretty awesome but we could never remember all the calls, and the actual binder Coach used is locked in the trophy room. What were some of them?"

"I'm onto you, kid." He glanced over at PJ, who just grinned.

"I told you, I'm Coach's secret weapon. I'll never be an all-star cornerback, but I'm good enough for the position. I only play football so I can go into coaching. Defensive coordinator's what I'm going to be. I can read people and plays like nobody's business."

"I think ours will give you a little trouble," Chase said. If they actually had any. Pretty hard to read plays that didn't exist. He suspected there would be a lot of scrambling on Sam's part due to trying to find a receiver who'd run in the right direction.

"Take a left and then slow down," PJ instructed after glancing down at the list. "Does your friend Alex have a GPS with him?"

"No. Why?" That didn't sound promising.

"He's got Ronnie with him, and he doesn't know where anything is. I think he got lost going from his math class to the cafeteria last year."

"It's an old school, with a lot of hallways. It always takes a month or so to learn your way around."

"He was a junior."

Damn. "If Alex doesn't show up for the spaghetti dinner, I'll see if the rental agency can track the car."

"Good idea."

They cruised the roads of Stewart Mills, covering their assigned area and ensuring everybody who'd entered the decoration contest had an entry and that every entry had a photo. PJ talked the entire time, about everything from algebra to zephyrs, which Chase had never even heard of.

"Hey, cop ahead," PJ announced suddenly. "It looks like

Officer McDonnell. She's really nice. You must know her since she's the coach's daughter, right?"

Chase beeped the horn and waved as he rolled past her. It looked like she was taking pictures of a dented mailbox. A few seconds later, his cell phone rang and he pulled it out to see her number. Even as hit the button to answer it, PJ pulled an iPod from his pocket and a second later was bobbing his head to music Chase couldn't hear.

"Officer McDonnell, what a surprise."

"Was that PJ in the passenger seat?"

"Yeah. PJ and I have been driving around town for two hours on behalf of the Eagles decoration contest."

She laughed for so long, he debated hanging up on her. "Did you draw the short straw?"

Chase wasn't having any part of the conversation. There was a good chance PJ was pretending to listen to music while really using some state-of-the-art eavesdropping device. "I'm learning a lot."

"Ask him about the history of the mills."

"No."

She laughed some more, and then finally quieted. "Here comes the homeowner. I need to take his complaint."

"I'm going to see you at the spaghetti dinner, right?"

"Yeah, but I'll be busy, so I'll be lucky if I get to wave."

That was disappointing. "Oh, before you go. PJ asked me if Alex has a GPS, because his navigator is a kid named Ronnie?"

"Shit. How did Jen let that happen?" He heard her sigh through the phone. "Alex travels a lot, so hopefully he's got a good sense of direction. And I'll keep an eye out for the rental."

"I'll see you tonight. Hopefully we'll see Alex, too."

Once he was off the phone, PJ took out the earbuds and told him he'd be taking a right in about half a mile. Then he started talking about meat processing, and after five minutes of way too much detail, Chase's stomach did a long, slow roll.

"Hey, kid. Do you know anything about the history of the mills?"

Kelly felt as if every single citizen of Stewart Mills was staring at her as she used tongs to plop spaghetti on plate after plate before handing them to Cheryl to add her red sauce and meatballs.

It was her imagination, of course. Not every citizen was even there. And the ones who were seemed too busy talking to each other and eating to stare at her. But she'd seen more than a few speculative glances sent her way. And conversations cutting off in midsentence to be replaced by an overly bright *oh hey, Kelly* meant people were talking about her.

Because she was Coach's daughter and everybody in town knew her, she'd been very careful since being hired by the Stewart Mills police department not to give them anything to talk about. Now she'd gone and had sex with arguably one of the most talked-about people in the town for the time being.

The line finally trickled out and, after nabbing some spaghetti for herself, she made her way outside to the picnic table where Jen was saving her a seat. Don and Cassandra Jones had offered up O'Rourke's for the benefit, since it wasn't easy to cook massive amounts of spaghetti and meatballs on a grill in the town square, but they couldn't seat everybody. Borrowing the same tables and folding chairs the Eagles Fest committee had used for the yard sale, along with a few picnic tables, they'd spread the seating out onto the sidewalk and down into the elementary school playground.

And then they'd have to return them all, she thought with a weary sigh as she sat down. Picking up her fork, she twirled it in the pasta.

She had no regrets when it came to the Eagles Fest, because her parents and her community were everything to her, but she was exhausted. The physical labor was the easy part, too. The constantly scrolling to-do list in her head and putting on an air of unwavering optimism had wiped her out. When it was over, she might take a couple of vacation days and do nothing but sleep, get up and eat, and then sleep some more.

Thinking she heard her name, she glanced up and caught two members of the board of selectmen watching her from a table diagonally across the way. Dan Jarvis turned his face abruptly, but Judy Faring gave her a very prim, pursed-lipped look of disapproval before slightly turning her body away.

Great. It wasn't bad enough the chief was in her business. She needed the town government judging her, too.

"How are you not stuffing your face with this spaghetti?" Jen wiped a smear of red sauce off her lip with her napkin, seemingly oblivious to what was happening around her. "It's like a free pass for all the carbs you can eat, and nobody makes meatballs like Cheryl Decker."

"I feel like everybody's talking about me."

"They're probably wondering why you've been twirling your fork in your pasta for ten minutes without taking a bite. I hope you realize that can't possibly fit in your mouth now."

"I meant talking about me and Chase, smart-ass."

"Which reminds me, tell me about you and Chase."

"There's nothing to tell."

"Interesting." Jen pointed her fork at Kelly. "If there's nothing to tell, what do you think people are saying about you?"

"I meant, *you* already know everything there is to tell."

"Seriously? He's not sneaking out of your parents' house every night and waiting for you to pick him up at the end of the block?"

"Nope. Between Eagles Fest and work, I have erratic hours, and he's been with the guys. And I live right in town, which isn't exactly private, and he's staying in my old room. It's not an easy thing to manage."

"You could meet in Gretchen's barn. Wouldn't that be romantic?"

"You've clearly never had straw poking your naked ass. And the barn cat hates me. She starts hissing the second I walk through the door."

"There has to be a way." Jen shoved another forkful of pasta in her mouth and looked thoughtful while she chewed. "You could always . . . wait. When did *you* have straw poking your naked ass?"

"You're not really paying attention."

"Oh, you have *all* my attention now."

Kelly laughed and used her knife to shove the wad of spaghetti off of her fork so she could start over. "Think about it. I'm the coach's daughter and, just like now, finding privacy was a bitch. Remember Kirby? He only lived here a couple of years before his family moved again."

"Oh, that's right. He was your first."

Kelly nodded. "In Gretchen's barn."

"I guess associating sex with straw poking you in the ass would explain the standing-up-against-the-wall fantasy," Jen said, and Kelly almost choked on her first bite of spaghetti.

"Very funny," she muttered when she'd managed to chew and swallow. "So what's going on with you?"

Jen froze with her fork halfway to her mouth. "What do you mean?"

"I don't know. Yesterday, Gretchen asked me if you were okay. She said you weren't being like you."

Something flashed across her friend's face but was gone before Kelly could identify it. "I had a headache yesterday. One of those that's not horrible, but won't totally go away."

"Those suck." She didn't think that was the entire truth, but Jen was the talkative one of the group, and big on expressing herself. If she didn't want to talk about something, there was a good reason, and she would when she was ready.

They ate their spaghetti, though neither of them cleaned their plates. That was the nice thing about spaghetti dinner fund-raisers. Everybody was willing to cough up the all-you-can-eat price, but very few people actually went back for seconds.

Once everybody had wandered off, the women and the high school team got to work cleaning up. Despite the expense, Kelly was glad they'd gone with disposable plates and utensils. Cassandra had volunteered her staff on her dime to wash the pots and serving spoons, but she couldn't do a town's worth of plates and silverware. Gretchen, who was a lot more used to physical labor than the rest of them, had suggested the three of them could wash by hand in O'Rourke's sinks, but Jen and Kelly had quickly vetoed that.

While going around with a garbage bag, picking up the napkins and occasional fork people had dropped, Kelly spotted Chase and was surprised to see him. She thought he'd left already, but apparently not. He was still there, directing the boys as they returned the picnic tables and various borrowed seating to where it belonged.

Because of the look he gave her, she wasn't surprised when he managed to corner her later in a small back room of O'Rourke's, where she was looking for a broom. There was no door, but somebody would actually have to step into the room and look to the right to see them.

"You're a hard woman to get alone," he said, reaching out to tuck a strand of hair behind her ear.

"I'm not making out with you in what's essentially Don and Cassandra's supply closet. Just to be clear on that up front. I see Alex made it back, by the way."

"He was back before I was, but I think they cheated. And I just put away three helpings of spaghetti and meatballs. I'm surprised I can walk, never mind make out."

"Three?" She shook her head. "You're going to crash hard in a little while."

"If those kids work a little faster, the crash should come when I'm facedown in my pillow." He moved forward, crowding her against the metal shelf unit. "But I wasn't passing up an opportunity to sneak a kiss."

Kelly wrapped her arms around his neck and pulled him

close. "I thought you'd left or I'd have dragged you back here already."

His mouth met hers, and the rush of desire hit her hard. When his hands slid up her waist, she couldn't hold back the small moan of frustration. She needed him, and this was definitely not the place.

Still, they were both breathing a little harder and their hands were roaming to the point that they were treading close to the definition of *making out*, when somebody called Kelly's name.

They parted reluctantly and she gave a breathy laugh as she made sure her shirt was in order. "I needed that."

"I need more."

She walked by him, but paused at the doorway. "We'll figure it out."

"Gretchen's barn?"

That made her laugh. "That's so not going to happen."

14

The next morning, Chase sprawled on his back on the high school football field and stared at the sky, waiting for the wind that had been knocked out of him to come back. He was seriously too old for this shit.

Deck loomed over him, hands on his wide hips and blocking out the sun. "You dead?"

"You're supposed to pull up in practice, not bulldoze me."

"Hell, I didn't even hit you, man. You ran the wrong way and hit *me*."

"And bounced," Sam added.

"You should try running the right route next time," Alex suggested, extending his hand to help Chase to his feet.

"I don't remember that play. Maybe because I'm supposed to be the running back and Briscoe's the wide receiver?"

"I can't catch all the balls," John protested. "We don't even have a tight end. You need to step in and catch some, too."

"What about Dan?" He was the custodian, who'd been in the band during high school, but he met the criteria for the alumni team. Except for the football part.

Dan shook his head. "Last time I tried to catch a ball, I was eleven and it broke my glasses. I'm going to stand in the line and try to knock down anybody who doesn't look old enough to drink."

"That's actually a good plan," Alex said.

"I go that way," Sam said to Chase, pointing to his left, and then he pointed off to the forward right. "And you go that way. I throw the ball. You catch it."

"I thought I went that way." Chase pointed straight down the field.

Sam put his hands on his hips and looked up at the sky as if praying for a lightning bolt to shoot down and end his misery. Then he waved a hand toward the end zone. "You just run somewhere and I'll throw the ball to you. If you catch it, try to fall down before they hit you."

"Sliding's for pussies and quarterbacks." Chase pointed straight down the center. "I'm going that way."

"Brilliant play calling. Those kids will never see what's coming," Briscoe muttered before going to take his position.

Chase thought of PJ, Coach's secret weapon, and laughed. He wasn't sure what the kid would make of this, although he was positive PJ wouldn't be shy about telling him. The other guys looked at him when he laughed, but he just shook his head and lined up. PJ really had to be experienced to be believed.

He made it barely ten yards before the ball hit him in the back of the head and he stumbled, tumbling to the ground again. "What the hell?"

"Ball slipped," Sam called.

It took Chase a few seconds to realize there was laughter coming from the sideline as well as the field, and he sat up to see Coach laughing and shaking his head. "You boys look like a bad movie out there."

"This is where you give us that inspirational speech about being in our prime," Chase said, "and how pride and perseverance and maybe some other P-words will overcome adversity and . . . stuff like that."

"Son, the only P-words that come to mind right now are perspiration and prayers that none of you need an ambulance before this is over."

"I'm blaming Cheryl's meatballs," he heard Sam say. "I must have eaten a thousand of them, and if I'd known she could make meatballs like that, I might have married her before Deck got the chance."

While Chase agreed with Sam's assessment of Cheryl's meatballs wholeheartedly, he knew there was more than an overindulgence of pasta at the root of his inability to get his shit together today. His mind didn't want to focus on trying to remember football plays from a decade and a half ago. It was too preoccupied trying to come up with a plan to get Kelly alone again. A hurried kiss in a restaurant supply room wasn't cutting it.

"Let's take a break," Alex said, and there wasn't a single objection.

They all walked to the sideline, where a cooler full of ice and bottles of water had been stowed under the bench. Chase cracked one open and sat on the bench, wondering what the hell he'd gotten himself into, because they had no chance at all of even competing with a bunch of teenage boys.

Just for fun, he reminded himsclf. The only thing on the line was money, and Chase was doing his part just by showing up and shaking hands. Who cared who won the exhibition game? The real winners would hopefully be the kids when they got to take the field in the fall.

As soon as the guys cleared the field, Briscoe's three boys and Decker's two were out there with a football. The ages varied, but they immediately launched into some kind of catch, keep-away hybrid game. Briscoe and Deck joined them, and Chase laughed when the kids ganged up to take their dads to the ground.

It would be nice to have kids to play ball with, he thought. He could picture the Briscoe family, gathered around the television to cheer on the Patriots, followed by a backyard game of their own.

He always thought he'd have that by now. A house. Some kids to toss a football around with, and it didn't matter if they were boys or girls. A house. A dog. Maybe if he'd given Rina the diamond ring when he bought it, he'd have had some of it by now.

And she probably would have then taken it all in a long, ugly divorce battle, instead of quietly boxing her things and having her new boyfriend carry them out. A wedding band wouldn't have changed things for the better.

Chase drank more water and watched the kids and their dads play. He still had time, he knew. No matter how it felt when he was out on that field, he wasn't old yet. But he was starting over, and things could get messier before they got better. Maybe when the ground was solid under his feet again, he'd find the right woman.

A woman like Kelly, maybe.

"The longer you sit, the harder it'll be to get back out there," Coach told them.

Chase put the cap back on his water. "Says the man whose sole job is to carry a clipboard and wear a whistle."

"And put up with you lot. Let's go, Sanders. Leavitt, you, too. Maybe a few laps will loosen you up."

They laughed at him and made their way back onto the field with no intention of running laps. Or even *a* lap. Sam stepped up behind one of the dads, who was filling in at center, and then pointed at Chase. "You run to the left and wave your hands in the air, and then I'll throw the ball to Briscoe."

"Just call a damn play," Chase growled. "I'm not that far gone yet."

"Keep telling yourself that, old man."

On Thursday afternoon, Kelly walked over to Eagles Lane to visit her parents. Because she'd seen the mail carrier up the street, she grabbed the mail from the box on her way into the house.

Her mom was in the kitchen, sorting through her coupon box. Helen McDonnell had watched a show about extreme couponing a few years back and, while she didn't go to extremes, she'd made something of a sport out of grocery shopping. "Hi, honey."

"Where's Dad?"

"He's working this afternoon. He'll probably be gone a couple of hours, at least."

Technically, there was still a McDonnell's Plumbing office downtown, and her parents visited it a few times per week. The paperwork was all there, as well as the ancient computer they both hated. But more often than not now, they stayed home. If somebody called, Coach went to work. If not, he worked around the house, taking care of the honey-do list his wife made out for him each week.

"I grabbed your mail." She set it on the counter, but slipped the weekly newspaper out of the pile and tossed it on the table. Then she poured a glass of lemonade, topped off her mom's, and sat down.

Her mom hummed while she sifted through the coupons, checking expiration dates and pulling any that corresponded to the week's shopping list. Kelly flipped through the paper until she came to an article about Eagles Fest.

The writing was fairly routine, which wasn't a surprise since the same guy had been writing the community articles for as long as Kelly could remember, but the photos drew her attention. They were more eye-catching than usual, with vivid detail even in black and white. Sure enough, when she looked closer at the fine print in the captions, the photos were credited to Alex Murphy.

She wondered if the editor of the weekly had an idea of who Alex was or if he'd just been offered high-quality photos and used them.

Alex had managed to get a shot of the dunking booth, catching Chase in the middle of his ridiculous windup. At the edge of the photo was the tank itself, and Kelly was laughing at him. Probably taunting him, too. Even as she admired Alex's eye for composition, the memory of Chase playing up to the crowd made her smile.

She traced her finger over his picture, thinking about the fact that he'd be stopping by later for a quick dinner. Earlier he'd texted her a photo of them all sprawled out on the football field, with a note that he should get some kind of special reward for working so hard.

"Kelly, I hope you're being careful."

She looked up, her face flaming when she realized her mom had been watching her practically stroking a picture of Chase Sanders. "Uh, what?"

"There's been talk, honey. And look at you." She pointed at the newspaper. "I know you're young and having fun, but the more I see you two together, the more I worry you're getting too involved with him."

"I'm not." She closed the paper and set it aside. Talking about Chase to her mom wasn't particularly high on the list of things she wanted to do, but she may as well face it head-on. "What does Dad think about the talk?"

Her mom sighed. "He's trying to ignore it because you're his daughter and he doesn't want to hear about certain details of your life. Plus, as I keep reminding him, it's really none of his business. But he worries about you. He doesn't want you to get hurt like last time."

Kelly swallowed a mouthful of lemonade. "There's a big difference between having a fling and getting divorced because your husband cheated on you."

"Broken hearts hurt no matter why they broke."

"Chase isn't going to break my heart, Mom. It's really not like that."

"Okay." Her mom slid a stack of coupons into a plastic sleeve labeled *baking products*. "Since everybody knows he bought condoms at the drugstore, at least I don't have to ask you if you're using protection."

Kelly laughed, even though she was totally sure she didn't want to talk condoms with her mother over coupons. "It's all under control, I promise. But do you think I should find him a different place to stay? Are you guys okay with him being here? Or is Dad, I guess I should say."

"We're fine. As long as you're okay and Chase is being respectful, your dad will stay out of it. You're his daughter, but Chase is important to him, too."

"I know." Kelly could kind of see where Chase had been coming from now. It was a little awkward, sleeping with the guy who was staying with her parents. It had to be even worse on Chase's end.

They visited awhile, making small talk and going through the coupons. Kelly had tried to show her mother how to find some online, but it hadn't worked out. Her mom liked gathering the coupon sections from the Sunday papers and clipping them while they watched television. Kelly thought it was as much something to do as it was about saving money, and using the computer and printer took the fun out of it for her.

"I have to stop at the store and grab some things for dinner, so I should go," Kelly said after an hour of reading tiny expiration dates started making her eyes hurt. "Tell Dad I said hi and that I'm sorry I missed him."

"I will. And I'll tell Chase you said hi, too. I don't think he's joining us for dinner tonight, though. Said something about grabbing a quick bite with a friend."

"Subtle, Mom." She kissed her mother's cheek and rinsed her lemonade glass. "Yes, I'm making Chase dinner, but just tacos. No meat or mashed potatoes."

"Is that how we separate flings from marriage material? Meat and mashed potatoes are for potential husbands?"

"And casseroles. Chase is definitely not marriage material, so no casseroles for him."

Her mom smiled, but it didn't quite reach her eyes. "He's leaving soon, so casseroles would be a waste of time."

As if she could forget. "Just tossing some ground beef and seasonings into a shell."

Kelly walked to the market for the makings of soft tacos, her mind now stuck on the fact that Chase would be leaving soon. The big game was tomorrow night, and then Eagles Fest would close out on Saturday with the parade. He'd never said when he actually planned to leave, and she'd never asked.

If he left Stewart Mills on Sunday morning, he'd be back in New Jersey and ready to start getting his life back on track for Monday morning.

Two and a half days, she thought, with a good chunk of that time already committed to the fund-raising activities. She backtracked through the store, putting back the groceries she'd already gathered, and then she went to the freezer section. After a moment's deliberation over toppings, she grabbed a couple of frozen pepperoni pizzas.

The less time they spent on supper, the more time they could spend in bed. And she liked being in bed with Chase a lot, so there was no time for tacos.

Chase waited for Kelly to let him in, determined to keep a tight leash on his raging libido. His balls ached even more than the rest of his body—so much that sitting on a kitchen chair was going to be brutal—but she was making him dinner, so he was going to show the proper appreciation and eat every bite before trying to get into her pants.

Then she opened the door and that fruity cop smell hit him, and he wanted to sweep everything off the table and take her right then and there.

But as the door closed behind him, he realized there were no food smells mingling with the aroma of fruit. No candles or place settings on the table. No food prep happening on the counter. If she hadn't even started cooking yet, that leash on his libido was going to start chafing in a big way.

"I haven't started dinner yet," she said, "but it only takes twenty minutes. I can start it now if you're hungry."

Chase hesitated, not sure how to ask what the alternative was. He didn't want to sit and watch the news with her first, if that's what she was asking. Then she tucked her finger under the neck of his T-shirt and tugged him closer for a kiss.

Any hunger for food was forgotten in the sharp resurgence of his hunger for her, and he put his hands on her waist to pull her up against his body. He'd missed her, and the kiss at O'Rourke's had only made it worse.

"I'd carry you to your bedroom," he said against her mouth, "but we practiced this morning, and I barely made it up your stairs. I'd probably drop you."

She laughed. "I had some fireman's carry training at the

academy and could probably carry *you*, but it's not really sexy, so it might be better if we just walk."

When she took his hand and led him toward the bedroom, Chase wondered how he'd been lucky enough to get lucky with this woman. "If you hadn't invited me over, I'd probably still be lying on the field at the high school, waiting for somebody to help me up."

"Is that your way of telling me I'm going to have to do all the work?"

"Judging by how long it took me to get my shirt over my head after my shower, I might need some help getting it back off." He hooked his arm around her waist and held her still so he could nuzzle the back of her neck. "But I think I'm getting my second wind."

She moaned, tipping her head forward so her hair slid out of the way, exposing the nape of her neck to his mouth. He kissed that soft spot, inhaling her soap or shampoo or whatever it was that made her smell so good. He loved her scent. The softness of her skin. Her sense of humor. The way she softened under his touch, liking for him to take charge. He couldn't think of a damn thing about Kelly he didn't like.

They helped each other out of their clothes, pausing now and then for kisses that turned him inside out. Her soft chuckle at his grimace when he lifted his arms so she could pull his T-shirt off made him laugh. "It's your fault I was on the football field this morning, you know. I think you should rub me down and make me feel better."

She ran her hands over his chest and then pushed until he was on his back on her bed. When she straddled him, he forgot all about his aches and pains, and dug his fingers into her hips. He'd tossed a condom onto the bed while they were getting undressed, and he needed to find it before she went too far.

But Kelly had other ideas and, when she began kneading the muscles in his shoulders and upper arms, he closed his eyes. "That feels so good."

She massaged her way down one arm until her thumb was pressing circles against his palm. Then her mouth closed over his finger, and his breath caught. His other hand fisted in the sheets when she sucked lightly.

He managed to hold himself in check as she showed the same attention to his other arm, but when her hands ran over his thighs, he buried his hands in her hair and growled her name in warning. It had been too long a wait to be playing games.

Being Kelly, she ignored him. He was barely aware of her hands massaging his sore thigh muscles as she ran her tongue up the length of his erection. All he could do was tighten his fingers in her hair and groan. He knew he should make her stop but when her mouth closed over him, he forgot why. All he knew was the warm, wet suction of her mouth and the soft strands of her hair that escaped his hands, tickling his thighs.

When he couldn't take it anymore and felt the end was imminent, he tugged at her hair. Kelly got a last quick flick of her tongue in before he hauled her up next to him and rolled over her, bracing himself on his elbows.

"Did that help?" she asked, a smile flirting with the corners of her mouth. She lifted her hand and he saw that she'd found the wrapped condom he'd tossed onto the bed.

"We don't need that yet," he said, trailing his fingers down her stomach. "You've been working pretty hard, too."

"I'm fine. Let's just—"

She stopped talking when he closed his mouth over her nipple and sucked hard. He kept it up until her back arched off the bed. "Let's just what?"

"I forget."

Chase laughed, then kissed his way down her stomach. Her shuddering sigh when he slid his hand up her calf was like a physical caress, and he hooked it behind her knee so he could bury his head between her thighs.

He took his time, savoring her and enjoying the way her body jerked when he ran his tongue over her clit. Her fist pounded on his shoulder as she got impatient, but he ignored her. He dipped his tongue into her sweet center, and then slid his finger inside her. She moaned and he swirled his tongue over her clit again as he worked two more fingers in, stretching her, as her breath shortened. Her fingernails raked his shoulders almost painfully when she came, and he nipped at her thigh.

While she caught her breath, Chase put on the condom and rolled her onto her stomach. Then he pulled her backward until her feet were on the floor and she was bent over the bed. He ran his hands over her back and her hips, making her shiver, before reaching between their bodies. There was no doubt she was ready for him, and he slid into her in one quick thrust.

Kelly gasped, her fingers clenching in the sheets, and Chase paused. He took in the moment—her body tight around his and the pounding of his heart and the curve of her back and the strands of blond hair over her flushed cheeks and her hands tangling the sheets—and then gripped her hips as he started to move. He wanted it to last forever, but it was too much. After her lips wrapped around his cock and her coming against his mouth, he was too close.

His pace quickened and he lifted her right knee to the edge of the mattress so he could thrust deeper and reach under her leg to press the heel of his hand against her mound. He came hard, pounding into her, and he heard her cry out his name as her body shuddered.

As the orgasm passed, he collapsed on top of her, both of them hanging over the side of the bed. It wasn't exactly comfortable, but neither of them seemed to care. He bit down on his lip as he tried to catch his breath, afraid he'd voice heat-of-passion emotions he couldn't take back.

"Now I'm starving," she muttered against the mattress after a couple of minutes. "When I can move again, I guess it's time to make that supper I promised you."

"Give me a few more minutes and then I'll help."

She laughed. "Trust me, I'm not going to need any help."

15

"I've never had a woman cook frozen pizza for me before," Chase said, picking up one of the slices Kelly had set in front of him on a paper plate. "I feel strangely flattered."

"Being flattered by frozen pizzas would be a little strange, yes."

He had to think about that one. "Well, it means you're comfortable with me, right?"

"Or it means I don't give a shit if you know I'm lazy." She grinned when he frowned at her.

"I'm going to stick with my theory."

"Hey, at least they're the kind that go in the oven. I almost got the little microwave ones." She sat down across from him, her hair still messed up from his hands being in it and her cheeks still rosy from the orgasms. "What do women usually cook for you?"

"Casseroles. They usually have ham in them. Or broccoli, which I don't get as a date food because it's the worst at getting stuck in your teeth." He took a bite of the pizza because he was starving. Once he'd chewed and swallowed it, he swiped at his mouth with a napkin. "Chicken, but not barbeque or fried chicken. Fancy stuff, like chicken cordon bleu and such."

"Because they're trying to impress you."

"And you don't care about impressing me?"

"Nope."

He waited while she ate a bite of her pizza to see if she'd expound on that resounding *nope* at all. Not that his feelings were hurt, but the transition from her naked body under his to her clearly not giving a crap what he thought of her was pretty abrupt.

When he didn't say anything, she shrugged. "Those women are showing you what you could look forward to in the future if you put a ring on it. You're leaving in a few days and, if you ever think about me again, it won't be the food that's on your mind."

"How could I forget frozen pizza?" he teased.

She was wrong when she said *if* he ever thought of her again. He'd think about her. He thought about her all the time now—what she was doing, how work was going, when he could see her again—and he didn't think a day's drive to New Jersey was going to change that. But wondering if she'd ever think about *him* at all bruised his pride a little.

Of course, if she did think about him it would probably be to wonder what she'd been thinking, sleeping with a guy who'd managed to screw up every aspect of his life before he even hit middle age and barely had a pot to piss in. He needed to keep reminding himself why this was a fling and not a relationship, or he was going to get in trouble.

"I had a choice," she continued. "I could make a nice dinner, which would take forever to cook and eat, or we could have frozen pizza and use that extra time in a better way."

"You made the right choice," he said. While he'd probably end up prowling around the McDonnells' kitchen in the middle of the night, looking for a snack, he didn't want to spend what time he could sneak with Kelly watching her chop vegetables.

They demolished one and a half pizzas while talking about the upcoming game and the other guys and the parade. When Chase expressed some concern about walking the parade route, Kelly laughed and told him she was sure Jen had a float arranged for them. They wouldn't make the honored guests walk circles around Stewart Mills.

"Have you heard anything from back home?" she asked, tossing her balled-up napkin onto her empty paper plate.

"Like what?" He hadn't really thought much about home in the last couple of days.

She shrugged. "I didn't know if they found your business partner or how things were going with work and stuff."

The question took a little of the shine off the evening. "They did find Seth, and at first he claimed he didn't take it. But everybody knows that's not true, so now he's claiming it was his money, too, so he was free to take it. There are lawyers involved and possible criminal charges, depending on how it shakes out, so it'll take a while to sort."

"But you'll be okay?"

"Yeah. Starting over sucks, but at least I won't be starting over in too big a hole. I'll manage whether I'm able to recoup any money from Seth or not."

"That's good news, then."

He tried to read her expression, but she gave him nothing but friendly curiosity. He wasn't sure what he was looking for. Maybe some sign her interest was more than friendly? She could be fishing to see if his life was in better shape than it had been before, which might give him a promotion into relationship material.

But it didn't matter. As he'd said, the hole he'd be digging his way out of wasn't too deep, but it was still a hole. The foundation he'd been basing his life on had been built on sand and collapsed. He had no interest in dragging anybody else into the rubble, especially Kelly.

He reluctantly pushed his chair back from the table. "I should get going. Even though I know it doesn't bother your parents, I hate being out late. It feels rude. Plus, you have to work early."

"And the big game's tomorrow." She stood, too, and walked with him to the door. "You have plans beforehand?"

"Nope. We decided if we try to do a pregame practice, we'll be too tired to actually play the game. Napping was mentioned."

She laughed. "Do you want to grab a late lunch after my shift?"

"I'll definitely need to eat."

"Good. I'll text you the time and place."

He kissed her good night, trying not to lose himself in it so completely that he ended up back in her bed. Only the knowledge her shift would start before he was even out of bed in the morning gave him the will to break it off.

"I'll see you tomorrow," he said, and she smiled.

Chase stepped out onto the street and, because he was paying attention to making sure the outside door locked behind him, almost ran into another pedestrian.

The man, who was probably a little intoxicated, looked from Chase to the door and back. "Kelly McDonnell, huh? Lucky bastard."

He had vague recognition of the guy's face, but he couldn't come up with a name, which meant they'd probably gone to school together but were in different years or different social circles. It had been happening to him since he'd arrived in town, though most people were quick to fill in the blanks. This guy was too drunk to care that Chase had no clue who he was.

"Tried to hit that last summer," the guy continued. "Figured I'd get out of a ticket and get laid at the same time. She went all ice princess on me, though. Stuck-up bitch."

Chase's right hand went so far as to curl into a fist, but he didn't plow it into the asshole's face. As satisfying as it would be, it wasn't worth it. And Kelly being dragged into a Stewart Mills police report about two guys fighting over sexual remarks made about her would be humiliating on both a personal and professional level.

"Guess she just wasn't that into you," was all he said, and started past him.

"Guess Coach's daughter wanted herself a washed-up football player," the guy called after him, but Chase didn't take the bait. He just kept on walking.

As always, the lights had been left on for him at the McDonnell house, but he was surprised to hear the television when he went through the front door. Coach and his wife hadn't gone to bed yet, and walking into the living room felt like walking into a brick wall of tension. Coach looked up from his television show long enough to nod, his jaw tight, but Mrs. McDonnell smiled.

"How was your dinner?"

"It was good," he said, not knowing if she'd guessed—or even knew for a fact—that his dinner had been with her daughter. It was obvious Coach thought it, so she must, too. Maybe she was just handling it better.

"Have a seat if you want. This show just started, but you haven't missed much. There's a dead body and they have to figure out whodunit."

"I'll probably go upstairs and settle in." Which was ridiculous. It was too early for him to go to bed and they all knew it. "The big game's tomorrow."

"Are you sure?" She set her knitting in her lap, looking concerned. "Are you feeling okay?"

"I've seen them on the field," Coach said. "Trust me, he needs all the rest he can get."

The smile took the edge off of the implication he wanted Chase to go away, but he got the message nonetheless. After saying good night, he went upstairs and stretched out on top of Kelly's bed to stare at the ceiling.

Apparently he hadn't done a good enough job of screwing up his life in New Jersey, so he had to continue on in Stewart Mills. People were gossiping about him and Kelly, which was the one thing she specifically hadn't wanted to happen. And Coach McDonnell wasn't happy one of his former players was messing around with his daughter, which was the thing Chase hadn't wanted to happen.

If he fumbled the ball tomorrow as badly as he was fumbling life, the alumni team didn't stand a chance.

The next morning, Kelly parked her cruiser next to Jen's car in the school parking lot and used her key to let herself in. The teachers and custodial team were in the building a lot during the summer months, but the doors were always locked because the office wasn't always staffed.

It was going to be a long day that started with an early shift and would end with the alumni game—and a late lunch with Chase in between—but she had to nail down a few details for the parade. Since she'd been driving by when she remembered Chase's concerns about walking, she decided to drop in instead of calling.

She made her way back to the guidance office and saw Jen bent over her desk, flipping through a folder. "Hey."

"Hey! What brings you here?" Her brows furrowed. "Please tell me none of the kids are in trouble."

"Nope. Nothing like that. They've been great, actually. I think seeing the town turn out the way it has to help them out is making a difference. They've been in better spirits and they're eager to help wherever they can. I just stopped by to say hello because I'm bored."

"Boring's probably a good thing in your line of work."

"Makes for long shifts, though."

"I'm just catching up on some reading. Sit down and tell me how things are going with you and Chase."

"Not boring." She sat in the visitor's chair with a sigh. Frozen pizzas had definitely been the right choice, since they were in bed less than two minutes after she let him in. It would have been a shame to miss out on an extra orgasm or two because she was shredding lettuce for tacos.

"What do you mean by not boring? Is it getting serious?"

"No. Not serious. Just fun. Very fun, actually." She shrugged. "Of course my mom's worried. I'm not sure she understands sex can have nothing to do with emotion. I've never asked because I do *not* want details, but I think my dad was her first and only."

"Of course sex can have nothing to do with emotion. It can be for fun or as a stress release. Or maybe it just happens and nobody can figure out why. But definitely no emotion."

Her friend sounded more agitated with each word, and Gretchen's concerns earlier in the week ran through Kelly's mind. "Oh my God, you had sex with Sam Leavitt, didn't you?"

Jen froze, and then her mouth tightened in a show of stubbornness. "Just because you're taking advantage of attractive men being in town temporarily to have random sex doesn't mean everybody else is."

"And bitchiness, too." Kelly grinned and leaned forward. "You're hiding something, Jen Cooper."

"No, I'm not."

"You'll feel better if you tell me."

"There's nothing to tell."

Kelly tapped her badge. "I've been professionally trained in this. Just confess already."

"Fine. I had sex with Sam Leavitt."

"Damn, I'm good at this job." She leaned back in the chair again. "When?"

"After the street fair. I was driving home and he was walking. I don't think he even knew where he was going. He was just walking along the side of the road."

"Did he see his mom? At the street fair, I mean." She thought she'd seen Sheila and had meant to say hi. And saying hi meant making sure she was still sober and was okay out in public. But it had been a busy night, and her time had ended up being split between watching Chase and trying not to die of hypothermia.

"Yeah. I told him to get in the car and we started talking, so I parked out by the dam. You know the spot."

Kelly knew the spot. Kids had been going parking there for as long as Stewart Mills had cars, but it had never occurred to her to meet Chase there. "So, talking and comfort and touching and . . . you had sex in your car?"

"*On* my car." Jen dropped her head into her hands. "I had sex with Sam Leavitt on the hood of my car."

"Wow. That's *really* not boring. So why do you look like you just dropped your ice cream on the floor?"

"Because why would I do that? With him, of all people. On my car."

Kelly was tempted to laugh, but she realized Jen was honestly upset with herself. "You said yourself sex can be a stress release. Maybe that's all it was. You both needed somebody, and you happened to be alone together."

"I just don't understand it, Kel. There's literally nothing about that man I should find attractive."

Should find attractive. It was a telling word. "Was it bad?"

"That's the worst part." Jen grimaced. "It was . . . amazing."

"Okay, I don't care how upset you are. I'm not offering

you condolences for having amazing sex with a hot guy on the hood of your car."

That actually made Jen laugh. "I guess there are worse things."

"Having bad sex with a guy on your car would be worse. Have you talked to him since?"

She shook her head. "Honestly, I don't think he's any more attracted to me than I am to him. It was just . . . one of those things, I guess."

"There you go. Just one of those things."

"Enough about me. Sam's leaving after the parade, and I'll never see him again. Let's talk about you."

Kelly wasn't sure she wanted to do that. In contrast to Jen's sexual escapade, what she and Chase had going on looked an awful lot like a relationship. They might not get to spend a lot of time together, but when they did, they enjoyed each other's company. They ate meals together and made each other laugh. They texted when they could. There was no denying the sexual chemistry was there.

And, if she was totally honest with herself, she was probably going to miss him when he was gone.

"I actually stopped by to ask you about the parade, not just because I was bored," Kelly said, diverting the conversation away from herself, since she knew Jen really wanted to know how things were with Chase. "Last I remember, we hadn't figured out the transportation for the team."

Jen gave her an *I know what you're up to* look, but leaned back in her chair. "The kids will ride in the back of three pickups like they usually do. The alumni team we're going to put on a float, so they can have chairs and they'll be waving the trophy around. Gretchen's loaning us the trailer her grandfather used for haying, and the cheerleaders are supposed to be decorating it today."

"Who's driving that truck?" An alumni player's chair tumbling off the float during a jerky start or stop would be a very bad way to close out Eagles Fest.

"Gretchen said she'd do it. It's a big-ass trailer, but she's been pulling it behind a truck since she was tall enough to see over the steering wheel out in the fields." Jen picked up her pen and started doodling on a sheet of paper Kelly hoped wasn't important. "I've been trying to estimate how many people will show up for the game."

"At a token dollar per ticket for something to do on a Friday night, I think we'll come close to filling the stands."

"It's going to be close."

Kelly nodded, feeling a profound sense of relief. She had some savings, so all she needed was close. Being *really* close would be nice, since it wasn't a huge savings, but she'd make an anonymous donation if she had to. "We'll make it."

"I believe you." Jen looked at her, a slow smile lighting up her face. "I think we might have saved Eagles football."

Chase pulled his phone out just enough to check the time without being too obvious. He was meeting Kelly for lunch, and this judging gig was taking forever. It had been Mrs. McDonnell's idea to have the alumni guys judge the Eagles Fest decoration contest, because Kelly, Jen and Gretchen had already given so much of their time. And while it wasn't possible to have *no* bias, the guys had mostly been away for long enough to mitigate the problem of judging one's neighbors.

So they'd all gathered at the town square gazebo to go through photos of the entries in what should have been a quick process. Unfortunately, none of the other guys seemed to have a hot lunch date, so there was more socializing than judging.

The football team was there to help keep things organized. There were so many entries, just going through and trying to narrow it down to three favorites of multiple judges seemed unwieldy, so they'd judge the photos individually. Each judge would give it a number between one and ten, and then it was just a matter of math.

It should have taken an hour, tops.

"We keeping you from something?" Sam asked with a pointed glance toward the phone Chase was sliding back into his pocket.

"Nope." Not yet, anyway.

"Oh, dude! This one's awesome!" Cody held up a picture of a scarecrow dressed in jeans and an Eagles T-shirt, holding what appeared to be a trophy made of gold-painted soda cans.

Chase had to agree. The scarecrow was nothing special, but the trophy deserved some points.

It took a lot longer than he'd anticipated to choose the top three entrants, and then there was some dissention in ranking those in first through third order. But they finally got it settled and wrote out their final decision, which would be delivered to Jen. Local businesses like O'Rourke's and the Stewart Mills House of Pizza had offered gift certificates as prizes, so she'd be handling the announcement and delivery of prizes.

Chase was going to make a run for it, but he saw Hunter

packing up the cooler they'd brought. The kid was alone, so Chase took the opportunity to see how he was doing. He knew the other alumni felt much the same about the kids as he did—they were reminded of themselves as teenagers—and he'd seen their attitudes improve over the course of Eagles Fest. He hoped it continued.

"How are things going, kid?" Chase picked up a couple of empty soda cans to toss in the garbage.

Hunter shrugged one shoulder. "Pretty good. My dad's had a couple of interviews, and one looks really good. He's not drinking as much. And my mom found a program that helps her get a degree online. It's still tight, but now everybody's kinda . . . I don't know."

"Hopeful?"

"Yeah." Hunter looked at him, nodding. "Like we'll be okay. And my dad talked to me about football. Like *really* talked. We're a small school and we're not in a really competitive class so, even if we get to keep the team, I can't count on a football scholarship. I can try for one, but no matter what, I need to get good grades. What if I screw up my knee or something? One bad fall and I could end up working for minimum wage because I pinned everything on football."

Chase hadn't known the kids long, but it stirred something inside him to see the change in Hunter from their first meeting until now, all because he'd realized people cared about him and his future. He wondered if it's how Coach had felt back in the day, when he'd taken a group of boys who needed that and helped them be champions. More than that, he'd helped them see a future beyond what they'd been shown at home, and they were all better for it.

Maybe when things were rough, Hunter would find strength in the memory of Stewart Mills rallying around him and his teammates, the way Chase had found strength in everything Coach had taught him.

It would be tough to leave them all behind, he realized. Not just Kelly, though *especially* Kelly. Even with the tension between them, Chase loved being a part of Coach and Mrs. McDonnell's lives again. And the kids. He'd seen them working to turn things around, and he wanted to know how they did. Not just the upcoming football season they all hoped would happen, but in life.

"I've gotta run," Hunter said, hoisting the cooler. "My ride's leaving. See you on the field."

"Yeah. Have a good one."

He watched the boy walk away and then shook his head. Once he left, he didn't think he'd hear from Kelly again. She'd made it pretty clear she was looking for fun sex with a man there was no hope of a future with.

Maybe he'd keep in touch with Decker, he thought. Deck would know what was happening with the football team, and Cheryl would probably know what was going on in their personal lives.

He wouldn't ask them about Kelly, though. As hard as he suspected it was going to be, once he left Stewart Mills, he had to let her go.

16

Kelly knew her day was about to take a turn for the worse when she walked into the station and saw Edna Beecher and Selectman Judy Faring talking to the chief. And since they were gathered in front of her desk, there was no way she could avoid being seen.

All she wanted to do was finish her shift, run home to change, and meet Chase for lunch. She probably should have just told him to meet her at her place, but she'd gotten it in her head it would be nice to go out to a restaurant and have a real meal with him. Like a date. Only not a date, because they weren't dating.

When she got within earshot, her stomach sank.

"Those men did us all a favor by coming back here to help out our kids," the chief was saying. "We're not going to repay that kindness by hassling them over stop signs that weren't there before."

"I also heard there was a break-in at the high school and no charges were pressed," Judy added. "If laws are being circumvented because Officer McDonnell is having a personal—even intimate—relationship with the offender, that's a problem."

"It's *police corruption*," Edna added, and Kelly heard the glee in her voice.

"Even if I was going to treat that accusation as credible, which I'm not," the chief said, "this is not a conversation to have in the middle of the police station. My officers let our visitors off with warnings about the stop sign at my instruction, the same way we gave all of you warnings when they first went up. And as for the high school, that was a misunderstanding."

The chief must have seen her approaching from behind the women through the corner of his eye, because he made a very subtle *go away* gesture. Kelly reversed direction and ducked around a corner. She could still hear, but she couldn't be seen.

"Now, Edna, you know we appreciate how you've looked out for this town. And Judy, I respect that, as a member of the board of selectmen, you're making sure we're doing our job. But I can assure you there's no police corruption in Stewart Mills, nor has there ever been any inappropriate conduct from Officer McDonnell."

"I'll be watching her," Edna promised.

She was always watching everybody, so that came as no surprise to Kelly, but she was more interested in what Judy Faring would say. If she and Edna could whip the town government into a frenzy over a nonexistent scandal, Kelly's job could be in trouble.

Luckily, Judy wasn't leaving without putting in her two cents. "It's your reputation on the line here, Chief, so I'll leave it in your hands. But if more citizens express concern, we might have to look into the situation more. In an official way."

"I understand. But I'll vouch for Kelly McDonnell both personally and professionally any day of the week, Judy."

Kelly leaned her head back against the wall and, from her hiding place, watched the two women leave. What a mess. And the very thing she'd been trying to avoid all along.

"You can come out now."

She turned the corner and walked to her desk, which her boss was leaning against. He looked more bemused than upset, which she took as a good sign.

"I'm really sorry about that, Chief."

"Nothing to be sorry about. You haven't done a damn thing wrong." He cleared his throat. "I got caught up in the wife's gossip and almost crossed a line I shouldn't have, but this is ridiculous. Your personal life is your own business."

"Thank you. And thank you for covering on the stop sign issue. And the school."

He shrugged. "If you'd come to me and asked me how to handle it ahead of time, I would have told you to do what you did, so therefore it wasn't really covering."

"Hopefully Edna will let it go." She winced. "You know she might call the FBI, right?"

"I'd expect nothing less from Edna Beecher. But trust me when I tell you she's not going to get the satisfaction she's looking for. She's probably part of their training on how to identify credible reports." They laughed together and then he shrugged. "Besides, Sanders and the other guys will probably all be gone by Monday and it'll be a moot point."

It was a good thing her boss chose to walk away, because emotion suddenly knotted in her throat, and she wasn't sure she could have continued the conversation. Logically, she knew the guys—including Chase—would probably all be gone by Monday, but she hadn't allowed herself to think too much about it. And now it wasn't some random time in the future. Monday was right around the corner.

It was in the shower, preparing for her lunch with Chase, that it hit her. *Maybe he would stay.*

He liked being in Stewart Mills. She could tell. He'd rekindled old friendships, and he genuinely cared about the people, especially the teens he'd gotten to know through Eagles Fest activities. He wasn't particularly close to his parents, and he wouldn't be so far away that he'd never see his sister or her family.

She wouldn't mind going home to Chase at the end of a long shift.

But even as the thought tried to take hold in her mind, she tried to squash it. Of course he liked being in Stewart Mills. It was like a vacation from the mess he'd left behind in New Jersey. She was his vacation fling. People liked going to Las Vegas or the Bahamas and having a couple of carefree, fun-filled weeks, but that didn't mean they pulled up stakes and moved there.

And even if he did, he wasn't in a stable place, and that scared her. His life was currently a mess, so he couldn't really make life decisions with a clear head. What if it seemed like settling down in Stewart Mills with Kelly was a good idea, but once he had his feet back under him, he realized that wasn't what he'd wanted, after all?

She'd married a man who came to that realization. Or more accurately, she'd been absolutely devastated by a man who'd realized too late that a life with her wasn't what he really wanted. She was never putting herself in a position to be hurt like that again.

If and when she put her heart on the line a second time, it would be for a man who had a stable life and knew exactly what he wanted his future to be. Right now, the only man she could imagine might be Chase but, as the chief had said, by Monday he'd be gone. Eventually she'd get over him and find the *right* man for her.

But today was only Friday, so she grabbed her keys and went to meet Chase.

Something had changed in Kelly between last night and being seated at a quiet family restaurant about fifteen minutes south of town. Chase couldn't put his finger on it, but her smile seemed a little strained, and there was tension in her body.

"Rough day?" he asked, wondering if maybe something had happened at work. Although, if something happened in Stewart Mills of a magnitude to cause a bad day for the police department, he probably would have heard about it. Unless it was a domestic issue. He knew there had been a few of those calls since he got into town, and they weighed on her.

"Not really." She picked up the menu. "Early morning, though. I could use a nap."

"Instead you had to drive down here just for lunch." Maybe that was all it was. "It seems like everybody knows—or at least thinks they know—what's going on. We could have just met at O'Rourke's."

"It's one thing to know people are talking about us. It's something else to have them all staring at us while we eat."

"I guess. It's not a big deal, though. I mean, you being seen with me."

"Tell that to Edna Beecher, who showed up at the station today with a member of the board of selectmen to accuse me of police corruption for allowing you to run stop signs and break into the high school because I'm having sex with you."

He knew his jaw dropped open like a cartoon character's, but he couldn't even make sense of the words coming out of her mouth. "You're kidding, right?"

"No, I'm not. Never underestimate the determination of a small town to start a scandal if there's sex involved."

"Holy shit, Kelly. You're not in trouble, are you?"

"According to the chief, no. He knows they're being ridiculous. And it's Edna. Very few people take Edna seriously."

"According to the chief? So that means you could still be in trouble with somebody else?" He couldn't believe this was happening. When she'd first mentioned the possibility her reputation could be damaged by sleeping with him, he'd thought it was a joke.

"It's fine. The worst that could happen is that Edna or Judy actually brings it up at a meeting, and then it's in the minutes and I'd probably have to make some kind of statement. But I'm not going to lose my job or anything."

"No wonder we left town to eat."

She smiled at him over the top of her menu. "I picked this place before that happened so, no, I'm not hiding you from anybody. I just wanted to have a nice meal with you without being interrupted by a bunch of people."

And without the good people of Stewart Mills staring at them, as she'd said. And not staring at them, apparently, but taking notes to be used against her. Anger made him tighten his grip on his water glass, so he set it down and picked up his menu.

"You won't be able to eat anything with your jaw all clenched up like that," she said, her voice light and teasing.

"It's stupid," he said.

"Yes, it's stupid, but I knew it could happen. The slight on my reputation, I mean. I didn't see the accusation of police corruption coming, though, because I didn't know three of you would decide to do a little breaking and entering."

"I'm really sorry about that."

She laughed. "I was kidding. Like you said, the whole thing is stupid."

"You know she's going to call the FBI, right?"

"Of course she will. Even though they're just going to blow smoke at her until she goes away, there will be an official record buried somewhere that states Officer Kelly McDonnell of the Stewart Mills Police Department had sexual relations with one Chase Sanders of New Jersey."

That struck him as nothing short of horrifying, but she looked amused, so he chuckled. "If you do have to give a detailed statement, it'll make for good reading."

"It would make some bored, low-on-the-totem-pole

agent's day, for sure." She grinned and he let go of the anger. As long as she was okay, there was no sense in spoiling the time they had together.

"So what did you do today?" she asked after they'd ordered burgers. "Weren't you guys being roped into judging the decoration contest?"

"We did that this morning, and one of the kids emailed the results to Jen, so that's done. I talked to Hunter a little bit."

"Really?" Immediately, he saw the change in her expression and was struck again by the depth of her feelings for their hometown. "How's he doing?"

"Good." He told her about his conversation with the boy, watching her relax again as he assured her things were looking up in the Cass household.

She was telling him about a rumor going around that there was a potential buyer for the old mill, when he caught himself wondering what she'd think of New Jersey. It wasn't too bad an area, where he lived, and it was close to the ocean.

But just as quickly, he discarded the idea. Stewart Mills was her home and not in the place-of-residence sense, but the place where her roots ran deep, and it was a part of who she was. Besides, what would he say to her? *Hey, I'm barely employed and technically don't have any place to live, but you wanna go to Jersey with me?*

There was no way she would walk away from everything she had here just because they'd had great sex, and he wasn't going to ask her to. Her trying to turn him down without wounding his pride would just be painful and awkward for both of them.

"Are you even listening to me?"

He gave her a sheepish grin, totally busted. "Sorry. I know you were talking about a potential buyer for the mill. I hope that works out, for the town's sake."

"Me, too. I think the rumor's a little flimsy and people are making it a bigger deal than it is in order to grasp at straws, but you never know. But where did your thoughts go?"

"Where my thoughts usually go when I'm with you," he lied.

"Aren't you supposed to abstain from sex before a big game?"

"I think that's before you go into battle. And if you'd seen us on the practice field, you'd know there's a good chance I won't be able to have sex *after* the big game."

She laughed, shaking her head. "By the time we get everybody off school property, clean up and then lock the gates, *nobody* will want to have sex."

The server brought their burgers and they dug in. When she was done, Chase finished the last quarter of her burger and all of her fries, too. He wouldn't eat right before going on the field, so he'd fuel up while he had the chance.

"Tell me about your sister's kids," she said while watching him polish off the rest of her meal. "Three girls, right? Do you see them a lot?"

"Not a lot, but regularly. They love me." He grinned and told her about his three nieces, who were quite a handful, just as he and Kathy had probably been.

There were a lot of stories, but he shared the best ones. Like the incident with the teddy bear and the toilet. And the inevitable run-in with Mom's makeup bag. Or the time they'd tried to convince their uncle Chase, who volunteered for babysitting at times, that fast food was medically necessary, because if they didn't eat fast, they got sick. He'd taken them through the drive-thru just because their story was so beautifully crafted, and he felt as though they'd earned it. Kathy had disagreed, of course, but those were the risks you took with a free sitter.

Then he showed her the photo his sister had texted him of the girls dressed up for a birthday party, and Kelly smiled. "They're beautiful. I like watching you talk about them, and I've seen you with the boys from the team. It's too bad you don't have kids, because you'd be a great dad."

The compliment was like a punch to the gut. He'd wanted kids, but lately he'd been grateful he didn't have any, because they'd just be caught up in the mess the end of the building boom and Seth Poole had helped bring about. And if he had a wife and kids and a mortgage, he might not have been able to juggle enough to keep himself out of bankruptcy.

"Maybe someday," he said. "Once I've got my life back on track. How about you?"

She shrugged. "I had planned to have kids, but I guess I wasn't married long enough. I was starting to think it might be time to start a family, when it all blew up in my face, so I'm glad now, of course. As much as I'd like to have children, I'm glad I don't have to maintain a relationship with my ex for the rest of my life for their sake. He's just gone from my life and I never have to see him again."

"I know what you mean." He'd dragged the conversation down, and he didn't like it when she talked about her ex-husband. Her eyes grew sad, and it made him want to find the guy and punch him in the face. "Do you want dessert?"

She smiled. "I didn't even finish my lunch. Do you want something?"

"Since I ate my lunch and then yours, hell no." With his stomach full, he leaned back in the booth and failed to stifle a yawn. "I can't believe I have to play football tonight."

"Maybe you should come home and take a nap with me," she said in a low, suggestive voice.

And just like that the tiredness was gone, and he wanted her so badly it hurt. But he remembered the story she told him and tried to force it down. "After what you told me about your day at work, I'm not sure that's a good idea."

Her stubborn face was almost a carbon copy of her mother's, which he'd seen often enough during the time he spent at the McDonnell house. "My private life is just that. Private. Plus, you can park out back in the town lot and it's only a few feet to the door. There are a dozen trucks just like yours in town."

So she might claim her private life was nobody's business, but it was obvious she wanted to minimize the chances of anybody seeing him at her apartment. No matter how much he wanted her, he wasn't willing to risk her job. "Kelly, I . . ."

Her calf brushed the inside of his, and she reached across the table to run her thumb over his palm in a way she knew drove him crazy. "Kelly what?"

"I don't suppose it's legal for you to give me a lights-and-sirens escort to the town lot?"

"No, but I know a shortcut that'll shave five minutes off the drive."

He signaled for the check. "That's five minutes more for *napping*."

"That wasn't a shortcut," Chase said from behind her as Kelly unlocked her door and walked in. "That was a cow path through the woods."

"You have a truck." She didn't see the problem. A sports car wouldn't have made it, but he had four-wheel drive.

"Yeah, but it's a *nice* truck. And it'll stay nice because I don't drive it down glorified cow paths."

"If your truck had been born with balls, it would be a gelding now. You know that, right?"

"But a nice gelding."

She tossed her keys on the table, shaking her head. "I can't believe you're carrying on about going through a few mud puddles and splashing dirt on the outside when the inside of your truck looks like a garbage disposal that stopped disposing about two years ago."

"Nobody sees the inside," he said, as if it were all perfectly reasonable. Then he stepped up behind her and wrapped his arms around her waist. She nestled against him, feeling the hard line of his erection through their jeans. "But I don't want to talk about my truck anymore. Or geldings, to be honest with you."

"What should we talk about?" she asked, although she already knew the answer. Conversation time was about to be over.

He pulled her shirt up and over her head and then slid his hands up to cup her breasts. "We can talk about how much I love touching you."

When he pushed down her bra and ran his thumbs over her nipples, she shuddered and sucked in a breath. In the past, men hadn't given her breasts a lot of attention because they were on the smaller side, but Chase didn't seem to mind at all, and she liked that.

She liked it even more when she turned to face him and he bent his mouth first to one breast, then the other. Sliding her fingers into his hair, she held him there, wanting more.

She unclasped her bra so she could slide it off and then unfastened her jeans. Before she could push them down, he captured both of her wrists with one hand. The other, he slid over her stomach and under the waistband of her underwear. Then he stopped, just letting his hand rest there, so close and yet still so far away.

Kelly made a sound of desperation low in her throat, but Chase refused to be budged.

"Are you in a hurry?" he asked, his breath hot against her neck.

"I'm not very patient when it comes to getting what I want, and right now I want you."

He pushed her back onto the bed so he could pull her jeans and underwear off and toss them aside. Then he made quick work of adding his to the pile.

Kelly heard him set a wrapped condom near the pillow, but apparently he wasn't finished tormenting her yet. He teased her until her fingernails dug into his back hard enough to make him wince, his mouth alternating between her lips and her breasts while his hand slid between her legs.

He made her come for him with his hand and his mouth before she heard him tear open the condom wrapper. With her breath still ragged and her heart racing, she opened her legs and pulled him close.

He slid into her slowly, the friction so delicious that Kelly actually sighed. She lifted her hips as he moved in an easy rhythm, urging him deeper.

His thrusts picked up in pace, and he hooked his hands under her knees to pull her close. Each stroke came faster and went deeper, and she arched her back as the orgasm shook her. He groaned and she felt him pulsing inside her, before he dropped her knees and pushed deep as the last tremors shook them both.

Once they could breathe again and their hearts stopped racing, Chase tossed the condom in her trash can and pulled her into his arms.

"That was worth getting my truck dirty," he admitted, and she laughed. "I'm a little disappointed you haven't handcuffed me to anything yet, though."

"I really don't get the whole sex and handcuff thing. Sorry."

"You don't think they're sexy?"

"They're a tool of my job and, if I have to use them, I'm probably not having a very good day. So, no, I don't think handcuffs are very sexy. You're a builder. Would you think it was sexy if I wanted to bring a tape measure to bed?"

"The last thing *any* man wants near him when he's naked is a tape measure," he said, wincing. When she was silent for a few seconds, he scowled at her. "This is the part where you assure me I have nothing to worry about."

"Oh." She widened her eyes and gave him a totally fake smile. "You have nothing to worry about."

He reached down and pinched her ass, making her jump. "Smart-ass."

She let her body relax into his and closed her eyes. It had been a nice day, she thought. Lunch with Chase in a restaurant and then a little afternoon dessert, so to speak, to top it off. And maybe there was still enough time for an actual nap before she had to get up.

"Okay, maybe you *are* supposed to be abstinent before a big game," Chase said after a few minutes. "All I want to do now is sleep."

"Oh, no you don't. Everything we've done has been leading up to this night. Jen did all the details for the game, and I don't know if she shared with me or I forgot, but what time are you supposed to be there?"

She felt him shift and assumed he was looking at her alarm clock. "Sooner than I want to be there, that's for damn sure."

"Damn." With a sigh, she disentangled herself from his arms and the sheet. "If you cut it too close, everybody walking to the high school to get the best bleacher seats will see you sneaking out of my apartment."

"Don't want anybody knowing your dirty little secret?"

She gave him an arched eyebrow. "As secrets go, you're not little, but you're probably a little dirty."

"Complaining?"

She wrapped her hand around the back of his neck and pulled him down for a kiss. "Definitely not."

"You have to let me go, or I'll be so weak Coach will bench me. And since I don't know if we even have enough guys in the first place, it'll be pretty noticeable if I don't play."

"Fine." She let him go and watched him get dressed. "I have to shower and put my uniform on, anyway."

"I'll see you there." He leaned down and gave her a quick kiss, wisely not lingering long enough to let her get her hands on him again.

"I'll be the blondc with the handcuffs," she said, and he was laughing when she heard the door close behind him.

17

Chase stood in the middle of the football field, looking up at the blur of faces as the last bars of the national anthem echoed through the stands.

For a moment, he felt seventeen again, geared up and under the lights and ready to do the only thing he thought he was good at back then. The thing that made him feel strong and confident and in control. And the one thing that had brought Coach into his life and given him the guys who'd been like brothers to him. Football had made him who he was today.

But he certainly wasn't seventeen anymore, since all the standing around before the game was getting to his back. And they weren't exactly geared up. After much discussion with Coach and an equipment count, they were playing a slightly modified game. It wouldn't be flag football, but it wouldn't be full contact, either, and they'd play shortened quarters. They were all in practice jerseys, blue for the team and white for the alumni, and they'd basically be playing a glorified version of backyard football.

It was still going to hurt.

The crowd sat, but then Jen walked out onto the field with a microphone, and Chase groaned. He should have brought one of those collapsible camp chairs, because he was seriously getting too old for this shit. Through the corner of his eye, he saw Alex shifting his weight from one foot to the other and knew he wasn't alone in wishing they could get on with it.

Then Gretchen and Kelly joined her and he didn't mind so much. Kelly was technically on duty, but she was wearing cargo pants and a SMPD T-shirt instead of her full uniform, with her ponytail pulled through the matching ball cap.

"Hey, Eagles fans!" Jen yelled. Whatever she said next—even with the microphone—was swallowed up by the cheers, so she paused until the noise subsided. "The Eagles Fest committee wants to take a minute to thank everybody who's given time or services or donated goods to the fund-raiser. As you know, saving Stewart Mills football means every single dollar counts. Actually, I can honestly say every single quarter counts."

She stopped talking and the crowd quieted, as if every person in the stands was holding his or her breath at that moment. Chase did, too, even though he was certain good news was coming. He couldn't imagine the women would interrupt the pregame to announce they'd failed and there would be no more Eagles football in Stewart Mills.

Jen turned to Coach and held out the microphone. He

shook his head slightly, but she just smiled and kept it extended until he finally took it. The microphone picked up his throat clearing, and Chase got nervous. Coach didn't often get emotional.

"It seems like forever ago and yesterday at the same time that I stood on a field like this one and watched my team win the championship for the first time." He paused, clearing his throat again. "Not many people thought it could happen. But I believed. And those boys believed. And now they're men and they're standing here with me today to help me keep teaching boys to believe in themselves."

He turned to face them. "I want to thank every one of you who came back to help us out. It means the world to me and to this town and to Eagles football."

The crowd added their thanks in the form of applause and whistles, which Coach waited out before speaking again. "To the boys playing for me now: on Saturday, the eighth of August, at nine A.M. sharp, I want you on this field, ready to play some football."

It took a few seconds for his words to sink in, and then the crowd erupted. The people of Stewart Mills were on their feet in the stands, but Chase turned a little so he could see the teenagers. They were overjoyed, jumping up and down like little kids and screaming. Watching them lifted Chase's spirits and made him thankful that, back when he'd been having one of the worst days of his life, he'd answered the call from the 603 area code.

The energy in the stands was infectious so, when everybody but the players had left the field, Chase was revved up and ready to play some football.

By halftime, he never wanted to play football again.

"I'm not getting shut out," Sam said, once they'd reached the visitors' locker room for a short break.

Alex snorted. "Unless you're playing for some other team, yeah, you're getting shut out."

"Right now we are, but I mean that I'm not going to let this game *end* with us being shut out. Even Coach McDonnell doesn't have a speech that'll inspire us into a win here, but we're going to put some damn points on that scoreboard if it kills me. Or you."

"The golden boys of fall," Chase said with a chuckle. "Determined to get our asses kicked with as much dignity as possible."

"I think I lost my dignity in the second quarter," Deck said.

Alex nodded. "I'm pretty sure having to use a time-out because you were laughing so hard you fell down and couldn't get back up will make the highlight reel. *Their* highlight reel."

"I'm sorry, but that was the worst kick I've ever seen."

Philly threw a towel at him. "My foot slipped."

"Okay, here's what we're going to do," Sam said. "At some point I'm going to say the word *Texas*. When I do that, you take off running to the left and deep, Briscoe. Make it look like you're going for a burst of speed to surprise them."

"They'd definitely be surprised," their wide receiver said, rubbing first one calf muscle and then the other.

"Sanders, I'm going to hand the ball off to you, and you'll go off toward the right. Don't step out of bounds, and don't stop running or fall down until you're in the end zone."

"You're a great coach," Chase said. "Really. Your plays are so sophisticated, I think you missed out on your true calling."

"I'd go back to washing cow manure off the walls of a barn before I coach football. You want to end this game with a zero on the board?"

"Hell, no." Chase stood and twisted from side to side, stretching his back. "Run and don't stop. Got it."

"And don't drop the ball."

They were halfway through the fourth and thankfully final quarter before whatever conditions Sam was waiting for came together. They were close enough to the end zone that Chase probably wouldn't have a heart attack and die ten yards short. The teenagers were pretty much goofing off and had let their guard down many plays before.

As they lined up, Sam took his position for the snap and said, "I really wish I was back in Texas."

As soon as the ball was released, Briscoe took off running and Chase almost missed his mark because he was so impressed by his speed. Startled, the boys realized one of the old guys was actually making a break for it, and they all took off after him like an entire peewee baseball team chasing down a ground ball.

Chase tucked the football and started running. He could hear the crowd going nuts, but he wasn't sure if they were cheering him on or trying to alert the boys to his escape. Keeping the chalk line in his peripheral vision, he focused on the end zone and tried to pretend he was seventeen again.

The first hand grabbed at his shirt right around the five-yard line, and Chase dug for a burst of speed. They'd won the first championship for Stewart Mills, dammit, and they weren't going down in a shutout.

Arms wrapped around him and he tripped, falling to the ground in a tangle with the kid who'd tackled him. The ground was hard and he was going to feel it in the morning, but he rolled, looking for the white line and whether or not the ball had broken the plane.

Then Don Jones from O'Rourke's, who was acting as a referee, blew his whistle and threw his hands in the air to signal the touchdown.

Chase pushed himself to his feet, feeling an adrenaline rush he hadn't felt in years. His teammates swarmed him, patting his back and slapping him in the side of the head as the people in the stands roared their approval.

He saw Kelly on the sideline, laughing and cheering with everybody else. Her cheeks were red with excitement and she looked so beautiful he couldn't resist. He jogged over to her and, before she could see it coming, kissed her.

Her hands pushed against his chest at the very second he became aware of the shift in the crowd's reaction. Whistles and catcalls joined the cheers, echoing through the stadium, and he knew he'd screwed up big-time as Kelly backed away from him.

Not only had he just kissed her in front of the entire town, but she was on duty, too. Even though she was in the more casual version of her uniform, it didn't change the fact that she was at the game in a professional as well as a personal capacity, and he'd just made a huge mess of things.

"I'm sorry," he mouthed, but she just gave him a flat look and waved back toward the field as a whistle blew.

"Smooth," Sam said as they lined up in defensive positions they still had no clue how to play.

He glanced over at the sideline and saw Coach watching him with a blank expression, arms folded across his chest.

Yeah. Real freaking smooth.

Kelly couldn't count all the times she'd sat under the lights on a Friday night, watching her dad's teams play football. She'd practically grown up on the Eagles sidelines. But this was the first time she'd ever felt as if the lights were shining on her like spotlights.

"That was . . . something," Jen said.

"Yeah." It was something, all right. Something exciting and scary and very, very public.

Because of the alumni team's rally—which put them down by only five touchdowns with a few minutes left on the clock—and the kiss, the crowd's flagging attention had rallied, too. They were loud, yelling and whistling and stomping their feet on the bleachers, which made it too blessedly loud for further conversation.

She didn't know what to make of the kiss. It was obviously a heat-of-the-moment thing, but the look on his face when their eyes met had made her heart rate quicken. In that triumphant moment, he'd looked for her and, when he found her, that sparkle in his eye and grin had become just for her. Then he'd been there, kissing her, and she hadn't known what to do.

Now she adopted her cop stance—as her friends and family called it—with her feet slightly spread and her arms crossed. It was like armor, she supposed, keeping personal conversation at bay while they watched the clock tick down on the alumni exhibition game.

When it was over, the high school football team—buoyed by their decisive win and the news they'd play another season—did some showboating on the field, much to the amusement of the spectators.

Kelly chose to get a head start on the cleaning up, and that's how she ended up being as close to alone as was possible by the watercooler. Plastic cups littered the ground, and she was bent over to pick them up when Chase found her. She looked at his sneakers for a few seconds before taking a deep breath and standing up straight.

"I got carried away. I shouldn't have done that." He definitely looked contrite, which was both nice of him and also slightly disappointing. So he'd been carried away by the moment, not making a public declaration of his feelings for her. Part of her almost wished he'd done it deliberately, with forethought.

She forced herself to laugh. "It's not *that* big a deal, Chase, so don't beat yourself up about it."

"Your reputation's taken enough hits this week without me planting a kiss on you in front of everybody."

"My reputation can handle a little fling. Once you leave, everybody'll forget and it'll be behind me."

His forehead furrowed for a few seconds, and he nodded. "That'll be good, then. Like it never happened."

For the rest of Stewart Mills, maybe, but not for her. She had a feeling she was going to miss having Chase around for a good, long time. "Yeah."

"I should go. The guys are heading for the locker room, and Coach will probably head in there and say a few words."

"Sure. And nice touchdown."

He laughed, a self-deprecating sound without a lot of humor behind it. "At least it wasn't a shutout."

Once he was gone, Kelly went back to cleaning up around the bench, not really caring what anybody else was doing. She was exhausted and now that the intense drive to make

Eagles Fest a success was over, she felt drained. There was still the parade to do, but they'd managed to time everything to take advantage of the town's Fourth of July parade, so most of the prep work was already done.

She was surprised to see her dad walking toward her, and she held up her hands as if in question. "What are you doing? You should be with the guys."

"And miss a chance to thank my best girl?" Once he was close enough, he held open his arms and she stepped into his hug. "What you did for me and my boys is pretty amazing. I know it wasn't easy, but you didn't give up. None of you did."

"You don't give up when it comes to people you love," she said, pressing her cheek to his chest.

"I love you, too, pumpkin." He pulled back so he could press a kiss to her forehead. "I guess I should go do a tour of the locker rooms. I have a feeling my alumni are just sprawled on the benches, groaning, but I should make sure the kids don't get too carried away."

"I'll be cleaning up for a while. I know it's late and Mom'll be waiting for you, so if I don't see you again tonight, I'll see you at the parade tomorrow. Did Mom get the candy for the boys to toss? I was going to, but she said she had some coupons."

"Yeah." He smiled. "She got candy and, yes, she had coupons. She has coupons for stuff we don't even use."

"I guess it's like you and your shed full of tools you don't use. What is it you say? You never know what you might need."

"Just like your mother," he said. "Good thing I love you both so much. And I'll see you tomorrow if not before."

She watched him walk away, liking the way his head was held high and the spring in his step. It made all the work they'd done worth it. But the work wasn't done, so she went looking for garbage bags. And for Gretchen and Jen, because there was no way she'd let them weasel out of helping.

And she wondered about Chase. She wouldn't see him tonight. If he did anything besides fall into bed, it would probably involve a hot bath and a muscle rub cream. But she didn't like the awkwardness between them as he'd walked away tonight. Something had changed when he kissed her, and she wasn't sure if it was her or him.

Once the chaos died down to a dull roar, Chase started walking. He was exhausted. Besides the physical toll the game had taken, his mind was tired of worrying over Kelly McDonnell and her dad.

He'd been so caught up in the fun atmosphere and the high of making a great play, he hadn't even thought twice about what he was going to do. Kelly had been right there on the sideline, laughing and cheering, and he'd had the urge to kiss her.

What he should have done was consider the fact that Edna Beecher and various selectmen would probably be in the stands, and that particular fire didn't need any more fuel. He could have remembered she preferred to keep her private life private, because it was hard enough to get people to respect her. Instead he'd given in to his first instinct and kissed her in front of most of Stewart Mills. And her parents.

By the time he got back to Eagles Lane, he wasn't surprised to see Coach sitting on the porch, waiting for him. It was obvious he had something on his mind, and Chase was about to get a talking-to. It was a look he'd seen before, on the rare occasion he screwed up at school after making the football team.

Rather than pretend he didn't know it was coming, Chase crossed to Mrs. McDonnell's rocker and sat down. "I guess I've disappointed you."

"It's not me I'm worried about. And you outgrew having to worry about disappointing me a long time ago."

"Not really."

Coach rocked slowly, the old wood creaking. "You plan on staying in Stewart Mills, son?"

"It hadn't really crossed my mind, to be honest. My business—such as it is—is in New Jersey and so is my family. There's nothing for me here."

"No, I guess there isn't."

Too late, Chase saw the flashing neon danger sign. If he hadn't been so exhausted, he would have detoured into a change of subject or at least navigated through the conversational hazard a little better.

Coach McDonnell had been asking his intentions toward Kelly and, even though they'd been skirting the issue, Chase hadn't seen the connection until the crash. *There's nothing for me here.*

Chase cleared his throat. "Coach, Kelly and I . . . we're not . . . I'm going back to New Jersey."

"The sooner, the better, from the looks of it," the man said, and his words sliced through Chase's heart.

"I know I caused her some embarrassment at work," he said. "And kissing her in front of everybody means people won't forget as fast, but once I'm gone, it'll blow over."

Coach turned to look at him. "You think I give a damn about her job or Edna Beecher or that Faring woman?"

Chase wasn't sure what to say, because he wasn't totally sure what the other man was getting at. "I don't understand."

"All that matters to me is Kelly's happiness. Maybe there was a time when I would have been happy to see you and my daughter together, but that was before I saw what a broken heart does to her. When she came home after leaving that bastard and got out of the car, her shoulders were drooped and her head was hung low. I'd never seen her like that, so I went out to meet her and she fell apart. I sat in my goddamn dooryard for a half hour holding my baby girl while she cried for a man who didn't deserve her."

"I would never cheat on any woman."

"It wasn't just the cheating. He didn't know what he wanted in life and neither do you. What I want for Kelly is a man who has his shit together and knows exactly what he wants. And it better be her."

Chase wanted to explain the situation, such as the fact that Kelly knew exactly what she wanted, too, and it wasn't Chase. But he couldn't think of a way to tell a man he loved and respected that his daughter was having sex just for fun—with no plans for a future—that didn't sound crude somehow, so he didn't even try.

"I thought I had my shit together," he said quietly. "But all I had was a business partner who stole from me, a diamond ring I never got around to giving my girlfriend before she left me for another guy, and a whole lot of people who are disappointed in me, so . . . what the hell do I know, right?"

"When you get knocked down, you get back up."

Great. It was inspirational-quotes time. "Or maybe when

you get knocked down, you make sure you don't drag anybody else with you."

"That's a sad way of looking at things, son."

A car pulled up to the curb, horn honking, and Chase turned to see Sam leaning out the passenger window of Alex's rental car while Briscoe waved from the backseat. "Sanders, let's go!"

"Not in the mood, guys."

"Bullshit," Alex yelled from the driver's seat. "Get in the car. Owner of the pizza place said there's a pizza and a pitcher of beer waiting for us, on the house. All we have to do is pay for the four other pizzas and two pitchers of beer it'll take to feed us all."

"That's a helluva bargain." Now that they mentioned it, a beer would hit the spot right about now. And he hadn't had any supper. While he wasn't really hungry, he should probably force something down. "Coach, you mind?"

He shook his head. "Go have a good time. But do me—and yourself—a favor and don't do anything that'll drag my daughter any further into your mess."

There was no chance of that, he thought as he shoved Briscoe over so he could get in the backseat. He'd already dragged Kelly down far enough.

18

Kelly shoved a soda can into the half-full garbage bag she was dragging around and cursed when some of the sticky fluid ran over her hand. The school administration had agreed to the exhibition game, but not to paying staff to clean up the inevitable mess afterward. In order to make it happen, they'd volunteered to take care of it.

She'd thought the bench area was a mess, but the stands were ten times worse. It's a good thing she wasn't handing out tickets for littering tonight, or they would have had to host another fund-raising festival so the good sloppy folks of Stewart Mills could pay their fines.

As far as Kelly was concerned, they should *all* get trophies when it was over, although Jen's should probably be the biggest. The town had pulled together and dug as deep in their pockets as they could—and it *had* made up the bulk of the fund—but they wouldn't have made it without Jen's tireless pursuit of gifts and donations from outside Stewart Mills.

Screw trophies, she thought. Maybe her mom would bake them a cake. A big chocolate cake with not a speck of blue, white or gold to be seen.

"Hey, Kel, take a break," Gretchen said, patting the spot on the bleacher next to her when Kelly got close enough to hear her. "Talk to me for a few minutes."

Kelly didn't want to talk about that kiss anymore, so if that's what Gretchen was after, she might as well keep picking up garbage. Half the town had asked her about it or commented on it as they made their way out of the stands. She'd even gotten a few congratulations, as if his kissing her in public meant they were engaged.

"I just want to be done with this."

"I have a question, and now seems like a good time to ask it, since we're alone."

With a weary sigh, Kelly surrendered to the inevitable and sat down. "If it's about Chase, the answer is *I don't know.*"

"It's not about Chase, but we can circle back to him and that kiss afterward." She glanced sideways and caught Kelly's expression. "Or maybe not. But I wanted to talk to you about the farm."

That sounded serious, and Kelly set the garbage bag down next to her feet. "Is everything okay?"

"As okay as ever, I guess." Which meant on the verge of losing everything, but never quite hitting rock bottom. "But Gram's medicines are starting to add up, and there are more doctor appointments. Even with her assistance, her medical costs are going to nickel-and-dime us out of house and home. So I was thinking about renting out a room."

"Renting it out to who?"

"Anybody who needs a room." Gretchen shrugged. "I'd advertise it. But I wanted to ask you if there's a way to do . . . like a background check or something on people? I don't know what you're allowed to do as favors for people. Or if there's an organization that does it for a small—very small—fee, maybe you could point me to it."

"The chief really liked your grandfather—hell, he even worked on the farm for a while when he was a teenager, if I remember right—so I'm sure he could help you a little, but are you sure you want to do that? How does Gram feel about having a stranger in the house? She's not a woman who takes well to change."

"It wouldn't necessarily be a stranger, though. There are a lot of people losing their homes right in our town, never mind surrounding ones."

"Because they have no work, Gretchen. They're losing their homes because they can't pay their mortgages or rent. If you rent a room in your home to somebody you know and then they can't pay, are you going to be able to evict them?"

"I just need a little more income coming in, and I think that would be the easiest way to do it. If I move into the room next to Gram's and rent my room, it has its own bathroom and everything. No kitchen, obviously, but you know how Gram loves to cook. Maybe there could be an extra charge to eat with us and not worry about kitchen privileges."

"I'll be honest, Gretchen. It makes me nervous. Especially if you just get random strangers answering an ad. I can't decide if I'm more worried about you renting to a friend who can't pay you or renting to a total stranger."

"I'm just thinking about it right now. I can only do it if Gram thinks it's okay, and if I know you or the chief can warn us about any red flags. I'm not going to have somebody potentially dangerous in the house with her. But it's not something I'm planning to do tomorrow or anything."

"We can talk about it again, and we'll do up an income projection and a pros and cons list to make Jen happy, and see if the risk and inconvenience is really worth it."

"Thanks. Now let's circle back to Chase and that kiss."

"I'm always circling back to Chase," Kelly said in a quiet voice. "I can't believe he did that."

"I thought it was sweet. And very romantic, like a scene out of a movie."

"And that's bad."

"It is?"

Kelly sighed and gave her friend a *really?* look. "Of course it's bad."

"Oh, were you two not doing the fun sex thing anymore?"

"We were doing the fun sex thing earlier today, as a matter of fact. But we weren't doing the *flaunting our fun sex in front of Stewart Mills* thing at all. Or we weren't supposed to be."

"So you haven't taken your relationship to the next level? Like the actual calling it a relationship level?"

"No, and that was never the plan. You know that."

Gretchen leaned forward, resting her elbows on her knees. "I assumed your original plan would go down in flames. I mean, it's obvious you guys like each other. You're always looking for each other and laughing together. And there's the fun sex thing. Why not call it what it is?"

"Because it can't be that." She'd been annoyed with Chase since the kiss, but now it gave way to a sense of loss. "Yeah, it's been great and we've had a great time, but it was temporary. He got to leave his life in New Jersey behind for a while, and even I've been out of routine with this whole Eagles Fest thing. It's like a vacation fling that can't be sustained back in the real world."

"You don't sound like somebody having a fun vacation fling. You sound like somebody who's trying to convince herself that's *all* she's having but doesn't really believe it."

"I'm going to miss him," Kelly admitted. Saying it out loud was both a relief and torture. It made his leaving seem even more immediate.

"I hate to state the obvious here, but you could always just . . . have a relationship. So he has to go back to New Jersey for a while. You keep in touch. Call, text, video chat. Maybe meet in the middle at a nice hotel once in a while for the fun sex thing, until you figure out what and where the future is."

"I'm not taking a chance on an unsettled guy again, and he doesn't even know what he wants. Been there, done that, paid the lawyer fees." Kelly shook her head. "It's better to part ways now, before we get all emotionally wrapped up in each other."

"I hate to say it, but I think you're too late."

Kelly shook her head but didn't waste any more breath denying it. At some point, yeah, her emotions had seeped in, and she cared more about Chase than one probably cared about a random vacation fling.

But that didn't mean she could just lay out her emotions for everybody to see. She'd been a mess after the divorce, and her friends and family had seen it. She never wanted to be smothered in that much pity and helpfulness ever again. Her time with Chase was coming to an end, and she was going to accept that with dry eyes and her head held high.

"You don't look like a man who's celebrating," Alex said, pointing a slice of pizza in Chase's direction.

They'd lost the game, so he was a little confused as to what Alex meant by that. "What, exactly, are we celebrating?"

"It's over. All we have to do now is get paraded around town on a float and then we're free to go."

Sam nodded. "I, for one, am celebrating the fact that I never have to play football again. I'm too old for that shit."

Chase laughed. "I can't argue with that."

"It looked like Chase might have more of a reason to celebrate than some other guys," Briscoe said, raising his eyebrows as if to emphasize the point.

Chase groaned and bit into his pizza. He knew where this was going, and it was nowhere he particularly wanted to go.

"I don't think it was exactly a secret," Alex said.

"No," Briscoe admitted. "But it seemed like they were trying to pretend it was."

"It wasn't a secret," Chase said. "It wasn't anybody else's business, either."

"Has Coach said anything about it?" Alex asked. "You were always one of his favorites, but she's his only kid. And a daughter at that."

"He didn't say much, until tonight when I pretty much

forced him into acknowledging what was going on by kissing her in front of the entire town."

"And what did he say?"

"I can sum up his thoughts on the matter as the sooner I leave town, the better."

Sam winced. "Ouch."

"Yeah."

"What family thinks is important, but it's what Kelly wants that really matters," Briscoe said, probably pulling from all the wisdom that came with being a married man.

Sam must have thought the same thing, because he gave him a dark look. "I know you're doing the 'til-death-do-you-part thing, Briscoe, but not all sex ends in happily ever after. Sometimes it's just sex."

Briscoe shrugged, not intimidated by Sam at all. "And sometimes it's not."

Chase didn't tell them Kelly wasn't looking for happily ever after, either. At least not with him. Briscoe had family in town, and Chase didn't want any more gossip going around about Kelly than already was. He'd rather everybody think he was the dumb schmuck who had a shot with her and blew it than have them hold their ridiculous double standards regarding sex against her.

They'd barely finished the pizza when Briscoe was summoned back to his parents' to help wrangle kids while his wife started packing for their trip home. They were hitting the road early in the morning, so he said his good-byes with a lot of handshakes and backslaps, and then it was just Chase, Sam and Alex.

"So what's next for you guys?" he asked them, and they both shrugged.

"I'm heading back to my glamorous life in Texas," Sam told them, holding up his soda glass as if he were making a toast.

"How the hell did you end up as an oil-field electrician, anyway?" Chase asked.

He shrugged. "I just drove around the country, doing whatever jobs they were hiring for. Ended up in Texas and I like it there. Worked on a ranch when I first got there, but then I found out I don't like cows very much. So I decided to get some education and bump my paychecks up a bit. That's it. How 'bout you, Murph? What's next?"

Alex shook his head, staring into his beer mug. "I'm not sure. I'll head home and do some research. Catch up on the world news and brainstorm a new story to tell. Then try to sell it."

"You don't get assigned stories to take pictures for?" Chase asked.

"Sometimes publications contact me to ask me to do a story, but I'm freelance, so I can do what moves me. It's getting tough, though. We used to give the world the photographs that illustrated news around the world. Now people on the street are using their phones to upload pictures to social media while the news is still breaking."

"That sucks." Sam covered a yawn, but it spread until they were all yawning. "So you looking for a new line of work?"

"No." Alex was definitely starting to slump in his chair, and Chase knew they weren't much better off, no matter how much he wanted to put off going back to Coach's house. "I don't know how to do anything else, for one thing. And the photos I like to take aren't necessarily breaking news, anyway. I like to use the camera to tell stories, and those stories don't always have splashy headlines. They're more than a quick flash in the social media pan and sometimes in-depth is still as important as immediate."

Chase wasn't sure he totally grasped what Alex did, although Mrs. McDonnell had showed him a scrapbook that had some of his pictures, but he knew Murph was good at it. He'd even won some awards. And he traveled a lot.

"You ever think about a wife and kids?" Chase asked him. "Settling down, I mean."

Alex shook his head. "I had a wife once, actually. She didn't like my lifestyle and, when I wouldn't give up my career, she left me. I've learned it's easier not to have a wife than it is to keep one happy."

Sam nodded. "What about you, Sanders? What's next on your agenda?"

Not a wife, that was for sure. "I'm heading back to New Jersey. I've got some jobs lined up, and I need to find a new apartment that's substantially cheaper than the last one I had. Downsizing all the way around, I guess."

Sam gave him a solemn look. "At least you've still got your truck."

That made Chase laugh. "You've gotta get out of Texas more, my friend."

He shrugged. "It's a nice truck."

Chase remembered the way Kelly had teased him about gelding his truck and took a swallow of beer. That was probably one of his favorite things about her. She made him laugh, and he liked that even more than he liked her legs.

"We're heading out about six o'clock Monday morning," Alex said, "because dumb-ass over here wanted a morning flight. When are you leaving?"

"Not at six in the morning," Chase said, and they all laughed. "I haven't really thought about it."

He should think about it soon, though. It was time to go, and no amount of dragging his feet would make it any less painful. Getting up and on the road first thing in the morning would be like ripping a bandage off—it still hurt, but it faded faster.

"The parade's at ten tomorrow," he said, "which kind of kills it as a travel day. Maybe Monday morning."

But if the parade started at ten and everything was over by noon, maybe he'd head out then. He could drive until he got tired and then find a cheap motel somewhere to spend the night. If he stayed, he might try to see Kelly, and he wasn't sure that was a good idea.

Maybe things were best left the way they were. They'd had fun. He'd made it awkward, and now it felt as if there was a distance between them. It seemed like a natural segue to the very real and substantial distance about to be between them.

He'd do the parade, say his good-byes and then hit the road. And, no matter how much he might want to, he wouldn't look back.

Kelly stared at her ceiling, feeling the lack of Chase beside her in an almost physical way. It had been a long day and, though she couldn't say she was in the mood for sex, she wouldn't mind nodding off wrapped in his arms.

Her mom had called her shortly after she got home, wanting to thank her again for all the work she'd put into Eagles Fest on Coach's behalf. During the conversation, she'd casually mentioned that Chase had gone out with the guys to celebrate their parts in the successful fund-raising, so Kelly didn't bother reaching out to him. And she didn't hear from him.

Now, unable to sleep and with nothing better to do, Kelly replayed the night over and over in her mind, wishing she'd handled it differently. He'd been hurt by the way she'd laughed off their relationship. She could see that now, but she wasn't sure exactly what it meant.

The possibility that his emotions had gotten tangled up in their fling like hers had was terrifying. Her putting on a fake smile and waving good-bye to him was one thing. If he offered her more, it would be so hard to walk away. But not walking away would be messy and hard, and she wasn't sure she was strong enough for that. The thoughts ran like circles through her mind, frustrating her and not bringing any clear answers.

Only when the annoying tone of her alarm clock woke her did Kelly realize she'd finally slept. Not long or well, judging by how groggy she felt, but she got out of bed and walked across the room to flip the switch on the clock. It was the only way she kept from hitting the snooze button multiple times every morning.

Parade day meant all hands on deck for the police department, which was all three of them. The chief always led the parade in the marked SUV Kelly usually drove, signaling the start with a blast of the sirens. Dylan would walk back and forth along the parade route, ensuring nobody got out of hand or strayed too far off the sidewalk. She was on traffic duty this year, which was her least favorite.

Because the Stewart Mills parade route included the

short stretch of the state road that ran through town, it had to be closed off for the duration of the parade. She'd park Dylan's sedan across one end with a sign explaining the brief closure, and then she'd stand at the other end with wooden barricades and another sign. Then she'd spend the entire parade listening to horns honk and people yell about how they had to be somewhere important.

Kelly showered and put on her uniform before braiding her hair, and then looked at herself in the mirror. She looked like crap. Her skin was pale and there were shadows under her eyes. And besides looking tired, she looked really unhappy.

Why was she doing this to herself? She was making herself miserable trying to fend off the possibility that she could end up miserable.

She was in love with Chase Sanders. That was the bottom line. It wasn't an emotional tangle. It wasn't slightly messy. It was the L-word. She loved him.

Bracing her hands on the cool vanity top, she closed her eyes and tried to get her head on straight. Chase liked her. He liked spending time with her and making her laugh. He'd been hurt when she carelessly laughed off whatever was between them as a fling.

If there was a possibility he loved her, she had to take the chance. So what if it was messy and hard while they sorted out how to make a future together? If they were meant to be, they'd get through it.

And if he didn't feel the same way, that would hurt. But either way, letting Chase go was going to hurt. At least if he knew what he was walking away from, she'd never have to ask herself *what if?*

Her mind made up, Kelly opened her eyes and took a deep breath. She even managed to smile at her reflection. After the parade was over and things had died down a little, she'd manage to find a quiet place to talk to Chase, and she'd tell him things had changed. She knew he had to go, at least for a little while, but she wanted him to come back to her.

19

Chase could only describe the parade's staging area in the school parking lot as utter pandemonium. He wasn't sure who would be watching the parade since it looked like most of the town's population was actually *in* it. All of the band members seemed to be tuning their instruments with no rhyme or reason. There were antique tractors jockeying for position, and a horse that really didn't seem to like people very much.

He could barely think straight, and he couldn't imagine how the chaos was going to exit the parking lot in an orderly line in exactly fourteen minutes, according to the person running around yelling a countdown like it was a nuclear launch.

When he spotted Deck in the crowd, he made his way over. "Is it always like this?"

"Sometimes it's worse. Trust me."

"Where are we supposed to be?"

"Toward the back, on the big float. The kids will be in pickups behind us. Cheryl's going to drive the wrecker up front so I can have my moment of glory, as she put it."

"Who's got the trophy?"

"Gretchen has it in her truck. Once we're all on board and it's time to take off, she'll hand it up so we can wave it around. Don't forget to smile."

"Yeah." Because smiling was just what he wanted to do today, when he'd be leaving Stewart Mills—and Kelly—in a few hours.

He'd already put his bags in his truck, telling the McDonnells he wanted to be home early the next day to help his sister out with something. He was pretty sure they both saw through the excuse, but neither called him on it. He'd find them after the parade and say a proper good-bye, though, because he couldn't just disappear on them after they'd opened their home to him.

"Hey!" Jen ran up to them, looking frazzled. "You guys need to be on the float. We have to make sure the chairs all fit without any being too close to the edges."

Chase did as he was told and made his way to the float. He stopped short when he saw it, and then smiled. Their championship banner had been taken down from the gym and was strung on what looked like clothesline above the chairs. Blue, white and gold balloons and streamers were attached to every possible surface of the trailer, as well as tied to the mirrors and antenna of Gretchen's truck.

"That must be our ride," Sam said, stepping up beside

him. "Jesus, there can't be a streamer left anywhere in the county."

"They certainly know how to make a float." He looked sideways at his old friend. "Does this feel as weird to you as it does to me?"

"Being celebrated as a hero by a town I've barely thought about in fourteen years because I came back, ate spaghetti and played a half-assed game of football?" Sam nodded. "It's a little weird."

As he watched the boys climb into the beds of the lined-up trucks—and waved to Cody, who'd spotted them—Chase knew they'd done more than that. They cared. And Sam, maybe more than any of them, should know that mattered. At first they'd come for Coach's sake, maybe with a sense of obligation, but he knew they'd all come to care about the kids.

Gretchen stuck her head out the truck window. "I didn't go through all this trouble to haul an empty trailer through town. Quit screwing around and get on the float."

Once they'd all been seated—which required multiple adjustments to ensure everybody could see, be seen and wouldn't fall off—Jen grabbed the trophy from Gretchen and handed it up to Sam. "Don't drop it."

The last person to climb onto the float was Coach McDonnell, and he gave them all a smile. "Fine day for a parade, boys."

Chase hadn't expected to see him again before he said good-bye but, now that he thought about it, it made sense that Coach would ride with them. They had chairs and a cooler stocked with sodas and water. The boys no doubt had coolers, too, but they were stuck standing on hard metal truck beds.

Coach didn't make eye contact with him, and Chase busied himself looking around at the last-minute preparations going on around them. Maybe with a little distance, Coach would come around to the idea that Chase was doing the right thing, but right now all he could see was his misconception that he'd disrespected the man's daughter. Since Chase wasn't going to clarify the situation, all he could do was accept Coach's silent disapproval.

Far up ahead in what was beginning to look something like a line, they heard the chief's siren sound and knew the parade was starting. Because they were toward the end, though, it seemed like forever before Gretchen's truck started rolling and the trailer lurched.

"Smile, everybody!" Jen was on the ground, timing departures, and she waved as they went by. "Enjoy yourselves."

They all did as they were told, smiling and waving as the parade made its way from the school, into town and around the square. They passed the trophy around, taking turns holding it high and making the crowd cheer. The boys were tossing candy from their helmets behind them, and the cheerleaders walked alongside the float and trucks, leading Eagles chants.

Throughout the entire route, Chase did his part, but he couldn't help looking for Kelly. While he wasn't ready to talk to her, he was surprised he hadn't seen her from a distance. He knew the parade meant she was probably on duty but, even if she hadn't been, she wouldn't miss it.

It wasn't until they turned onto the state road toward the

end of the route that he saw her. She was manning a barricade erected to stop traffic, which gave her an excellent vantage point of the parade as it passed by.

As if she sensed him watching her, she turned her head and their eyes met. Her expression changed, the friendly and open smile fading, and her gaze skittered away. Deflated, he turned back to the people lined up on the sidewalk and forced himself to wave.

When their float reached the corner, she once again went out of her way to avoid eye contact with him, even though he was the alumni player waving the trophy around at the time, and he felt the dismissal like a fist to his gut.

Kelly didn't want to see him.

Whatever had been between them was over and she was already putting it, and him, behind her. As she'd said, once he was gone, everybody would forget all about what had happened between Chase Sanders and Kelly McDonnell during Eagles Fest.

He gritted his teeth and suffered through the rest of the parade with a smile. But once they pulled back into the school parking lot and began to disband, he faced the other alumni players before they could escape the float and told them he was leaving.

"Something came up at home and I'm going to head out."

One by one he shook their hands, and he realized he was going to miss these guys. They'd all exchanged contact info as they arrived in order to reach each other about activities, and now they promised to keep in touch. He wasn't sure how long it would last, but for now they all seemed sincere about it.

When he got to Coach, he extended his hand. "Thank

you for taking me in, Coach. And for everything. I hope your team kicks ass this year."

"So you're really leaving?"

Chase wasn't even sure how to respond to that. The night before, this man basically told him to get out of town, and don't let the door hit him in the ass on the way out, and now he looked disappointed Chase was going.

"I have to go," was all he said, because the explanation was too long and too personal, and Kelly's dad would probably be the last person who'd want to hear it.

"I'm sorry to hear that." Coach took his hand and then pulled him in for a hug. "No matter what, my door's always open to you, son. Always."

Chase choked up then, and all he could do was nod and climb down off the float before his vision blurred up. Then he almost ran smack into Gretchen.

"Did I hear you say you're leaving?" she asked.

"Yup. I need to get back."

She looked at him for a long time, and then gave him an obviously forced smile. "We all appreciate you coming back to Stewart Mills, Chase. I hope everything works out for you at home, and Kelly was heading toward the station to put the barricades away if you want to say good-bye."

He thanked her, and then made a beeline for the last place he'd seen Mrs. McDonnell. That good-bye was even harder, because she got emotional and wouldn't let go of his neck.

"Promise me you'll keep in touch," she said when he'd finally untangled himself from her arms. "Even if it's just an email. I want to know how you're doing."

"I will," he said, wondering if he really would. Eventually, maybe. It would be a while before he'd be able to handle hearing about Kelly without remembering how much this was hurting.

Once he'd said good-bye to almost everybody, he walked away from the milling crowd. When he reached a junction in the sidewalk, he stopped. His truck was one way, and the police station was in the other.

He didn't want to say good-bye to her. He was afraid she'd see the truth of his feelings on his face and reject them. She hadn't even wanted to look at him earlier, so he wasn't going to get the response he desperately wanted from her.

He walked to his truck and jammed the key into the ignition. When he'd been driving for a little while and stopped for coffee and gas, he'd send her a text. Nothing heavy or serious. He'd give her the kind of good-bye that ended meaningless flings.

After firing up the engine, Chase pointed the truck out of Stewart Mills and, after coming to a complete stop at the sign, hit the gas.

Chase was gone.

Kelly stared at her phone, reading the text for what felt like the hundredth time. Had to hit the road. Thanks for a great time, and I'll never forget the frozen pizza.

He'd never forget the frozen pizza? She knew on a logical level he was trying to be funny but, on an emotional level, she wished she could reach through the phone, grab him by the throat and shake the hell out of him.

She was going to tell him she loved him.

When she'd seen him on the float, she'd been so afraid the intensity of her emotions would show and scare him off, she'd avoided looking directly at him. There would be time after the parade to talk. To really talk seriously about what was between them because, the more she thought about it, the more sure she was he felt the same for her.

Then she'd run into Hunter and Cody, who told her he'd said good-bye to them and that they were pretty sure they saw his truck leaving town.

She hadn't wanted to believe it. She'd continued looking for him, sure that even if he was in the process of leaving, he was taking a long time to say good-bye and just hadn't gotten to her yet. Then she'd crossed paths with her dad.

"Have you seen Chase?"

He'd given her that fatherly look that said he wanted to wrap her in a quilt and keep her safe from what was about to come. "He said he had to go. He said his good-byes before we even got off the float."

"Oh." She refused to believe it. "He must be looking for me. For a small town, it can be awfully hard to cross paths with a person at times."

"Let him go, honey." His face was somber, but she could see the love he had for her in his eyes. That didn't mean she wanted to hear what he had to say. "That boy's not capable of giving you what you deserve."

"I don't know about *deserve*, but he's capable of giving me what I *want*. Which is him." She held up her hand to fend off whatever parental platitude he had lined up. "I'm going to take a walk around the square again."

Ten minutes later, her phone had chimed.

Anger was the emotion that rose to the top. That's what their relationship was worth to him? Not even a good-bye in person? Hell, it wasn't even a decent text message. He'd basically cracked a bad joke while showing her that he had no respect at all for her or what they'd shared.

She tried to cling to the anger, to armor herself with it, but the tears kept rising up, and they were getting harder to blink back. She made her way to the covered bridge, which was blessedly empty as people were still milling around the parade route and the school, chatting and picking up stray candy off the ground.

Without thinking, she went to her spot and sat on the support beam as tears began streaming down her face. She'd give herself a few minutes, to release the pressure of this first wave of tears, and then she'd go back to the station. If she couldn't pull herself together there, she'd tell the chief she was sick and go home to bed.

Reaching down behind her, she traced the outline of his initials and the heart she'd carved into the wood so many years before. If only she'd known that someday Chase Sanders would actually look her way and truly see her. And then he'd break her heart.

A tissue appeared in front of her face, and she looked up to see her mom. She had an entire travel packet of tissues in her hand, which was good because as soon as Kelly saw her face, the crying began in earnest. Her mom sat beside her and put her arm around her shoulders as they shook.

"He left," she managed to say between sobs.

"I know, honey. He didn't say good-bye?"

Kelly hit the screen on her phone and held it up to show her mom. After a few seconds of silence, her mom swore, which she almost never did.

"That little bastard. I never should have invited him to stay with us."

The need to defend him rose up in Kelly, taking her by surprise. What happened was as much her fault as it was his, and it wasn't fair to let people believe he'd callously broken her heart. He hadn't known he *had* her heart to break.

But then she thought of the text, and the words died before she could speak them. Screw him. He didn't even have the balls to look her in the face and say good-bye.

The anger returned, which helped dry up the tears. The last thing she wanted was for anybody to see her crying on the covered bridge right after Chase left town. The sideways glances of speculation and pity would be too much to take.

"It's his loss, sweetheart." Her mom stroked her back, saying almost the same words she had when Kelly returned home after the divorce.

And just as she had then, Kelly tried to believe it was *his loss*, but she was the one who felt as if she'd lost. She'd allowed herself, despite her better judgment, to believe Chase might be the one she could make a life with, and now she was paying the price.

20

In a diner slightly closer to New Jersey than New Hampshire, Chase sat in an uncomfortable booth and watched the sun rise while he drank strong coffee, ate shitty pancakes and missed Kelly.

He'd spent the night in the motel next door, but he hadn't gotten a lot of sleep. After nodding off shortly after he hit the bed, he dreamed of her and woke before dawn with a hard knot of emotion in his chest. There hadn't been any going back to sleep.

If he'd known missing her would hurt this much after just one night, he might not have been so quick to leave.

He was a chickenshit. There was no way around that fact. He'd been afraid of being rejected by Kelly—of not being good enough or stable enough or enough of anything else she wanted in a man—so he'd run away.

"You look like you got run over by a truck and just about the time you started getting up, it popped into reverse and backed over you again."

Chase looked up at the waitress as she refilled his coffee cup. The tag pinned to her T-shirt said her name was Barb, and there was a note of sympathy in her voice that tugged at him. She was a stranger and he'd never see her again.

"I'm a chickenshit."

"Well, at least that's something easy to fix. Suck it up and do what it is you're afraid to do."

That made him laugh. "You've never coached high school football, have you?"

"No, but I had three sons play. You pick up stuff."

He dumped sugar and cream into his cup and gave it a more thorough stirring than was probably needed. "My life fell apart on me a little, and then I met the woman I've been waiting for."

"Having somebody makes putting your life back together suck a little less. I can speak from experience on that." She didn't sit across from him, but she leaned her hip against the back of the other bench in a way that signaled she'd be sticking around for a minute or two.

"She's looking for somebody whose life is already together." The words were painful to say. *I love her, but she doesn't want me.*

"Oh, that's too bad. But if you asked her to be a part of your life, no matter what's going on, and she said no, then she's not the right person."

"I didn't actually ask her."

Barb put the hand not holding the coffeepot on her hip

and gave him a look. "So that's where the chickenshit part comes in?"

He ended up telling her a condensed version of the story, feeling safe in baring his feelings because, again, she was a stranger he'd never see again. When he got to the kiss on the sidelines, she actually smiled, but she stopped once he got to the aftermath. Especially the part about the parade and her unwillingness to look him in the eye. And his text message.

"There are other ways to look at that, you know," she said. "She's there at the barricade, in her uniform, so a lot of people are looking at her. Maybe after your little public display of affection on the sidelines, she was trying to look like she wasn't looking for you and ended up trying too hard."

He wanted to believe her, but he couldn't figure out how to explain how her expression had been different. It wasn't just that she wouldn't look directly at him. She'd looked as if she was hiding something—like there was something there she was afraid he would see.

"If nothing else," she continued, "you should have said good-bye. The text was a mistake and the tone of it was even worse."

"It would have been too hard to hear her tell me that, basically, I was good enough for a fling, but not for anything more."

She shrugged. "Harder than wondering for the rest of your life if being a chickenshit cost you the woman you love?"

He took a sip of the coffee, considering. "I thought so. But now you're making me doubt what I thought I saw."

"There's really only one way to find out." She stood up and started walking away, but paused to look over her shoulder at him. "And not by text."

Once he'd reached his limit of coffee—which was roughly when it started burning the lining of his stomach—Chase paid his bill and went out to his truck. Once again, he was faced with a decision. He could continue heading south and try to work hard enough rebuilding his life that he'd forget the piece that was missing. Or he could turn the truck around and head back north. No matter what happened, he'd know he had looked her in the eye and told her what was in his heart. No questions and hopefully no regrets.

After backing out of the parking space, he made his way to the parking lot exit and sat there for a few minutes without turning his blinker on. Then, calling himself every kind of an idiot, he headed north and set the cruise control for five over the speed limit.

When he finally, after several stops along the way—including a half hour or so spent at a truck stop cleaning out his truck—reached the Stewart Mills town line, he adjusted his speed down to exactly the speed limit. He wasn't going to start his second trip into town on the wrong foot this time.

Even over the music blaring from his radio, Chase heard the siren behind him and he slammed his palm on the steering wheel. That damn stop sign.

Kelly slammed the cruiser into park and popped the latch release for her seat belt. If Chase Sanders thought he could send her a lame-ass text, sneak out of town, make her spend a whole night crying into her pillow, and then run the stop sign coming back, he had another thing coming.

She got out, not untethering her weapon even though it was protocol because, as tempting as it might be, she couldn't shoot him. Especially since there were people out and about, and the sirens had attracted attention. Now they were watching, and she was over the Chase and Kelly show being their entertainment.

The truck door started opening and she kicked it closed. "Stay in the vehicle."

"Kelly, I want to talk to you."

"License and registration."

"What?" She braced herself and looked directly into his face, seeing nothing but confusion.

"I asked for your license and registration."

"You're going to give me a ticket?"

"You ran the stop sign again. You were let off with a warning the first time. This time you're getting a ticket, yes."

"Oh." He looked around and then nodded once, as if things made sense all of a sudden. "We don't want Edna thinking you're letting me off easy."

"I'm giving you a ticket because you ran the stop sign and that's the only reason. And now you're walking a fine line toward failure to comply."

He frowned. "I know you're upset, but—"

"Give me an excuse," she said in a low voice. "Give me a reason to drag you out of that truck here in front of God and everybody and put you on the ground and show you that handcuffs are, in fact, the unsexiest thing you'll ever wear."

"Okay, you're *really* angry. And that's actually a good

thing because it must mean you care, right? So just let me explain."

"Send me a text if you have something to say. All I want from you right now is your license and registration."

She'd gotten out of the cruiser on a wave of hurt, anger and disbelief, but looking into his face was harder than she'd thought. It took everything she had to stand there with her cop face on and not let him see how utterly devastated she felt.

When he leaned over to get his paperwork out of the glove box, she realized something looked off and stretched up onto her toes. "You cleaned your truck out."

"Yeah." He handed her his papers. "I don't know why. Show of faith, maybe? Some way to prove I'm capable of cleaning up my act."

She clenched her jaw and walked back to the cruiser, where she wrote out the ticket. Recognizing it was a petty way of lashing out at him, she might have let him off with yet another warning, but word had gotten around, and there was now a substantial crowd trying to pretend they weren't watching her and Chase. There wouldn't be any special treatment this time.

When she walked back to his truck and handed his license, registration and the ticket through the window, he gave her a look that threatened to tear down the wall she was barely keeping in place.

"I just drove for hours, Kelly. Please. Give me ten minutes."

He was a hard man to say no to. "No."

"Five minutes. I came back to say something to you, Kelly McDonnell, and I intend to say it. If I have to stand in the middle of the street and yell it after you while you drive away, so be it."

She'd managed to hold her head up while people gossiped about her and Chase. She'd survived Edna Beecher sticking her nose into it. But there was no way in hell she would take the chance of breaking down in tears while in her uniform, doing her job, in front of everybody.

"I'll meet you in my dad's driveway. Leave your truck running, because you won't be staying long."

She took a different route than Chase, mostly so people wouldn't know they were going the same place. As ridiculous as it sounded, she wouldn't put it past some of them to find a reason to walk down Eagles Lane, and she didn't want an audience for this.

By the time she pulled into the driveway next to his truck, she felt as if she had her emotions mostly under control. Or the tears, at least. She didn't think she'd cry. After killing the engine, she took her time getting out of the cruiser, making him wait.

He was leaning against the passenger side of his truck, where he knew she'd have to park, but he didn't look relaxed. She walked to the front fender of the SUV and basically mirrored his posture. "Okay, five minutes. Go."

"I'm sorry."

"You're going to have to be more specific."

He held up his hands. "I'm sorry about everything, but mostly that I left without saying good-bye. It was a chickenshit move."

"So you drove all the way back to say good-bye? I'm surprised you didn't text me."

"I'm definitely sorry about the text message."

"And what you said? What the hell was that?" She wanted to shove him, so she put her hands in her pockets instead. "You'll never forget the frozen pizza?"

"That was stupid and I'm so sorry. I was trying to be funny. To keep it light because I thought that's what you wanted from me. And the frozen pizza was special to me, actually. It'll always remind me of that night, so it wasn't as idiotic as it sounded."

No, she guessed it wasn't. The frozen pizza night had been one of her favorite evenings with him, so she could see where he was coming from. She guessed if he'd stayed gone, it would have been a long time before she passed the frozen pizzas in the grocery store without thinking of that night, and of him.

"Why did you leave without saying good-bye?" she asked, since that seemed more important than analyzing his text to her.

He rolled his shoulders a little, and she realized he was nervous about what he was going to say. "Because you wouldn't look at me during the parade. I felt . . . dismissed. Like I'd screwed up so badly kissing you on the sidelines that you couldn't even stand to look at me."

Kelly closed her eyes for a moment, willing them not to tear up. She'd never for a moment imagined she'd come across that way, and the only way to explain why he'd been wrong was to confess how she felt about him.

Her heart had taken a hard knock, and she wasn't sure about making herself that vulnerable, but the man had to have made it at least halfway home to New Jersey, and he'd come back just to talk to her.

"I was trying not to look at you because I'd made a

decision to tell you something, and I was so intensely emotional about it, I was afraid you'd see it. I didn't want to scare you off."

She watched his face as she spoke and could almost see his mind turning as he tried to make sense of what she was saying. "What were you going to tell me?"

"That I . . ." *What the hell,* she thought. If he didn't like what she had to say, he could put a few more miles on that truck of his. "That I didn't want you to go. I mean, I know you have to go for now, but that I wanted you to come back to Stewart Mills. To me."

"Why?" His look was so fierce, she thought she might melt.

"Because I fell in love with you," she said, surrendering to saying it first. Assuming that's what he'd come to say. "I love you."

All the breath rushed out of his body and he seemed to sag against the truck's door. "I came back to tell you I love you, Kelly."

Tears prickled at her eyes again, but she blinked them away. At least they were leaning toward happy tears now. "You should have led with that and closed with the frozen pizza joke."

"I was afraid to tell you. I was afraid you wouldn't want me because my life's not really in order."

"It's scary," she admitted. "But we'll figure it out, because being with you means more to me than having all of our ducks in a row."

"Like you said, I've got a few things to take care of in New Jersey. I might even have to do four days there and three days here for a while, but everything I do will be working toward being here with you."

"What will you do here?" She knew things were still tight in the building market.

"Whatever it takes. I'll find work, or I'll drive down to the southern part of the state every day because there's new building going on there. The commute will be worth it if I get to come home to you every day. Eventually people will start buying all the houses for sale and want them remodeled. I'll find work."

She laughed, wiping a tear from her cheek. "Listen to me. I'm being all practical and ruining our romantic moment."

He crossed the distance between them and cupped her cheek in his palm. "Practical things are important to you. I'll stand out here and make spreadsheets and pie charts if it means you'll take a chance on me."

"I'm ready. No matter how messy it gets."

He rested his forehead against hers. "I kept thinking I didn't even have a solid foundation in the ground to offer, but I was wrong. Loving you is my foundation, and we can build on that. I *want* to build on that. I don't know what that building will look like, but I know it won't ever shift out from under us. It'll stand forever."

"I love you."

"I love you, too." He kissed her. "I'm sorry I took off. Trust me when I tell you I'm seriously kicking myself in the ass right now for not at least trying to talk to you first."

"Don't do that again." She wrapped her arms around his waist and held him close. He was hers. Forever.

When she thought about how close they'd come to losing each other because of bullheadedness, she shivered. He held her tighter and kissed her neck. "I'm going to love spending the rest of my life with you."

They heard the screen door slam, and she wasn't surprised when Chase took a step back from her in reflex. She saw her father on the front porch, one eyebrow raised as if waiting for some kind of explanation as to why Chase Sanders was back in his driveway.

Chase took a step toward the porch, and Kelly slid her hand into his to walk with him. "From now on, we're a team."

He grinned and squeezed her hand. "Then I've already won."

Coach met them at the bottom of the stairs and gave Chase a hard look. "I was beginning to wonder about you, son. I was pretty sure I'd taught you better than to give up on what you wanted most."

"I always had to learn the hard way."

Coach turned to Kelly, and she smiled for her dad. "I'm trying to think of a football analogy that doesn't sound weird in front of you. Scoring drive. In the end zone. They all sound a little inappropriate, though."

He chuckled. "I'll just say welcome to the family, son."

Kelly's throat tightened as she watched the two men she loved shake hands. Then her dad went back inside to give them more privacy.

"You should probably shut your truck off before it runs out of gas," she said, wiping away the last wetness from her cheeks.

"Uh, yeah." He did that, then pulled her into his arms again. "I really do have to go back. I was thinking I could spend a couple more days here, though. With you."

"I want that more than anything. I'm on duty for a few more hours, though."

"I can sit on the curb in front of your apartment until you're done. That'll give people something to talk about."

She slapped his shoulder. "Or I can give you the keys."

He kissed her until she could barely breathe. "I'll be waiting for you when you get home. I'll make us a frozen pizza."

Happiness curled through her, and she laughed as she threw her arms around his neck. "It's a date."

Please turn the page for a sneak peek at

Defending Hearts

The next book in the Boys of Fall series
by Shannon Stacey

Available November 2015 from Jove Books

Dodging bullets had a way of making a man realize he wasn't young anymore. Dodging them for no good reason made the realization a lot harder to shove to the back of his mind.

Alex Murphy sat on the thin mattress in his shitty motel room and looked at the photo on his phone's screen again. It wasn't one of the many he'd taken during his week in the volatile region, using instincts and years of experience to capture on film a population on the brink of revolution. It was one some random passerby had taken with his cellphone and it had gone viral. It was the photo the world would remember.

Alex would still sell his pictures. They told the story in a way one viral camera shot couldn't. But times and technology were constantly changing, and sometimes he felt like a dinosaur. *Photojournalismasaurus.*

Burnout. As much as he didn't want to admit it, even to himself, a decade of freelancing and travel—only to be scooped by a teenager with a cellphone and Instagram account—took its toll, and it might be time to take a break. The idea of going back to Rhode Island didn't appeal to him, though. The apartment in Providence was a place to keep his stuff, but it had never felt like a home.

Using his thumb, Alex navigated to a recent photo album he'd set up on his phone, titled *Stewart Mills, NH.* After almost a decade and a half away, he'd recently spent about ten days there and, when it was time to leave, he'd found himself wishing he could stay a little longer.

He flicked through the photos, pausing over each one. Not with a technical eye, but to gauge his emotional response. Old friends laughing. People he'd known most of his life, but who were practically strangers. A town that had once been his entire world. And Coach McDonnell, who had taken the ragtag group of boys making up the Stewart Mills Eagles football team and made them men.

Alex had been on the first Stewart Mills Eagles football team to win the championship back in the day and, when the town cut the football team's funding, he'd been one of the alumni players who returned to help out with a fund-raising drive to save it. He'd gone out of love for Coach McDonnell, but rediscovering his hometown had also reminded him of how nice it could be to have roots. He hadn't felt grounded to any one place in a very long time.

He wanted to go back.

The plan was taking shape in his mind even as he closed out the photo app and pulled up his contacts. Calculating time zones was second nature to him at this point, so he knew it was safe to call Kelly McDonnell, the coach's daughter and a police officer for the town. She'd given him her cell number when he was in town, and he tapped it.

She answered on the third ring. "Hey, Alex."

"Are you busy right now?"

"Nope. I'm actually sitting in my cruiser, making sure everybody slows down and doesn't hit the power company guys replacing a transformer. What's up? Did you forget something?"

He laughed. "Nope. How are things in Stewart Mills?"

"Pretty good. Everybody's still on a bit of a high from Eagles Fest, for which I can never thank you enough."

"The Eagles are why I'm calling, actually," he said. "I was looking through the photographs I took while I was there, and the story's unfinished. I'm thinking about coming back for a while and following at least the opening of the team's season."

"Following them professionally, you mean? Like for a story?"

"If I can get releases from everybody, I'd like to do a story, yes. Or maybe even a book. There are a lot of towns going through what Stewart Mills has faced, and what you all did is pretty inspirational. And I'd like to broaden the angle, too. Make it about the entire town and not just the team, though that's the core story, of course."

"Wow." There were a few seconds of silence while she digested what he'd said. "That sounds really great, as long as you respect privacy where it's requested and recognize there are some things people wouldn't want shared."

He chuckled. “Don’t worry, Officer McDonnell. I won’t hurt anybody and I won’t share anything people don’t want shared.”

“Shouldn’t be a problem, then.”

“Perfect. I called you because I’m hoping, since you know the community in and out, that you could recommend a place to stay. I know the motel’s closed up, but maybe somebody willing to rent an apartment or even a house on a month-to-month, short-term basis?”

“With so many people losing their homes, the rental market’s incredibly tight right now.” She sighed and he gave her a moment to think. “You know, Gretchen was talking to me about renting a room at the farm. She hasn’t because she’s nervous about having a stranger living with her grandmother, but renting to a friend can end badly when there’s money involved.”

“I’m not a stranger, but I’m not exactly a friend, either.” He remembered Gretchen Walker from school, and he’d had a chance to talk to her a few times during Eagles Fest. She was an attractive woman, but she was definitely a closed book. “All I need is a place to sleep and it wouldn’t be long-term, so maybe I’m a good opportunity for a trial run.”

“That’s what I was thinking. The room has its own bathroom and you’d have access to the kitchen, not that her grandmother would let you go hungry. I’ll talk to Gretchen and have her get back to you. She’ll have to talk it over with Gram, too. Can she call you at this number?”

“The time zones will be a horror show for the next few days, so email’s the best bet.” When she said she was ready, he gave her his email address. “It sounds perfect on my end, so I’ll look forward to hearing from her.”

Once he hung up with Kelly, Alex flopped back on the mattress and stared up at the peeling ceiling. Maybe it was the professional version of a midlife crisis, but he needed a break, and Stewart Mills seemed like the perfect place to regroup and make a plan for his future.

Chronicling the current state of his hometown and the Eagles while rediscovering his roots would simply be a bonus.

"You have to stop trying to sit on Gram's lap," Gretchen Walker told the sixty-pound chocolate Lab looking up at her with adoring eyes. "You're not good for the circulation in her legs."

Cocoa tilted her head sideways and blinked before raising her paw for a high five. Gretchen sighed and gave her one. It seemed to be the only trick the newest member of the Walker family knew, so it was her answer to everything.

It had been the nurse at Gram's doctor's office who suggested a dog might be good company for her grandmother, since Gretchen had her hands full trying to work the farm, and Gram had immediately agreed. Gretchen had driven her to the shelter in the city, anticipating a fluffy little lapdog who would be content to curl up with Gram and watch her knit the days away.

Instead, Gram had fallen in love with a big Lab the color of rich hot chocolate, and Gretchen had to admit she felt an immediate connection with the dog, too. The entire household budget had to be recalculated to accommodate the beast's food costs, but it was nice to get a high five every once in a while. And Cocoa seemed to love the sound of Gram's voice, so everybody was happy.

"My rocking chair isn't big enough for both of us," Gram pointed out. "Maybe we should trade it for one of those leather love seats with the double recliner ends and the built-in cup holders."

Sure they should. What furniture store wouldn't want to trade a fancy leather love seat for a decades-old glider rocker with a cushion perfectly molded to Gram's skinny behind? "We'll see."

"You sound just like your grandfather when you say that. *We'll see* means we can't afford it and you don't want to flat out tell me no."

Gretchen didn't bother denying it. "For now, you need to train her to curl up next to your feet on the floor. She's too heavy to be on your lap. It's not good for you."

"Go wash up," Gram said without making any promises. "Breakfast is ready."

With a sigh, Gretchen went to the sink and washed her hands. She'd already gathered eggs from the chickens and fed the three horses they boarded for a family that lived in the southern part of the state. She'd have to clean their stalls and work in the gardens later, but for now she was starving.

"Maybe we can afford a new love seat now that the Murphy boy's going to be living here," Gram said while Gretchen took a seat at the table and took a scalding swallow of the coffee waiting for her.

"I'm still not sure this is a good idea." It had seemed like a great idea when Kelly brought it to her and through multiple emails with Alex over the last two weeks, but, now that it was actually going to happen, she couldn't help but have second thoughts.

Gram set a plate of biscuits and sausage gravy in front of her. "Wouldn't be fair to change your mind at this point. He'll be here in a few hours."

"I know. It'll be strange having a man in the house again." It had been nine years since her grandfather passed away, and it had only been her and Gram since.

"At least he'll have his own bathroom so we won't have to worry about falling in the toilet in the middle of the night if he leaves the seat up."

Yeah, Gretchen thought, he'd have his own bathroom. He'd have *her* bathroom, along with the bedroom she'd had for years. But giving him his own space, except for the kitchen, made more sense than sharing a bathroom with him. Gretchen had never shared a bathroom with any man, and it seemed very intimate. Intimacy was definitely not what she was going for.

"I was thinking about making a ham tonight," Gram continued. "And maybe my scalloped potatoes and creamed corn."

Gretchen never turned down her grandmother's creamed corn, but she didn't like the way this was going, and the man hadn't even arrived yet. "Alex isn't going to be a guest. It's a business arrangement."

Gram sat across the table from her with her own bowl of biscuits and gravy. "He's paying extra to eat meals with us. That's what you said."

"Normal meals. You don't have to cook anything special for him."

"I'll worry about what I'm cooking. Did you finish getting his room ready?"

Gretchen nodded, shoving a forkful of gravy-soaked biscuit into her mouth. She'd moved all of her belongings into the room next to Gram's, and everything from her bathroom into the one they'd be sharing. For Alex, they'd put on fresh bedding and put brand-new towels and washcloths in the bathroom.

Between Cocoa and Alex Murphy, they'd put out some cash recently, and Gretchen rubbed at the back of her neck. The room and board he'd be paying would help, but for right now, things were a little tighter than she'd like.

"You're going to come in early, right?" Gram asked. "You should clean up before Alex gets here. Maybe take a shower. Put on a little lipstick."

Gretchen stared across the table. "What are you talking about? I don't even own lipstick, Gram."

"You can borrow some of mine. Oh, Cherry Hot Pants would be a great shade on you with that dark hair of yours."

"I am not putting Cherry Hot Pants on my lips." Gretchen didn't even know what else to say about that. "I'll probably say hi and point him in the direction of his room, and then I'm going back to work."

"You're never going to get a husband."

Gretchen pushed her chair back and carried her dishes to the sink. This wasn't good. Not good at all. "I'm not putting on red lipstick. I'm not looking for a husband. Alex Murphy is going to be our tenant and nothing more. I mean it, Gram."

The older woman smiled. "My great-grandmother ran a boardinghouse in London, and she took in an Irish boarder who fell head over heels for my grandmother. It was very romantic."

"I don't have time for romance," Gretchen said, shoving her feet into the barn boots she'd taken off at the back door. "I've got horseshit to shovel."

Alex hit the brake pedal hard, and the used Jeep Cherokee he'd owned for three days skidded to a stop. The Jeep's nose was about three feet past the stop sign.

Now that he wasn't an honored fund-raiser guest and therefore exempt from minor traffic mistakes, he glanced around to make sure he wasn't about to be busted by any of Stewart Mills' finest.

Several stop signs had been added between the time Alex and the others had graduated and gone off to college and their return for Eagles Fest, and they weren't the only changes. The recession had hit hard, the mills had closed, and things had gotten really hard for the people of Stewart Mills. As he drove through town, he noticed again the number of empty storefronts and real estate signs. There seemed to be fewer foreclosure auction signs, though, which was hopefully a sign the worst was behind them.

He found the turnoff to the Walker farm by memory and drove slowly up the long and bumpy dirt driveway. The big white farmhouse needed a little TLC, but he knew from his last visit to town that Gretchen had been running the place alone since her grandfather died, and that her grandmother had had some health issues. Nothing serious, but basically it was a one-woman show.

He got out of the Jeep and was greeted by a chocolate Lab who made it clear they were going to be the very best of friends. Behind the dog was Gretchen Walker, though her greeting was a little more reserved.

"Welcome back," she said, giving him a tight smile.

"Thanks. I'm looking forward to spending some time here."

She nodded, folding her arms across her chest. Gretchen was tall and lean, with long, dark hair in a thick braid down her back. Old jeans tucked into even older barn boots hugged her legs, and she'd thrown a faded flannel shirt over a T-shirt.

Strong. As the dog sat at her feet, Alex composed a mental snapshot of her, and that was the word that popped into his head. Not only did she have physical strength, but she also had an air of resolve and determination about her. He had no doubt when something—anything—needed doing, Gretchen would quietly step up and get it done.

"Pretty dog," he said, remembering she wasn't the chatty type and it might be up to him to carry conversations.

"Thanks. Her name's Cocoa."

Alex smiled. "I can't imagine why."

"Yeah, it's not the most original name for a chocolate Lab, but she came with it and she seems to like it. Right, Cocoa?" The dog put up her paw and he watched Gretchen give her a high five. "She also likes high fives. A lot. She knows the basics, like sit or down. Stay is a little iffy. She has no idea what *get off the couch* or *no dogs on the bed* means, but if you're looking for somebody to celebrate with a high five, Cocoa's your girl."

"Who doesn't love a high five, right?" he asked the dog, who trotted back to him so they could slap palm to paw.

"Do you need help carrying things in?"

He shook his head. "I don't have much. I figured I'd say hello first and meet your grandmother. I'm sure we've met before, but it's been a long time."

"She's waiting inside."

Alex followed her around the house to the back door, which opened into the kitchen. He hadn't been away from New England so long that he'd forgotten the front doors were for company and political door knockers. After she'd kicked off her boots, she led him into the living room, where her grandmother was sitting in an old glider rocker. She set her knitting aside just in time for the big Lab to hop up in her lap. It took Cocoa a few seconds to wedge herself into a comfortable position, and he heard Gretchen sigh before she reintroduced them to each other.

"Sit for a few minutes," her grandmother said. "Let's chat."

He perched on the edge of the sofa. "Thank you for letting me rent a room in your home, Mrs. Walker."

"Call me Ida. Or Gram. Do you like scalloped potatoes?"

"Um." He tried to keep up. "Yes, ma'am. Ida. Gram. Yes, I like scalloped potatoes."

"I'm going back to work," Gretchen said. "Let me know if you need anything."

"You'll need to write the Internet password down for him," Ida told her before looking back to him. "Speaking of the Internet, you don't have any weird proclivities, do you?"

"Gram!" Gretchen stopped walking and turned back, holding her hands up in a *what are you doing* gesture.

"If he's going to live under the same roof as my granddaughter, I have a right to know."

"No, you don't," Gretchen said in a low voice.

"I guess I'd wonder what your definition of weird is," Alex said at the same time.

"Don't answer that, Gram."

Because they were technically his new landlords, the question could be totally illegal as far as he knew. But he wasn't particularly outraged by the turn in the conversation. "I've never received any complaints about weirdness with regard to my proclivities."

"Good." Ida gave him an approving look. "You can never be too careful."

"That's so true. So tell me, Gretchen, do *you* have any weird proclivities?"

"I am not discussing my proclivities with you."

"If I'm going to live under the same roof with you, don't I have a right to know?"

She shook her head, but he could see her struggling not to smile. "You have a right to know the dishwasher hasn't worked for almost a year and a half and where the extra toilet paper's kept. My proclivities, weird or not, are off-limits."

If not for the fact that her grandmother was watching them, Alex might have been tempted to poke at her a little more. He'd seen her during Eagles Fest, mostly from a distance, and he knew she had an infectious, musical laugh that seemed at odds with her stern exterior. When she was with Kelly McDonnell and their friend Jen Cooper, the high school guidance counselor, Gretchen had no problem letting her sense of humor show through. He could see glimpses of it now, and he wanted to draw it out.

But she escaped into the kitchen before he could say more, and a minute later he heard the kitchen door close with a thump. Alex turned his attention back to Ida, who was rubbing between a sleeping Cocoa's ears.

He would be in Stewart Mills for a while, so he had plenty of time to get under Gretchen Walker's skin and make her laugh.